Out of the Frying Pan

By

Jim Davis

Copyright © 2005 by James W. Davis

ISBN 0-7414-2351-0

Published by:

INFI◯ITY
PUBLISHING.COM

1094 New DeHaven Street, Suite 100
West Conshohocken, PA 19428-2713
Info@buybooksontheweb.com
www.buybooksontheweb.com
Toll-free (877) BUY BOOK
Local Phone (610) 941-9999
Fax (610) 941-9959

Printed in the United States of America

Printed on Recycled Paper

Published March 2005

This book is dedicated to my family.
Without them I would have very little to write about.

CHAPTER ONE

Jack Wallace pulled the zipper on his jacket a little tighter around his neck as he felt the cool breeze coming off the mountains to the west. He felt an involuntary shudder as he imagined how cold it would be up there this early in the year. Jack loved this part of the country but it seemed to take forever to warm up in the spring. He was almost to Big Piney, Wyoming, which, short of Alaska, was one of the coldest places in the continental U.S. in the winter. Ahead of him was the Wind River Range, colder and higher yet. He straddled his old motorcycle and pulled it upright off the side stand. He pulled the dipstick out by his right knee, noted the oil level, and replaced the stick in the oil tank; he never started the bike without checking the oil. The bike was a 1972 Harley-Davidson Sportster. It was too old and unreliable to be making a trip like this, but to Jack, that was part of the lure of it. In fact, everything about the bike was wrong. The shifter was on the right and the foot brake on the left. Harley was stubbornly hanging on to old conventions even that late in the game. Maybe that's why Jack and the old bike seemed to get along so well. Jack pulled out the kicker and put some pressure on it with his boot until he felt it engage the gear. His knee was still sore from the last time when the gear didn't catch. He kicked the old motorcycle to life and felt the intense vibration through the handlebars. That was why he had stopped here in the first place, to allow the numbness in his hands to dissipate. The exhaust note brought the heads up on several cows that were grazing alongside the road. Now, as he sat looking north, highway

1

189 seemed to wind away before him like a road in a child's storybook. The country was wide open and rolling. Jack could picture the snow blowing across these hills in the winter. He guided the bike out onto the highway and felt the chill of cool air leaking in around his neck and sleeves. Soon it wouldn't bother him, but right now it did. It was cold.

Jack Wallace was thirty-three years old. If he had been ten years older, people would have accused him of having a mid-life crisis, but it was more than that. Jack had always been looking for something in life that he could not seem to find. He had gone through the motions, done everything right. High school had been easy for Jack. Honor Society, football team, track, he had done them all without complaining. He had rebelled a little in his last two years, maybe partied a little too much. He had done very well in college, in spite of the fact that he had spent more of his time in the local bars and pool halls than in the library. His achievements were nothing short of legendary in his fraternity and throughout the rest of the Greek community. Most of the guys who worked that hard at playing, flunked out by their sophomore year. But Jack was a good student when he needed to be. He changed majors twice before he gained any kind of academic focus. At last he decided, albeit reluctantly, to study law. It probably had more to do with the fact that his girlfriend at the time was a law student, than with any profound interest in the subject. He applied and was accepted into law school at the University of Kansas at Lawrence, not far from where he was raised. This accomplishment had been a great relief to his parents, who had suffered the many slings and arrows of rearing a teenager who refused to grow up.

Although the relationship that had drawn him to law school in the first place evaporated after the first year, Jack continued in law and, in fact, did quite well and even enjoyed it, if that is really possible. His parents were pleased and proud. There was something to be said for that, but something was missing. Jack still felt as if he were floating along, playing someone else's game.

Jack's father had been a small town veterinarian with a thriving practice at which he worked way too hard (for too little money in Jack's opinion). His mother had taught school in the same little town for thirty years before retiring. His parents had retired while he was in college and resided on the old farm where Jack had grown up. Jack's sister, Jenny, three years his junior, had been the perfect child that all parents hope for but don't often get. Jenny had also gone to KU and had taken a fast and focused track to become a doctor. She almost beat Jack out of school. He should have been embarrassed. He wasn't. Jack took great pride in his sister and her family. She now had two rowdy little boys.

Jack had done well in law practice for a few years and had made a little money. He had lived frugally, since he still wasn't married, and invested what money he had made in the booming stock market of the nineties. By all estimates, he was pretty well off. But Jack was bored. When Jack had studied law in school it had been new and even exciting at times. Once out in practice, though, it became old and routine. You don't study the boring part when in school. Perhaps if they did, there wouldn't be such a surplus of lawyers in the world. Jack had begun to think that maybe Shakespeare was right.

A plan had begun to form in Jack's mind. He started it into fruition by bailing out of the stock market, much to the consternation of his longtime friend and investment manager Scott Williams.

"What are you doing Jack? You're leaving a lot of money on the table, man. You don't want to quit now. This thing's just getting started. The internet...."

Jack had cut him off. "I don't care. I don't want to have to worry about it any more. Besides, what am I going to do with all that money? Just put it someplace safe. You know, bonds or something. You're the expert." He had left it at that. It turned out to be a pretty smart move. Jack was mostly in cash when the bottom dropped out.

Jack had given his "two weeks notice" at the law firm where he had become a junior partner. A lot of jaws dropped

3

the day he walked out of there. But Jack had pored over all the abstracts and paperwork from quibbling spouses that he could stand. Life was too short. He packed up a couple of boxes of items and took them to his sister's place with instructions to send them to him if he called for them. Then he packed up his few "possibles" as the cowboys used to call them, strapped them on the back of his old motorcycle, and headed west. Possibles, to Jack, included a change of clothes or two, a sleeping bag, and a fly rod.

In the beginning Jack had taken a credit card and a sizeable amount of cash with him. The cash had run out and the credit card became a burden to Jack's mind, if not to his sister's; she had been receiving the bills. He cut it up.

Cool weather had driven Jack south into New Mexico where he had taken various riding jobs on ranches. He had grown up with horses and had spent enough time with the cowboys of eastern Kansas to feel comfortable with both. Cowboys were the same everywhere. As winter settled in, Baja seemed a likely place, so that's where Jack went. It was warm and dry. The beaches were beautiful. It was one of the loneliest places he had ever been. He loved it.

Money was easier spent than made down on the peninsula and the Sportster had balked at the gasoline a couple of times, so Jack made his way back north. Jack hadn't found out about September 11th until four days after it had happened. He felt a little guilty, but then, what could he do about it? He went back into New Mexico, back to the ranches, but he soon tired of planting juniper poles and stringing barbed wire. The restlessness within him was worse than ever now. He felt the need to move. Colorado, Utah, Nevada...he kept moving, always looking for whatever was over the next mountain, around the next curve in the highway.

Jack had spent the night on the ground in Beaver River State Park, near Evanston, Wyoming. The sign had said "No Overnight Camping" but no one had bothered to run him off in the night or even noticed him for that matter. He had awakened in the cold gray of dawn with just a hint of

4

frost on the drop cloth which he had pulled over his bag in the night. He had gone so far as to look at tents in the Walmart at Evanston, but it had seemed like too much trouble. Now, as he made his way north once again, he had warmed to the task, and was enjoying the feel of the bike beneath him and the open road. He met a cattle truck and he felt the sting of the little bits of grit and gravel that all big trucks kick up into the faces of motorcyclists everywhere...at least the ones that don't have the benefit of a windshield.

He made it to Big Piney, which didn't seem to offer much, but he saw, amongst the 1-ton diesel pickups, a sign that said "Café". A cup of coffee was perhaps Jack's most pressing engagement in the world at that particular moment, so he pulled off. Many heads turned as Jack walked in the door of the eatery. It was mid-morning and the local ranchers had finished chores enough to go to the coffee shop to get the latest local news and gossip. Jack shrugged out of his leather jacket and dropped into a booth where a newspaper lay open on the table. A used coffee cup and a dirty plate lay next to the paper, a cigarette butt was giving up its final tendrils of smoke in the ashtray. A single quarter lay beneath the edge of the plate. Jack looked up at the counter where a redheaded waitress was ringing up the ticket for a customer. The patron turned around as he stuffed the change into his billfold and fixed piercing blue eyes on Jack.

"I'll bet you like'ta froze your ass on that bike this mornin'," the man spoke in a loud voice around an unlit cigarette dangling from his lips.

"Something like that," Jack responded flatly as he met the man's stare with his own cool green eyes. The man was big, mid-thirties, somewhat fat but he carried the weight as if he were fit underneath. He cocked his head over and lit the cigarette with a lighter.

"You doin' any work today, Big John?" another local queried.

"You goddamn right!" replied the big man, looking up from under his sweat-stained hat.

"John Kirby!" fumed the waitress, turning crimson.

"If you're gonna' use that kind of language in here, you can find your breakfast someplace else!" The café had become silent as a tomb.

"Awe, I'm sorry Miss Flora, I didn't know you was so delicate," Kirby replied sarcastically. He looked at no one as he walked out the door. Jack saw him pause at the bike and look through the window to see Jack eyeing him. The man broke his gaze and strode off. Jack turned to find the waitress pouring him a cup of coffee.

"Sorry about that," she said, "coffee's on the house." She gathered the dirty plate and utensils in one hand and wiped the table with the other. "Can I get you anything to eat?"

"Sure," said Jack with a smile, "A couple eggs over well, bacon, and wheat toast."

"Comin' right up," she said, already heading for a pass-through that accessed the kitchen. Jack picked up the paper, a USA Today. It had a story about another Bin Laden lieutenant and one about what the CIA knew or didn't. Jack didn't want to see any more, so he put the paper down and surveyed the crowded little diner. No one was talking about the terrorist attacks out here. They couldn't do much about it anyway. The talk here was about calving and new foals and the lack of snowmelt, things that mattered to them, in the here and now.

"You headin' for Sturgis or something," the waitress said, setting a plate of food in front of Jack.

"No," Jack replied with a laugh. "I just want to do some fishing, if I can find enough work to support that nasty little habit." The waitress laughed.

"Well, hey, that feller that just left was talkin' about hiring some help for a pack trip. He's an outfitter, if you can put up with him," she said grinning. "Somehow I think that would be like oil and water." Jack thought that she was probably right. He ate, left a generous tip, and stepped out the door to straddle his bike.

"I wonder what his story is?" The waitress stared out the window at Jack as he once again headed north.

CHAPTER TWO

Jack was headed for Pinedale, Wyoming, the county seat of Sublette County. Pinedale is a ranching town, first of all, and, during the summer months, a jumping off point for the Bridger Wilderness Area. The population runs around 1400 people and the town lies above 7000 feet in elevation. The winter months see ranchers struggling to feed livestock in a country where the snow and cold are harsh to say the least, but summertime welcomes a hoard of backpackers, fishermen, and other tourists to the area. Not everyone welcomes them, but most do. These tourists bring in a good deal of money and excitement to the otherwise sleepy little town.

When Jack got to the junction of 191, he hesitated. Pinedale lay scarcely a dozen miles to the east, but first Jack wanted to see the Green River again, so he turned left towards Warren Bridge where the river went under the highway. The Green River runs through a lot of private land and the landowners protect the property vigilantly. You can drift a boat through their land on the Green, but you can't even drop an anchor to take a leak. The bottom of the river is theirs too. Fishing privileges are sold on these private lands for big money. The Green River north of Warren Bridge had numerous turnouts for public access. Jack knew this and figured he could find a quiet spot to make a camp on the Green. The country looked just like it had several years ago, when he had seen it for the first time. The air smelled good coming off the Wind River Mountains. Jack felt as if he were coming home.

He had not gone far when he saw an old blue Suburban pulled over to the side of the highway. Jack downshifted and came to a stop in front of the vehicle. Steam was seeping out from the grill and a young lady sat in the driver's seat with her face in her hands. As he pulled off his sunglasses and looked back at the girl, he could see a look of growing apprehension on her face. He walked directly up to the hood of the suburban and grinned at her through the cracked windshield.

"Pop the hood latch," he said pointing at the hood. She had a look something close to terror on her face now, but she complied. As he raised the hood a cloud of steam billowed out from underneath, like smoke signals from an old western. Fanning the steam away, Jack saw the problem immediately. The radiator return hose had ruptured next to the clamp. He heard the door on the old truck open with a loud creak, betraying its lack of lubrication, and the lady stepped out. As she peeked around the hood, Jack could see that she was not as young as he had at first imagined. She was older than he was, with a few crow's feet showing when she smiled.

"Is it bad? Did I ruin it?" She asked timidly.

"It's just a hose," replied Jack, pulling out his Leatherman tool. He used the screwdriver to remove the clamp, cut off the split portion of the hose and reattached it to the radiator. As he tightened the clamp, he looked up at her face. She was staring at him with a smile that made her whole face light up.

"Now how in the world did you know how to fix that?" she asked. "I'd have never thought of that trick in a million years."

"This one was easy," he said, "you're going to need some water though."

"I can take care of that," she said walking to the back of the Suburban. She reached in and pulled out a couple of two-liter soda bottles full of water. "Will this be enough? It's left over from a picnic."

"Should get you back to the ranch."

"How do you know where I live?" she asked, looking apprehensive again.

"Oh, I don't." he said, "it's just an expression."

"You aren't from around here are you?"

"No, just up here enjoying the country," said Jack.

"Vacation?"

"Sort of," he replied. "I'd like to stay the summer at least, if I can find a job."

"I'd sure like to pay you for your work," she said reaching in for her purse. "My name's Kate Wilcox, by the way." She stuck out her hand.

"Jack Wallace," he said shaking her small but calloused hand. "And no, you can't pay me for this. I'd be ashamed of myself if I took your money." He grinned.

"Look, Jack, I just live up the road here and I left my kids alone while I went to the store." She hesitated, and then continued her thought. "Why don't you come by for lunch? It's already past noon and I'd really like to pay you somehow."

"Well, I guess I would accept that kind of payment." He smiled. He didn't normally relish horning in on someone's family meal, but in this case it seemed all right.

"Okay then, great...Just follow me home then." She looked a little flustered, but quickly recovered and jumped back into the old Suburban. The starter whined and he could hear her pumping the accelerator. The engine came to life grudgingly, but finally smoothed out. Jack swung back over his bike and kicked it to life as well. He felt a trickle of sweat run down his back and began to second-guess his acceptance of the offer. After a moment he swung the Sportster out onto the highway and followed the smoky trail left by the Suburban.

They had gone perhaps a mile when Kate turned off on a county gravel that angled back toward the mountains. She soon pulled onto a rutted ranch road. Jack could see where they were going now. He could see kids in the yard of a small ranch house. The jagged, snow-covered peaks in the background gave the whole scene an air of serenity. The

9

kids seemed excited as the old Suburban's squeeling brakes brought it to a halt and the dust settled around it. A lanky teenage boy jogged up to the vehicle as Kate stepped out, but his eyes were on Jack, who was shrugging out of his leather jacket.

"Hey, Mom, what's with the biker guy?" asked the teenager as his mother pulled bags of groceries from the back seat. He either didn't know or didn't care that Jack could hear him. An old blue-heeler dog was cautiously sniffing Jack's pantleg.

"Reid, this is Jack...uh," she faltered.

"Wallace," Jack prompted.

"Sorry...Jack, this is my son Reid." She turned back to Reid. "The Suburban broke down and he got it going again...I asked him to eat lunch with us." You might have thought she was answering her father instead of her son. Jack shook Reid's hand, as the young man looked him over. Jack was clean-cut and did not sport the tattoos and body-piercings that would have labeled him a "biker", but he was used to people being suspicious just because he rode a motorcycle.

"Nice to meet you," said the teenager, smiling. "I'm Reid, that's Jesse, and out there is my younger brother, Bud," said Reid gesturing towards first a smiling blonde-haired girl, then at a boy just over the fence. Jack shook the hand of the girl, a youthful version of her mother, and then he looked back over the fence. An obviously frustrated youth was playing tug of war with the lead rope of a stout-looking yearling colt. Jack walked over and leaned on the top rail of the fence.

"Why don't you let him drag that rope a few days and get his head sore. He'll start easier," Jack said smiling. The boy looked over at Jack, dropped the lead, and walked over to the fence.

"Hi Mister. Hey, is that your bike?" The boy reached out to shake Jack's hand looking past him at the motorcycle.

"I'm Jack Wallace," he shook the strong little hand.

"Yes, that's my bike."

"Cool."

"You like motorcycles?" Jack asked.

"Absolutely!" came the reply.

"Cool," said Jack, imitating the boy.

They unloaded the groceries, Jack taking two bags and each child carrying something. The house was fairly old and almost square with a porch spanning it's entire width. Various feed tubs littered the porch. It appeared that this was where the yearling colt was fed. Other signs showed that perhaps more than one horse had the run of the yard. The home on the inside was neat but definitely had the lived-in look. The furniture was plain and mismatched, showing a good deal of wear. Several watercolor paintings adorned the walls, depicting wildlife and mountains.

"Who's the artist?" Jack asked putting the bags on the kitchen table.

"That would be Jesse," Kate replied as she began to put the groceries away. "She's the artist in this family. Takes after her dad. I know she doesn't get that from me." Jack was looking at one of the paintings when the screen door slammed behind him. He turned to see Bud standing on a rug just inside the kitchen door.

"Hey, Mr. Wallace, would you like to see my dad's motorcycle?" asked Bud excitedly.

"Call me Jack. Mr. Wallace is my father," Jack said smiling at Bud.

"Okay Jack, do ya wanta see it?" the boy asked eagerly.

"Bud!" the boy's mother scolded. "Don't pester him with that old bike."

"That's alright," said Jack, "I'd love to see the bike."

"Come on!" said Bud rushing out the door. Jack followed the youth out the door and around to the barn. It was a low-roofed structure, built into the side of the hill. Bud swung open one of a pair of huge old doors to reveal a rather dark interior. He turned on a light, which consisted of a single bulb with a pull chain hanging from a rafter. The barn smelled of dust and old hay. A well-worn workbench stood against one wall with an assortment of tools hanging behind it. The tools each had their place on a pegboard. It appeared that whoever had worked in this place had been orderly. Everything was covered in a fine layer of dust, suggesting that the tools hadn't seen much use in recent times.

Bud walked in past the workbench and pushed an old lawn mower out of the way. "Here it is," said Bud, gesturing to a fender peeking from under the corner of an old saddle blanket. Jack helped him uncover the dusty relic.

"Oh, my gosh!" Jack said, astonished. He was looking at an old Harley-Davidson Panhead that obviously hadn't moved in years.

"Isn't it cool!" the boy said. It wasn't a question at all.

"Oh, Bud, it's cool alright. This thing looks really original."

"Is that good?"

"It is in my book." Jack was poring over the bike. It was a '56 by the paint job. It even had correct leather saddlebags, although they were badly dried out. Jack surmised that it must have been in this old barn for years. The dry mountain air had done little to deteriorate the bike. The tires were flat and cracked and a dark oil stain marked its spot on the floor, otherwise it was like looking back in time.

"Mom said he used to give us rides on it, but I was too little to remember," the boy went on. Jack was still in awe. The chrome looked very good under a thick coat of dust. The only hint of rust was where the exhaust pipes came out of the heads.

"Bud," Jack asked quietly, "Where is your dad?"

"Oh, he's with Jesus," Bud replied confidently. "He died when I was real little." Bud got rather quiet. "I can't remember too much about my dad to tell you the truth."

"I'm sorry, Bud" said Jack sincerely.

"It's okay."

"This bike is worth a great deal of money. Don't sell

it, if you can keep from it," said Jack.

"I won't. Reid and I are going to fix it up some day."

"You do that. I'm sure your dad would be proud," Jack said. A call from the house diverted their attention. They covered the bike back up and closed the door to the barn.

At the house the whole family sat down together and prayed before the meal. There was a roast with potatoes, carrots, and onions cooked right in with it. Jack had smelled the food even before he had reached the house. It reminded Jack of home, and Sunday dinners after church, growing up in Kansas. The meal was the best Jack had eaten in months. He said as much to Kate.

"This is the last of the elk that Reid shot last fall. It was surely a good one." Kate was obviously proud of her son.

"Reid gets his license next week," Jesse broke in. "Then he's going to drive us to the swimming pool every day. Right Reid?"

"Not likely, Jess," said Reid. "I'll take you in some, but I've got a part-time job now too."

"Reid's starting at the parts store," Jesse offered.

"That's great Reid. I'm sure you'll do well," said Jack. A cherry dumpcake was brought out for dessert. Jesse had made it. It consisted of cherry pie filling dumped into the bottom of a cake pan, with a box of cake mix dumped on top of that. Butter was melted and drizzled on top and the whole thing went into the oven to bake. Jack's mother had given him the same recipe when he went to college. Everything about the meal reminded Jack of home, of family.

The boys excused themselves and went out into the back yard. Jack offered to help with the dishes but Kate and Jesse wouldn't hear of that. He stayed in the kitchen long enough to comment on how well-behaved and polite the children were. He saw Bud and Reid playing with a fly rod outside and excused himself to join them.

The two boys were taking turns doing practice casts with little success. "Can I see that?" Jack asked. Reid

13

handed him the rod sheepishly. Jack looked the outfit over. "I've got an old Cortland just about like this. I still use it for a backup." He stripped out a little more line, made a couple of false casts, and let the line go. It settled out gently in front of him about forty feet out.

"Wow!" Bud exclaimed. "Can you teach us how to do that?"

"Sure thing, Bud. It just takes a little practice." He handed the rod back to Reid and showed him a thumb-on-top grip. "Try it now," said Jack, "and remember that you're throwing the line, not the lure. You have to finesse it, not force it." Reid made a couple of casts with Jack giving him a few more pointers. Bud tried it also and soon both boys had made dramatic improvements. "That's it, just don't bend your wrist, and wait until the line straightens out on your back-cast. You see how that helps." Jack looked at Bud. The boy was beaming. They spent an hour or more talking and casting.

Inside the house, Kate and Jesse had finished the dishes and could see the boys out the window. Jesse was working on a drawing of Bud and the yearling teaching each other to lead. She looked up. "What's wrong Mom?" she asked, seeing that her mother was a little teary eyed.

"Nothing Jess," she said sniffing. "I just wish..." she broke off.

"I know," said Jesse, "we all miss Dad." She gave her mother a hug.

"Let's go outside," Kate said. They walked out to where the guys were.

"I'd better be going Kate," said Jack. "I think I've overstayed my welcome."

"I doubt that," she said, looking at the boys still fiddling with the fly rod.

"Thank you for a perfect afternoon and a great meal," Jack said sincerely.

"Well, thanks for fixing the car," she said. "We've all enjoyed your visit. You can come back anytime." She paused. "I feel like we've known you for ages already."

14

"Reid tells me that Circle "A" needs hands, so I may see if I can hit them up for a job. But either way I'm going to hang around Pinedale for awhile."

"Well, come on back next Sunday, if you want, and have dinner with us again. I'm sure the boys would love another lesson in fly fishing," said Kate.

"I might just do that," said Jack. They talked a little longer, and then Jack said his goodbyes and started the motorcycle. He waved as he pulled out onto the county road, looking back at the picturesque setting. He got to the highway and abandoned his original plan of camping on the banks of the Green. He headed on into Pinedale and got a room at the Pinedale Inn. The shower felt exceedingly good and he even shaved since the water was hot, even though he would probably do it again in the morning. He turned on the television and flopped down on the bed. He thought back on the day, not really watching the TV. He was a bit ashamed of himself. He hadn't even known it was Sunday until Kate had said it, right as he was leaving. The news came on and it was more of the same. Locally it was snowmelt in the mountains and water; national news was about politics and stock market woes and, of course, the war on Terror. He would hear it all again in the morning. With the TV still on, he fell asleep wishing he at least had a dog.

CHAPTER THREE

The next morning found Jack up early. He grabbed a cup of coffee at a small quick shop where he filled the tank on his motorcycle. He had been on reserve coming in the evening before. He backtracked west on 191 and smiled when he passed the road that went out to the Wilcox place. The air was crisp and he was not dressed for a long ride. At the next county road he came to, Jack turned off, and before long came to the driveway to Circle "A" Ranch, just as Reid had described. He pulled under the rather fancy entryway, which had a big "A" in a circle between the words "Circle" and "Ranch", all done in bent sucker rod. The lane split off shortly. One fork of the road was paved and angled up towards a sprawling new and very modern home. The house looked out of place, Jack thought. Behind the house Jack could see a long, paved runway that reached back out to the road and a large airplane hangar near the house. The other fork in the drive went down to an older house sitting next to some barns and corrals. He could see activity at the barns, so he took the left fork. A number of horses stood lazily in the pen made from pine poles. Several cowboys were saddling horses at a low shed next to the corral. All heads turned toward Jack, horses and cowboys alike, as the loud motorcycle approached. Jack pulled up and stopped, shutting off the ignition. He leaned the bike on its stand and approached the nearest cowboy. He was quickly relayed to the foreman, who was saddling his horse just outside the low shed.

"I hear you need hands," said Jack. The man turned around and looked Jack over.

"Can you ride a horse? We don't use motorbikes."
The man was not smiling.

"I can do whatever it takes," Jack offered.

"You wanta' start today?" the man asked.

"Sure."

"Catch the buckskin gelding and put a saddle on him.
You don't have your own saddle I take it?"

"Not today," said Jack pulling a halter and rope off a
hook in the barn. He walked into the pen of horses. There
were two buckskins in the pen, but one was a mare. The
gelding was a little fidgety, but Jack approached him slowly
and backed him into a corner. Jack eased the rope around
the big horse's neck and soon had the halter slipped over its
head. He led him back to the shed. Another cowboy handed
him a bridle, which Jack slipped on the horse. He then
quickly applied the blanket and saddle, tightening the cinch.

"Try him out," the foreman said with a wave toward
a large corral next to the horse pen. Jack led the horse out,
pulled the reins around its neck, and climbed aboard. He
knew what was coming. Sure enough, he was barely in the
saddle when the horse laid its ears back and went into an
impressive bucking fit. Jack kept the horse's head up as well
as he could, but the big buckskin came down hard with his
front feet together and twisted sideways. The buckskin spun
and bucked, but Jack kept his balance and held a tight reign
on the horse's head. The gelding made a few more hops
around the pen and finally decided that his rider was there to
stay. The horse snorted and was breathing hard with nostrils
flared. Jack trotted the horse around the pen a couple of
times and reined up where the foreman and other cowboys
stood grinning.

"He's energetic," said Jack. They all laughed.
"What's his name? Buck?"

"Of course," said the foreman as Jack dismounted.
"Mine's Jim Palmer. You got a name?"

"Jack Wallace." He shook hands all around as the
other cowboys were introduced.

"You've got a job, Jack," said the foreman. "You
can stow your gear in the bunkhouse." He pointed toward a

17

newer looking building with a small satellite receiver on top.

"Thanks," said Jack, walking toward his bike to get his duffel.

"Don't you want to know what it pays?" the foreman asked after him.

"Nope...just that it does," Jack replied, smiling.

Jack pulled his bedroll and duffel off the back of the bike and walked toward the bunkhouse where Jim Palmer met him at the door. Jim was about fifty or so, with a little bit of a potbelly and short-cropped gray hair underneath a bone colored Stetson. He opened the door for Jack and stepped inside behind him. For a bunkhouse, this place was nice. It had a kitchen area, a refrigerator, and a small lounge area with a 36" TV with a satellite receiver box on top. The bunks were solidly made of wood and one of the bottom ones contained a sleeping figure. Jack could see an earring and a tattooed arm protruding from under a wadded sheet. Jack looked at the foreman as he spotted the cowboy in the bunk. A look of rage came over the man's face and his jaw tightened. Jim walked over to the bunk and kicked it hard with his boot. The figure stirred and an oily head glared through squinting eyes.

"Get yer ass outa bed. There's work ta do," Jim growled, then he turned to Jack. "Find an empty bunk. My wife cooks meals up to the house. You'll eat there." He stalked out, grumbling. Jack threw his gear on a bed and turned to go. The man in the bunk sat up, threw his legs over the side of the bunk, and reached under his bed. He pulled out a pint of Jim Beam, cracked the cap, and took a long pull on the bottle. The man stared at Jack menacingly. Jack walked past him and out the door, hearing the slosh of the bottle once again. "Takes all kinds," Jack thought.

Jack walked the short distance to the corrals to join the others. He heard the whine of a jet aircraft and looked toward the runway just in time to see a puff of blue smoke and hear an echoing chirp from the tires as a sleek business jet touched down at the far end of the strip. "Yep," he said aloud this time. "It takes all kinds." He gathered Buck's reins and mounted up.

CHAPTER FOUR

Yuri Aleksandrov stood alone in his study, surrounded by dark mahogany bookcases and cabinetry. He sipped a glass of Manavi wine as he gazed out the large picture window that overlooked the ranch buildings below. Yuri was distinguished looking, if not actually handsome; he carried himself with an air that seemed to command respect. He was gray at the temples, but still had most of his hair and he smiled often and had the laugh lines that go with that condition. Whether or not the smiles were genuine was anybody's guess. He was sixty-three years old, but he didn't show it like many Russians did. Although he drank often, he did not drink excessively, and he did not have the ruddy complexion and broken blood vessels in his face that many of his comrades displayed.

Yuri held the wineglass up to the window and admired the straw-green color against the backdrop of the Wind River Range. The dry Georgian wine reminded him of old times, good times. Although he preferred the California wines, he had picked up a case of the Manavi while in Washington D.C. a few days ago, on a nostalgic whim. Sometimes he missed his Russia, but he loved this rugged Wyoming country. It was so much different from the cities, especially those of Russia and Eastern Europe. The air was clear and clean. No smog. The people here didn't have that hollow-eyed, hopeless look. The cowboys and their horses were just like the ones he had seen in movies when he was still in the Soviet Union...when there still was a Soviet Union. It was almost like having his own aquarium, but,

19

instead of fish, he had cowboys. It would be difficult to leave this place. He wrinkled his brow at the thought. A soft knock on the door interrupted his thoughts. "Yes?" he queried in English, not bothering to turn around. He had been thinking in Russian.

"It is me," came the reply in an Eastern European accent.

"Please come in, Sasha," said Yuri, losing his scowl. A tall, square-shouldered man dressed in an Armani suit and black collarless shirt entered the room. "You return, my friend. With good news I hope?"

"Mostly good, Yuri." The man was dark-complexioned with a thick black beard. His shiny black hair was pulled back into a ponytail, giving him a striking appearance.

"And this would be?"

"We are very close," the man said pouring himself vodka from a well-stocked bar. "We will get what we ask, I am thinking."

"Then why did you say 'mostly'? You are telling me there is a problem?"

"Nothing that cannot be overcome," Sasha replied.

"Well?" Yuri was again looking out the window, waiting for an answer.

"Al-Rahman requests to pick up the package here," said Sasha.

"You told him where it was?" Yuri asked anxiously.

"No, Yuri, you know I would not do that. He knows that it is in a remote place. That is all he knows. He wishes to take delivery and send it on to where it will be deployed immediately." Sasha took a sip from his glass. "We would not have to move it ourselves that way."

"That is not possible. Someone might recognize the aircraft as having left from here. No. I cannot accept this." Yuri spoke with finality.

"It could work, Yuri. We could bring them in at night. Our airstrip can handle the jet they will use. It is the

20

only way we can get the money transferred without delay. This way they will give us all that we have requested."

"This I must think about," Yuri replied. Both men fell silent. Sasha poured more vodka in his glass and walked over to the large window. He peered at the cowboys saddling their horses below.

"Things are increasingly more difficult for them," Sasha added. "Accounts are being frozen. Some disappear altogether."

"I am in agreement with you, Sasha," said Yuri. "Time is short. But we must be careful. We would not want to find ourselves in that same position."

"What about your headman, Palmer, is he going to be a problem?" Sasha asked, turning to face Yuri.

"He will not be a problem for long, but, yes, I under-estimated the man. He has become suspicious and disagree-able."

"Then how...?"

"Marion will take care of the problem," Yuri said abruptly.

"Do you think it wise to do such a thing now, Yuri?" Sasha voiced his concern. "Besides, Marion is a thug. Can he do this thing without arousing suspicion? Is he capable?"

"He has discussed it with me and I approve of his plans. No suspicions will be raised. If it does not work, it can be easily aborted without compromise to our larger plan." Yuri put down his empty glass as if to say that the conversation was over. "Go now and rest, you have had a long journey. You no doubt have jet lag. We will talk more in the morning when I have had time to think."

"Of course, Yuri, I will see you tomorrow then."

Sasha left the room and Yuri walked over to the bar and poured himself a large vodka. He also thought of Marion as a thug. The man was simply an asset and quite disposable.

After leaving the study, Sasha passed through a short hallway and into the great room of the luxury home. The

21

architecture and furnishings were something one might expect in Malibu or Beverly Hills. The art that adorned the place was modern and impressionistic. The furniture was a complex mixture of glass, stainless steel, and leather, with odd bits of Eastern European items scattered here and there. Somehow it all came together and was tasteful and elegant. The decorator had pulled out her hair trying to make it work; given the things her client had insisted that she work with. As Sasha passed through the great room, he looked out the back of the villa. The entire wall on that end of the room was of windows and the view was spectacular. The mountains hardly looked real, stretched out against the blue sky with their snow-capped peaks. The view closer to the house, Sasha thought to himself, was just as spectacular. A bronze, slender form moved slightly, adjusting her position on a lounge chair by the pool. The lady was wearing a white two-piece bikini. It contrasted well with her bronze skin. Her hair was very dark, almost black and cut rather short.

Sasha slid open the door leading to the pool. The lady craned her neck to look up at him. Recognition flashed in her eyes and she jumped up. She glanced around like a schoolgirl caught cheating, then dashed to Sasha and pulled him behind the edge of the wall. They embraced and she kissed him passionately. When at last she allowed him to pull away, she begged, "Please, don't ever go away from me again."

"I think I shall not need to very soon my dear." He looked back toward the house. "Does Yuri know?" he asked.

"I don't know. I don't think so. It doesn't matter anymore." She looked up into his dark eyes.

"Come." He led her away.

Yuri walked silently out of his study and into the greatroom. He could see the couple disappearing around the wall outside, toward the guest wing. He had suspected that Anna and Sasha were lovers for some time. Now he knew. It did not upset him. Perhaps he was relieved. Anna must be lonely out here. Yuri had never loved Anna. She had been loyal to him long after their days together as Soviet spy and master were over. Yuri had cultivated her from a Czechoslovakian street girl into one of the KGB's most valuable agents. Her Chechnyan heritage and brown skin had made her an outcast until, on the streets of Prague, he had rescued her. She was the perfect girl to infiltrate the Americans. The Americans with all their technology and all their lust, it was the lust that made them vulnerable. She looked nothing like a Russian, none had ever suspected. Anna also had a certain naiveté that could be wholly disarming, a quality that proved to be ever so useful. No, Yuri did not mind Anna enjoying Sasha's company.

As a KGB handler in the days of the old Soviet Union, Yuri had made a name for himself. He had climbed a difficult ladder and had reached the top only to find that the building it was leaning against was imploding upon itself. Glasnost or Perestroika, whatever name you gave it, had brought an end to a monopoly on commerce for many in the KGB. But, Yuri was resourceful, as always, and used his connections to broker arms and technologies both ways. Why spend years of research and engineering to build something that had already been built? He had taken a lesson from the playbook of the Kremlin and simply pirated patents and copyrights. He had manufactured in the budding republics everything from copies of Russian AK 47 rifles to American missile guidance systems and sold to the highest bidder with ready cash. And all that time Anna had stayed with him. Sasha too. Yuri was their safe harbor in the storms that came after the fall of the great leviathan, the Soviet Union. He would not deny them each other. After all, his one love had been taken from him all those years ago, never to be replaced.

Anna slipped into the door behind Sasha and followed into the room. Her white terrycloth robe was pulled tightly around her slim waist. She pulled herself close to

Sasha as he took off his suit jacket. He was looking in the mirror. She looked around his shoulder and stared into the mirror also.

"Will you shave off the beard?" asked Anna. "It makes you look like one of those horrible terrorists that are on the news all the time. Sometimes it scares me."

"The beard scares you?"

"Sometimes."

"I will shave it off soon." He looked down when she met his eyes in the mirror. She slid her arms around his waist, but he continued to look down and did not meet her eyes in the mirror.

"It is lonely here," she said softly. "Yuri is preoccupied and he hardly notices that I am around. And Tino is not much company at all." She looked at him in the mirror. Sasha too seemed preoccupied. "I went to Jackson yesterday."

"Shopping?"

"Yes," she said, glad to get some response. "But I didn't buy much. Even with all those people around I was lonely. I want someone to go shopping with."

"Things will be different soon," he said, turning to embrace her. "I think we will be going on an extended vacation. Perhaps in the Caribbean." He yawned and sat down on the bed.

"You are tired from your trip," she said, "and you talk about leaving again. Why don't you get some rest." She smiled at him and walked toward the door. He watched her but did not respond. She opened the door and slipped out into the hallway.

Anna went back outside to the pool area. She sat down on the lounge chair where a radiant heater glowed, warming the spot to a comfortable temperature. Steam rose from the surface of the water. She slipped off the robe. The contrast between the cool air and the warmth of the heater was strange. Her relationship with Sasha was much the same. He was warmth in a cold place, yet the cold was still there also. The heater warmed her skin without touching her. The air was still cool. She walked to the edge of the heated pool and dived in. She swam a few strokes and felt the warm water engulf her. She had driven by the community pool in Pinedale a couple of days ago and she had seen all the children laughing and playing, the sun bright on the surface of the water. Anna had felt that she was missing something. Perhaps she was missing everything. The water of the pool concealed her tears, but there was no one to see them anyway.

CHAPTER FIVE

Life on the Circle "A" was good. After the first week Jack had acquired a great deal of respect for the foreman, Jim Palmer. Palmer was a bit gruff but he was a top hand and was not to be outworked by any of his cowboys. He seemed to have a good eye for stock and a good head for efficiency in using the available labor. Jack had helped work what seemed like an unending number of calves; they were preparing to move several herds onto some higher pastures on BLM land as the grass became available. The work was hard, but Jack was in as good a physical shape as he had been since he played football in high school. The slight paunch which had begun to develop while Jack was in law practice had disappeared well over a year ago. As a working cowboy he had spent as much time doing groundwork as he had on the back of a horse. Flanking calves was hard work and, as the week came to a close, some of the cowboys were talking about heading into town for a beer. "You better go with us Jack," said Charlie. "My wife went to visit her sister and I can stay out all night if I want to." Charlie Silvers was a big man with a mustache and hat that made him look like something out of a Louis L'Amour novel. He didn't stay in the bunkhouse but lived on a small rented tract near Bondurant. The older couple that owned the place came but rarely to visit their property.

"A cold beer sounds like just the thing to relax my aching muscles," Jack answered. "I don't think I can stay out all night though."

"Aw, me neither. These young bucks can have that

stuff all to themselves." He indicated the other two smiling young men who were in on the conversation. "We can play pool while they try to pick up women."

"What do you mean, Charlie?" Jack asked. "You think I can't pick up women?"

Charlie laughed. "With a mug like yours? Not a chance." The others guffawed. Jack had never had a problem getting dates. Women had fawned over him in school and even more so after he got out and the available bachelor sources were drying up. Of course that worked both ways. Most of the women that Jack considered to be of appropriate age were looking for their second husband by now. He had enjoyed some semi-serious relationships over the years, but, so far, none had panned out.

"Well, I hate to disappoint you boys," came the high nasal voice of Abe Cain, "but I can't go. I've got a date."

"Does your wife know that?" asked Charlie.

"Well of course she does ya' darn fool!" said Abe indignantly. "Who do ya' think the date's with...Aww, you're pullin' my chain again. Ain't ya'?" Charlie laughed and shook his head. Abe was a little slow and everyone liked to tease him. He always took it well.

"I'm goin'," said Billy, a young cowboy out from Missouri for the summer.

"I'll hitch a ride with you then Billy. Do we ask Wade?" Jack indicated a cowboy who was just now unsaddling his horse. Wade was the one Jack had seen still in the bunk his first day.

"He can get his own ride," said Billy, seriously. No one cared for Wade. In fact, Jack had noticed that most of the other hands referred to him as "that asshole" when Wade was out of earshot. Wade was mean to horses and cattle alike. Even the Palmers' border collies growled at him and they seemed to like everybody.

Billy and Jack had reached the bunkhouse and Charlie had come in with them to wash up before going to town. "You haven't got much for clothes," Charlie said, pointing to

27

Jack's duffel. "I can loan you some if you need 'em."

Jack laughed. "I'd have to roll up the pants legs," he said. "Besides I have some more coming. My sister's sending some of my stuff out."

"She from Kansas?" Billy asked, as he turned on the shower.

"That's right. She's a Doctor in Topeka." Jack spoke loudly over the sound of the water.

"Now we know who got all the brains," said Charlie loud enough that Billy would hear also. Charlie was combing his bushy mustache in the mirror.

"Don't waste your time on that, Charlie," parried Jack. "A comb isn't gonna help your looks any."

Just then the door opened and Wade Archer walked in. The banter stopped and Charlie picked up his chaps and started for the door. "Later, Jack," he said and slipped out. Jack lay back on his bunk in his underwear waiting on the shower. The bunkhouse was littered with well-worn paperbacks of various authors, but Jack didn't feel like reading at the moment. He thought back to the conversation with his sister, Jenny, a few nights ago at a payphone in town.

"You're in Pinedale?" she had said it in an envious tone. "Are you staying at Ethan's?" Jack had explained that he had a job at a ranch owned by some rich oil guy or something. "You had better get over there and see them this weekend or I won't send your stuff out," she scolded. "You give Ethan and Betty each a big hug for me." Jack promised to give Betty a hug and shake her husband Ethan's hand. "I wish we were able to get away. We'd love to take the boys on another pack trip. Jimmy was too young to go last time," she had said. They could have talked until his phone card was used up, but someone needed the phone, so Jack had told her to send the stuff to Ethan's address and he would call again soon. He missed seeing his family.

Jack's thoughts were interrupted as he heard the now familiar slosh of a bottle from Wade's bunk. Jack's turn came for the shower and he took a quick one as most of the hot water was used up. He grinned, figuring a cold shower might do Wade some good. Jack and Billy were soon heading to town in Billy's old Toyota pickup.

The evening was a typical one for a town like Pinedale. Jack and Billy had arrived at the Stockman's bar before Charlie, who had made a stop at Faler's, a large store that had groceries on one side and hardware on the other. Faler's had everything, including a pretty good selection of dry flies as Jack had discovered the first time he had come to Pinedale.

The bar was practically empty. It was a little early yet for the nightlife to get going. They ordered some food and a beer. Charlie showed up and they were able to talk while the bar was quiet. Jack always thought that it was funny how you could spend all day working with somebody, then go to a bar or restaurant with them and still find something to talk about. He guessed that a different atmosphere made it possible. Jack and Billy were introduced to a few more friends and acquaintances of Charlie's as they drifted in. The click of pool balls in the next room caught Billy's attention and he challenged the others to a game of eight ball.

After two or three games and several beers, Billy sat down on the long bench that stretched the length of the room past all the tables. After the first game Charlie had suggested that they partner Billy up with Jack to even things out. Billy was more of a liability than an asset, so Jack agreed. Jack had continued to win. He would let Billy break, Charlie would get in a few shots, then Jack would clear the table. Jack was only on his second beer and it sat on a shelf with a pool of condensation growing around its base. He noticed that Charlie was still nursing his first.

"You're not hitting that stuff very hard," said Jack, indicating the bottle in Charlie's hand.

"I gotta' keep my faculties about me if I'm gonna beat you," replied Charlie. "You had better do the same, if you want to get home tonight." Jack followed Charlie's eyes to the bench where Billy was slumped. The kid's eyelids were draped halfway across his irises.

"He looks like he's about ready to close up shop," said Jack, as he sunk the eight ball securing his victory.

"Remind me never to bet against you, Jack."

"I'll do that," said Jack. He turned to Billy and said, "You ready to go home?" Billy just leaned forward until he could stand and headed for the door, leaning in the direction of travel. Jack and Charlie followed him out. Billy jerked the passenger door open and fell into the seat. He tried to slam the door, but the end of a lariat rope had drifted out and wouldn't allow the door to shut. Billy gave the door a couple more slams against the end of the rope, but it wasn't going to latch.

"Hang on, Billy. You're gonna' bend the hinges," said Charlie, pulling the door open to get the rope out of the way.

Jack got in the driver's seat and felt for the keys, which were still in the ignition. He started the truck. Billy just slumped down in the seat and pulled his hat over his eyes.

"Don't know why it is, but they all think they're in a race when it comes to tossin' beers down at that age," said Charlie leaning in the open window of the pickup.

"He'll figure it out after a while," said Jack. "I guess I'll see you Monday, Charlie."

"Yeah, have a good weekend, Jack," Charlie replied, pushing away from the truck. "Good luck if you go fishin'."

"Thanks."

Jack drove to the bunkhouse and was relieved to find it empty. He woke Billy who stumbled inside, stripped down to his boxers and fell into bed like a downed tree. Jack walked back outside.

"You fellers are back early." The voice belonged to Jim Palmer, who had walked up to where Jack was standing.

"Billy was in a hurry," said Jack with a chuckle. He was looking toward the big house, which was flooded with lights. After a moment of silence, he asked, "Who owns this place, Jim?" The older man lost his smile.

"Guy's from Russia," began Jim. "Name is Yuri Aleksandrov. Most folks call him Mr. Alexander."

"What's he do for a living? Oil man?"

"No, he's some kind of import export bigshot, or some such," said Jim.

"You sound like you don't care for our boss, Jim," said Jack with a hint of sarcasm.

"Well, Jack," Jim said, confiding, "I just kind of doubt that a Rooskie like him come by all his money honestly." Both men were quiet for a moment.

"What does he sell, or import export as you say?" Jack asked.

"I don't really know. He's got offices in New York and San Francisco, that's why he needs a jet I suppose; but I think he made his money overseas," Jim replied.

"He could be legitimate," said Jack. "A lot of money to be made from one country to the next I suppose."

"Maybe so," said Jim, "but I saw a suitcase full of something one day that I don't think I was supposed to see."

"Drugs?" Jack said apprehensively.

"No, no. It was either foreign money or bonds or something. It was all in bundles, but it didn't look like greenbacks. I didn't see any drugs, but I'd be willin' to bet that's what the money was from. They just looked guilty when I walked up and they slammed the case shut."

"They?" Jack asked.

"Yeah, Yuri's got a couple of sidekicks. One long-haired, pretty boy and an exotic-looking woman. They're both about your age I'd say." Jim was sounding tired.

"Relatives?" Jack asked.

"I don't know... maybe. Alexander's only owned this place for five or six years. I wish the Carsons still had it," said Jim. Jack had heard this place called the 'Old Carson Place'. "I'll hang around a while longer and then retire I guess."

31

Jack and Jim bid each other good night. Jack walked into the bunkhouse and flopped down on his bunk. He lay awake awhile wondering why, when things seemed so good, they usually had to change. That's all he needed was to be working for a drug dealer. Who knew, maybe the Feds would bust them and Jim would have a new boss. Sometimes that's the way it worked. The hands and the foreman didn't change, but the owners did. He fell asleep to the sound of Billy snoring.

CHAPTER SIX

Saturday morning was chilly but clear. Jack was up early and dressed. He walked out of the bunkhouse and pushed his bike around the side of the tractor shed to start it. He figured Billy might have a headache and didn't want to wake him. Wade's bunk was still empty this morning. He let the bike idle a few minutes to warm the oil, and then he headed for town. The morning sun was low in the eastern sky and was turning some of the mountaintops a bright orange. Other peaks, still covered in snow, just looked incredibly clean and white. He caught a whiff of pine smoke coming from someone's woodstove. Even the dust rising from the gravel road smelled good to Jack. He liked riding a motorcycle so he could smell all the smells and feel the temperature changes from valley to hilltop. These things were easily missed in a car. Once he got to the highway he opened up the throttle and shifted to fourth. A half dozen antelope jerked their heads up and trotted away from the fence when they heard the noise of the bike.

Jack's first stop was the local auto parts store. The proprietor was open early and already doing business. Jack looked at various tools and accessories while he waited his turn. After a bit he stepped up to the counter. "I need a radiator return hose for an '83 Chevy Suburban with a 350 in it," he explained.

"I ought to have that one," the man behind the counter said, punching it up on a computer. He disappeared into the back and came out with the shaped hose. "Anything else? Clamps? Antifreeze?"

33

"A gallon of antifreeze," Jack replied, "and can you get me an oil filter for a '72 Harley-Davidson XL 1000."

The man punched it in his keyboard. "Be here Tuesday morning."

"Thanks," said Jack paying for the items. "Is this the place Reid Wilcox works?"

"It will be Monday. That's when Reid starts."

"I'm sure he'll be good help," said Jack. The man agreed.

"Since Lawrence died of cancer, Kate has sure done a fine job of raising those kids alone," said the man. Jack admitted that he hadn't known them long but he would have to agree.

The ride out to the Wilcox place felt good to Jack. The day was beginning to warm up and it was a nice one to be out riding. He pulled in to the ranch and the blue-heeler, "Freckles", came out to check him out. Jesse met him at the door.

"Hi, Jesse, how are things going?" Jack asked.

"Hi, Mr. Wallace," said Jesse smiling.

"Call me Jack," he corrected.

"My horse's name is Jack," she said. "I can't call you Jack without thinking I'm talking to the horse. Can I call you Wally?" she asked.

Jack didn't like the sound of it, but he didn't expect it to catch on. "I guess," he said, "but only *you* can call me that." She thought that was funny.

Kate came around the side of the house. "I thought that was you riding up," she said, seeming pleased. "Jesse and I are leaving to take a pie to a neighbor lady. The boys are out back, though. They'll want to show you what Reid bought."

"It's a jeep," whispered Jesse as if revealing a secret.

Jack watched them leave and walked to the back yard. Bud came bounding up to him so fast that the dog barked at him. "See Reid's jeep!" Bud spoke excitedly and pointed to the jeep sitting in the middle of the back yard. It was a late seventies CJ7 with no top, a bent bumper, and plenty of rust.

"Looks like a project, Reid," said Jack.

"I'm sure it will be," replied Reid, "but it runs and drives okay as it is." He hopped in and started it to show Jack.

"Two fifty eight?" asked Jack, listening to the motor.

"How did you know?"

"I have a '78 CJ5 in my parents' barn back in Kansas," Jack admitted. "That was my first vehicle."

"That's cool," said Bud.

"I paid eight hundred for it," said Reid.

"You'll have fun with it. Just be careful," said Jack. "And it's a good thing you work at a parts store," he said with a smile.

Jack and the brothers played with the jeep and practiced fly-casting all morning. Jack had tied his pack rod tube to his bike, so he was instructing both boys at the same time. They were getting along well and improving rapidly.

"I'll admit that I'm not really a very good fly fisherman," Jack admitted when the boys had tired of casting. They were now passing a football back and forth. "But, I'm a heck-of-a lot better than either of you!" Jack yelled, as he jumped up and intercepted Reid's pass to Bud. Both boys immediately attacked Jack and tackled him. This started a genuine free-for-all wrestling match.

"What was that?" asked Reid, suddenly finding himself on his back.

"That's a major outer reap," said Jack. "O Soto Gari."

"What?" asked Bud puzzled.

"It's a judo throw. A major outer reap," said Jack. "I shouldn't have done that to you. You could have been hurt." He helped Reid up.

"That was amazing!" said Reid. "Can you teach me?"

"I'm not really qualified to teach you," said Jack. "First you have to learn how to fall without getting hurt."

"What do you mean?" asked Reid.

"You have to learn to tuck your chin." He fell back tucking his chin and slapped the ground with his arms at a 45-degree angle. "You kind of roll down, while your reflexes are telling you to catch yourself. That way you don't get hurt or bounce your head off the ground."

Bud tried it and landed hard on his back.

"Tuck your tail, Bud." Jack showed him again. This time he rolled back up and assumed a fighting stance.

"Cool!" said Bud. "How'd you learn to do all that?"

Jack told them about taking a self-defense course with his sister. She had wanted him to take it with her when she was a freshman and he was a senior in college. They had both enjoyed it and had taken more lessons together. He told of hiding behind doors and attacking his sister; more often than not ending up with a black eye or bloody nose to show for his trouble.

"Your sister sounds pretty cool for a girl," said Bud.

"She is," said Jack, "she has two boys of her own now."

"I'll bet they think you're the coolest uncle ever!" said Bud.

"They're probably mad at me. I need to get back there and harass them soon."

Kate and Jenny finally returned. They invited Jack to eat with them again. He started to decline and then said, "I'll make a trade with you." He ran over to his bike and pulled off the sack from the parts store. "Come on Reid, you can help me."

Jack showed Reid how to drain out the antifreeze solution into a bucket. "Dogs will drink this stuff and it will kill them, so don't leave it sitting in a bucket somewhere," he cautioned. He let Reid replace the damaged hose and refill the radiator with a mixture of new antifreeze and water. "Fifty-fifty mixture," Jack instructed.

They finished and washed up to eat some lunch. When they went inside, they found that the food was put away. Kate, Jesse, and Bud had already eaten. Kate got them each a sandwich from the fridge and they ate them hungrily. Jack had not realized it was so late. He apologized for staying so long and started to leave.

"Would you go to church with us tomorrow?" asked Kate.

"Well...I can't this time," he said sheepishly. "I promised to do something else. I'd love to go next Sunday though."

"That's alright. Next Sunday then."

Jack said his good-byes and mounted the motorcycle. This had been a great day. He wished he could have gone to church with them, but he had no suitable clothes. He also had a promise to keep. He rode back into town and found the payphone again. Sitting on the sidewalk beside the phone, he used up a thirty-minute phone card talking with his parents. He then went back to the ranch.

The bunkhouse was empty when he pulled up outside it. He looked at the sun as it angled toward the hills to the west. He decided there was still plenty of daylight left, so he quickly changed into his running shorts. He went through a short stretching and warm-up routine, and he set a pace down the driveway toward the county road. He checked the watch on his wrist. It was a cheap watch that he had gotten at Wal-Mart, but it had a timer so he set it for twenty minutes.

He had gone about a mile, he guessed, when he met a Jeep Cherokee in the road. It slowed down as it got close to him. Jack stopped running and leaned on his knees, breathing hard. A thickset man with a bushy, red mustache leaned out the open window. "Who the hell are you?" he asked in a heavy accent that was unmistakably Australian.

"Jack Wallace," he said between breaths, "I work here." He was walking in small circles while he caught his breath. Suddenly he walked right up to the window of the car and said, "Now, who the hell are YOU?" He stared the man in the face. The Aussie bristled.

"A wise ass are ya" the man reached for the latch and started to open the door. When it was open about six inches, Jack grabbed the door at the bottom of the window with both hands and slammed it shut again. The Aussie was knocked back into his seat. He sputtered and began to curse, starting for the door handle again, when a big hand grabbed his shoulder from the passenger side.

"Easy Mick," said a gravelly, deep voice from the other side of the car. "This one is one of our cowboys." This guy sounded like a mobster right out of the movies. "So," the voice addressed Jack, "your name is Jack Wallace. I like that. I like it that you want to know who this stranger is," he said, patting Mick on the shoulder. "You're new here?"

"Yes," said Jack flatly, still staring down the Aussie.

"That's good. You got some spunk. You go on now and have a good jog, Mr. Jack Wallace." With his free hand he indicated to Mick to get the car moving.

The Aussie broke his gaze and threw the car in gear. Jack let go of the door and stood up just as the car took off. He stepped back further as the rear wheels slung gravel past him. He turned back down the road and resumed his run. "What have I got myself into?" he thought. He reached over and reset his timer.

CHAPTER SEVEN

Early Sunday morning Jack got up, shaved, and dressed. Billy was still asleep in his bunk snoring, as was Wade. He didn't know what time it had been when Wade had come in, but he had been awakened as much by the smell of liquor fumes as the noise the man had made. He and Billy had discussed throwing Wade in the irrigation ditch, if he didn't take a shower soon. Jack had kicked a pile of Wade's dirty clothes out onto the porch the night before in an effort to improve air quality in the bunkhouse.

Jack went outside as quietly as possible. It was early, but the sun was almost all the way up, so Jack rolled his motorcycle out, straddled it, and coasted it down the lane until he reached the ditch crossing where the drive started uphill again. There, he started the bike, let it warm up half a minute, and took off. Jim had offered to let him use one of the ranch pickups when he wanted to go to town. Jack had told him that he would do that if the weather was bad, but perhaps he should do it just because of the noise on these early morning trips. He cracked the throttle open a bit when he got to the road, enjoying the sound of the bike.

The town of Pinedale was quiet as he rode in. Someone was at the laundry mat. Jack had done his own laundry the night before at the bunkhouse. Large dips in the pavement, put there to funnel away water, crossed Pine Street, which was also 191, the main drag through the town. Jack slowed the bike at each of these and, in turn, opened the throttle slightly until he got to the next one. The sound of his pipes echoed off the buildings that lined both sides of the street. He passed on through the town staying on 191 until he saw a county shed where snowplows and various other items of maintenance equipment sat parked. He turned off on a gravel road there. The washboard surface of the road forced him to go at a snail's pace.

He soon came to a familiar ranch gateway and turned up the rutted lane. As he approached the house and buildings at the end of the lane, several dogs announced his arrival and came running to check him out. He parked the bike beside a white pickup that, judging by the fiberglass unit in the back, belonged to a veterinarian. Scattering a number of cats, Jack made his way to the door and, without knocking, walked in.

"Well I'll be damned, look what the cat dragged in," said a voice from the back of the room. "I could of used you a little bit ago. Would have saved Ross the trip." The older man doing the talking indicated a man sitting across the table from him dressed in dark green coveralls with a veterinarian's caduceus embroidered above the pocket. Both men were drinking coffee; the older man was smoking a cigarette. Jack walked over to the table and stuck out his hand, which the older man shook.

"Hello, Ethan," said Jack. He turned to take the other man's hand.

"Ross Daniels," said Ethan, "meet Jack Wallace." The two men shook hands. Jack estimated Ross to be about the same age as himself. "Jack's an attorney, but he's probably pulled as many calves as you have," Ethan said to Ross. "His dad's a vet and a helluva good one."

"Your dad drug you out on emergencies I take it," said the veterinarian, grinning broadly.

"Every time he could," said Jack, the emphasis on "every". Jack walked to the stove and helped himself to coffee. "Where's Betty?" Jack asked.

"She went to Jackson to pick up some girls at the airport," Ethan replied. "You want a little trail shortener in that coffee?" He waved toward a half-empty fifth of Jack Daniels sitting in the middle of the table.

"Better not," said Jack. "You're still doing the girls' camp then?"

"Still doin' the camp," said Ethan, "You'll have to come by in a few days. We'll have a dozen girls here. God, they'll get a kick out of seein' you ride up on that motorcycle. Is that a Harley?"

"Yeah, it's an old one. Barely made it out here."

"It sounded about like the one I had," said Ethan. Jack knew that Ethan had ridden a bike years ago. "Mine was a seventy four."

Jack looked at Ross. "He means seventy four cubic inches, not nineteen seventy four." Ross raised his chin in understanding.

"They made a smaller one, too," said Ethan.

"That was a sixty one," said Jack. "The one I'm riding is closer to that."

"What year was that Ethan?" asked Ross, interested.

"Late forties, I'd say. The motorcycle was a forty-seven." Ethan took a sip of coffee and a pull on the cigarette. He squinted in thought as the smoke rolled past his eyes. "I was working up close to Butte at the time. Bunch of us lived together and pooled our money. We all wanted to get motorcycles. We would keep the money in a drawer and when we got enough to buy a motorcycle we would draw straws to see who got it." He laughed now recalling. "I was the last one of the four to get one."

"What were you doing up in Butte?" asked Ross.

"Worked in a mine."

"I'll bet that was a rough life," said Ross.

"It was for us," said Ethan. "They wouldn't let us work together. They split us up and put us each with an older miner." He snubbed out the cigarette in an ashtray and continued. "The older guy would set the charges. Showing us how to do it, I suppose. You did that right before you quit for the day. That way the dust would clear in the tunnel, and when you come back the next day, you shovel all the shot rock into a cart and haul it out. The older guy was getting paid for however much ore he got out. So if he had some

41

young feller with him, doin' all the work, if he could work him hard enough, he got paid pretty well."

"Sounds like a hard way to make a living," said Ross.

"No harder than what you do," said Ethan. The older man laughed and said, "Everything was tough back then, but nobody knew any better."

"Was your motorcycle a Harley?" asked Ross.

"Yeah," said Ethan, "It had to be that or Indian, back then. Mine was the overhead valve kind, some of 'em got flatheads."

"That would be a Knucklehead," said Jack, "with the overhead valves back in '47." He had been listening intently. He had heard this story before, but never tired of it.

"I rode that thing working on ranches in this part of Wyoming for a few years. Got in trouble with it a few times." He laughed again as he lit up another cigarette. "I remember one time I was in a bar and I bet this guy that he couldn't stay on the back of the bike. It had a buddy seat where you could carry a passenger. We went out front of the bar and I started cuttin' didos and carryin' on to try to get rid of this guy. I ended up dumpin' the bike over and the clutch pedal went through the calf muscle on my leg."

"Did you get the guy off the back?" asked Ross.

"I don't think so," said Ethan. "He won the bet and my leg got infected. God, I was laid up for awhile during haying season."

The veterinarian looked at his watch and stood up, setting down his coffee cup. "Well, I better get home, Ethan," said Ross. "The wife will get mad if I don't help get the kids ready for church."

"You can blame it on me, Ross," said Ethan.

"We'll blame it on old Bossy out there. She's the one that decided to have trouble calving this morning," said Ross. They walked out the door scattering cats. "This place is looking more like a cat farm than a dude ranch," he said.

"Betty wants you to come out and cut all these little toms someday," said Ethan. "She won't spay the females though; she says the toms are the ones ought to get the knife."

"If you can hold them," offered Jack, "I'll neuter them. As long as Ross doesn't turn me in for practicing without a license."

"I'll tell you what," said Ross, "I'll give you some ketamine and you can work for me and do the job. Ethan won't get all scratched up that way." He walked to the back of his truck and pulled out two bottles of the anesthetic and added a cc of acepromazine to each. He handed the bottles to Jack with a couple of small disposable syringes and a scapel blade.

"Got a hemostat I can borrow?" asked Jack.

"There you go," said Ross, tossing Jack a small curved forceps.

"Let me see," said Jack. "A ten pound cat gets about a cc. Is that right?"

"Yep, most of these will take about half that," he said. "Be careful with that, it's a controlled substance now, you know."

"That's what Dad said. They use it for a date-rape drug," said Jack. He started to hand the bottles to Ethan.

"You better keep track of that until you get a chance to use it," said Ethan. Jack put the bottles in a zippered pocket on his jacket.

"Keep track of what you use and get the rest back to me," said Ross. "Cindy will throw a fit if the records don't match the inventory." Cindy was his vet technician.

"We'll even name all the cats and start records while we do it," said Jack. "If the camp girls haven't named them already."

Ross drove off, waving. Ethan turned to Jack. "You come out to go fishin'?" he asked.

"Mostly," said Jack. "I'm working out at the Circle "A".

"Is that right?" Ethan raised an eyebrow. "Some folks don't like the Circle "A" much."

"Because the owner's some rich foreigner?" asked Jack.

"Probably," said Ethan. "But Jim Palmer is a good

43

guy. He ran the place for Carsons for years."

"Yeah, I really like Jim," said Jack. "I've been riding a week already."

"You don't say," said Ethan. "Jim's got good horses. I'm sure you'll like working there. I knew you were comin'," said Ethan changing the subject. "Some boxes come yesterday addressed to you." He ushered Jack back inside. "You ain't gonna' be able to haul 'em on that motorcycle though. They're pretty big." He indicated two large boxes off in a corner.

"Jenny must have sent these the day after I called," said Jack.

"How is Jenny?" asked Ethan, "And that husband of hers...Mark?"

"They're all doing fine," said Jack.

"I believe that pack trip we took you folks on was the best one we ever had," said Ethan. "That Jenny is a tough girl," he added, "I'll bet she can outwork most men."

"Oh, I'm sure that's right," said Jack. They sat back down and poured more coffee. "I'll just get a few things now, and get the rest when I come over in a pickup," said Jack indicating the boxes. He realized he now had clothes and could still make it to church, but he didn't know which one the Wilcox's went to. Jack and Ethan reminisced about previous fishing trips that Ethan had taken with Jack's dad. They spent several hours talking and walking around looking at horses and cattle. Jack told Ethan that he planned to hike up into the Winds the next weekend if the weather looked good.

"You can take a horse from here if you want," said Ethan. "We've got plenty." Jack said that he thought he would just walk in. He needed the exercise. "There's not much graze for a horse up there yet anyway," said Ethan. "You going to Trapper Lake?" he asked.

"Either that or I'll start at Elkhart Park and see how far I can get."

"You're wanting to go back to Island Lake where you caught that big trout with the mice in it. Aren't you?" Ethan said with a laugh.

"I'd like to," said Jack, "but I doubt if I'll have time for that." Ethan's memory for details always amazed Jack.

Jack went through the two boxes and found his backpack. He stuffed it with items of clothes and a few odds and ends. He came across his Haynes repair manual for his Jeep. Originally he had planned to get the jeep when he got tired of riding the Harley. He put the manual in the pack, thinking he would give it to Reid when he saw him. He also came across his Colt automatic, wrapped in a silicone cloth. He decided to take the old 45 with him just to get it out of a house that would soon be overrun with teenage girls. The pack was heavy as he lifted it and he carried it out and tied it to the short sissy bar on the motorcycle. He didn't want to be in the way when Betty came back with a vanload of girls, so he told Ethan good-bye and headed back for the ranch.

When he was almost back at the ranch, as he passed the end of the runway, he met a beige sedan coming off an intersecting road. The man was looking toward the big house and driving slowly. The car sped up when the driver saw Jack, and he drove back toward the highway. Although the car was unmarked, it was unmistakably "official". Jack figured it was a BLM bureaucrat or something and didn't think any more about it.

CHAPTER EIGHT

"Man, you look tired, Bingo. You been having trouble with your dryers again?" asked a casually dressed white man on his way to work at a radio station in Los Angeles.

"It ain't the laundry, C. J., it's this damn place. I got no help all the sudden." The man behind the counter was a middle-aged black man with a stubble of gray beard showing and tired, bloodshot eyes. He had acquired the nickname of 'Bingo' after winning the bingo game five times in a row at the Knights of Columbus hall at St. Theresa's. He had come away with five hundred dollars that night and had started his own business, a corner newsstand, which he had parlayed into several businesses over the years. They were standing in a Seven-Eleven right at the edge of Inglewood, California in south central Los Angeles. Bingo owned this store and a nearby coin-operated laundry plus a dry-cleaning shop.

"What happened to Hadji and his brother Daryl," the man asked. He had always referred to Bingo's hired help as "Hadji" like the sidekick on Johnny Quest, even though the guy wasn't Indian.

"They drew their last paycheck and took off," the black man said with resignation. "Now I got two back-to-back shifts to fill and nobody wants to work. At least nobody that can make change for a dollar."

"Won't the cash register pretty well do that for them?" the man named C. J. asked.

"Yeah, but you still have to know a quarter from a nickel and be able to swipe a credit card. The idiots that come in here looking for a job only want one long enough to

46

get money for dope, then they party for a few days and don't show up for work."

"Hadji was here for a long time wasn't he?" asked C. J.

"Shoot yes," said Bingo. "He was here for ten years and brought in his cousin about four years ago. They didn't say much but they were good help."

"Why'd they take off, do you know?"

"Don't know. It was out of the blue for me. They'd been savin' their money though, because they drove out of here in a pretty new fancy car. It was a big black Jaguar. I never knew either one of them to drive."

"They had that kind of money?" asked C. J. drawing himself a Big Gulp of Diet Coke.

"I guess so. I asked them if they stole the car. They said they bought it off a used lot over in Florence. It was a couple years old. Maybe Jags don't hold their value. I don't know."

"So you're running this place and the cleaner shop without any help?"

"Oh, the cleaners will run itself with Jimmy there. Long as nothing breaks down. It's just that I had come to rely on Hamad to run this place. He was good. A reliable, conscientious man...even if he was a sand nigger. I even kind of miss the guy."

"Yeah, he was alright," said C.J. "He even tried to follow the Lakers, but maybe that was just to have something to talk about. He didn't seem like all that big a fan." The man paused and sipped his soda. "You think maybe they got spooked with all this anti-Arab stuff goin' around?"

"Shoot. What anti-Arab stuff? Those people got more rights than I do, what with all the politically correct bullshit that goes on," huffed Bingo.

"Yeah, but maybe they were afraid some gang-banger would have a flicker of patriotism and come by and shoot 'em for sport."

"More likely they'd shoot me, if they found out I was a Republican," said Bingo.

"Your secret's safe with me, Bingo." C. J. picked up a copy of the Times and perused the sports pages. "Were you here during the race riots? That Rodney King fiasco?" he asked, making conversation.

"You bet I was. I was protectin' my property from those idiots. They burned down a mini-mall right up the street where that damned Clean-and-Go set up shop in that tin shed they call a building." He was referring to a rival dry-cleaning establishment that had come in about three years ago. "Ol' Hadji was right here with me."

"You gotta be kiddin'," said C. J., astonished.

"He was right here behind this counter packin' my nickel plate three-fifty-seven. I think he knew how to use it too." Bingo took a sip of cold coffee from a paper cup he had next to the cash register.

"You gave Hadji a gun?" asked C. J., incredulous.

"You bet I did. We didn't have much choice. Those crazy people were burnin' and lootin' everything. It wasn't all blacks either. There was teenage white-boys and leftover commie-types from the hippie days joining in on the act. They just used the riots as an excuse to go nuts." Bingo laughed as he recalled. "You should of seen it. I was hanging out over at the laundry with the shotgun, when I saw this old, tall, hippie guy come runnin' up to the store. I figured Hamad might need a little help so I come over and snuck in the back door. That hippie guy come tearin' through the doors with a piece of pipe about four feet long in his hands. The guy must have been fifty years old. He cocked that pipe back and took a look at Hamad and that cash register and took about one more step, when old Hadji pulled that long barreled three-fifty-seven out from under the counter and said, 'Go ahead, punk...make my day!'. It was in that damn accent of his. Didn't sound much like Clint Eastwood, but it shore done the trick. That old hippie dropped the pipe and turned around and ran out the door. He got clear of gun range and started yelling, 'Anarchy Rules!'. Hadji come around the counter and followed him out the door. I think he would have shot him in the back if he hadn't

48

turned around to see who was laughin' so hard in the back of the store." Bingo was laughing so hard now he could barely finish the story. "Yeah, I'm gonna miss old Hadji."

Barely three blocks away Hamad Al-Busaid and his cousin, Fahad bin Rahman, were loading up the last of their meager belongings into the back seat of the shiny black Jaguar. They were both well-dressed in new suits from a nearby outlet store. If you did not look too closely at the two men, and didn't notice the mediocre quality of their suits, you would think that you were looking at a pair of misplaced oil sheiks from the Arabian Peninsula. They had dawned their traditional Arab headdresses for the first time in ten years for Hamad. They were ready to begin the journey of journeys, the trip of a lifetime, or maybe the trip to end one. By late tonight they would be in Boise, where the machinery was in motion for the next phase of the journey. They spoke to each other in Arabic, but any onlooker could have seen how excited they were that it was finally happening. It was all they could do not to high five each other as they turned up the on-ramp for I-110. Before long they were on I-5 headed north, riding in style with the cruise control on, and listening to soft rock on the radio. By afternoon they would be headed East on I-80 toward Reno, then north on 95 at Winnemucca. The sky was clear as a bell, it was a beautiful day, and they were headed for Paradise...by way of Wyoming.

CHAPTER NINE

Monday morning brought an overcast sky and a smattering of rain. The cowboys were catching horses and saddling their mounts. They were loading them onto a big aluminum-bodied gooseneck stock trailer hitched to one of the ranch's one-ton, dually pickups. A shiny new Ford Thunderbird, one of the retro-looking models that recently came out, pulled up to where Jim Palmer stood holding open the trailer endgate. The car was a pearl white color and had its removable hardtop in place with the little landau window. The driver's window came down and a distinguished looking, older man in fine dark clothes leaned his head out. "Mr. Palmer, where will you be working today?" the man asked.

"Be over at the Hollis place," said Jim, matter-of-factly, "Gotta' move some cows."

"Marion will follow you over there. He is going to get me some photographs of you cowboys, away from the vehicles of course, to send to a friend of mine in Europe," said the man.

"That'll be fine," said Jim. The man thanked Jim, gave him a big smile and drove off. As he wheeled the car around he slowed down and his passenger, a dark-bearded, somewhat younger man, rolled down his window and said something to Wade, who was just now saddling his horse. Jack could see that the passenger had a long, black, braided ponytail hanging over the back of the car's white seat. "Christ," said Jim, "This is a damn dog and pony show to them."

50

"I take it that was Mr. Yuri Aleksandrov," said Jack.

"That was him," said Jim, disgust evident in his voice.

"And the other guy was Marion?" Jack asked.

"No, Marion's older, this guy is the pretty boy I was tellin' you about," said Jim. "His name is Sasha. I guess that's short for somethin' in Russia."

"Sounds like a girl's name. Don't it?" said Charlie coming up to them.

"Sure does," said Jack smiling.

"Marion's Yuri's driver from Chicago or some such. He's nothing but a thug if you ask me," said Jim. The conversation stopped when Wade came up leading his horse. The horse stepped onto the trailer and Jim shut the gate.

They rode over to the Hollis place piled into the crew cab pickup. Jack could tell that Wade still hadn't taken a shower. The corrals where they would start their gather were within site of the headquarters, but it was quicker to haul the horses. You can see a long ways in Wyoming.

At the corrals they all piled out and began pulling horses off the trailer and tightening cinches, when the black Jeep Cherokee pulled up. Jack could see that it was the same two characters that had accosted him on the road the day before. The Aussie was not the driver this time.

"That would be Marion," said Jim. He had noticed Jack eyeing the newcomers.

"We've met," said Jack coldly.

Not wanting anything to do with those two, Jack mounted up, followed closely by Charlie, Abe, and Billy. They walked their horses, but moved steadily on out toward the pasture. Jack figured they could get pictures of his backside, if they wanted them. He heard the warble of a cell phone and turned around. He could see Jim reach into his vest pocket and pull out a phone. Wade was just now mounting up a little bit behind Jim. Jack turned back around and began scanning the pasture for signs of the herd.

Suddenly, Jack heard the squeal of a horse and a yell. All four of the riders turned around and saw Jim falling against the fence and Wade was on the ground between the two horses. Jack wheeled his horse and spurred him back to the corral. He jumped off the buckskin before it had even stopped and rushed to Jim's side.

"Jim! Jim! Are you hurt?" Jack asked, cradling the man's limp head in his hands. Jim didn't respond at first. Jack rolled him off his side, straightening out his legs so that he lay flat on his back. Jim's right arm stuck out at an odd angle.

"Call an ambulance!" he yelled at no one in particular. Charlie had dismounted and was helping Wade to his feet when both doors on the Cherokee opened. The men from the car walked up and surveyed the situation.

"Call a damn ambulance!" Jack repeated, infuriated by their attitude.

"Toss 'im in the Jeep," said Mick. "That'll be a hell of a lot quicker than an ambulance." Neither man moved a muscle towards helping Jack pick up Jim and carry him toward the vehicle. Jim moaned as Jack pulled him up by his left arm.

"I think his shoulder is dislocated," said Jack. He jerked the door open and laid Jim gently inside. By this time Charlie had come to lend a hand. Jack quickly moved to the other side of the vehicle, opening the door to get in. Mick pushed the door back shut roughly, staring Jack down.

"No passengers," he said. "Back to work. We'll take this man to town. He's not hurt that bad."

Jack was fuming. "Take him to the clinic in Pinedale, as fast as you can get there."

Mick got in on the driver's side and Marion on the other. Jack thought they moved with deliberate slowness. He watched them pull away down the drive. Jack winced as the Jeep bounced down the rutted lane past the corrals, thinking about Jim.

"Let's get these cows moved to the government land so we can get back to town," said Billy.

"I'm with you," said Charlie.

Jack was looking at the ground near Jim's horse. He

reached down and picked up the cell phone. He hadn't even known that Jim carried a cell phone. He had never seen him use it. When he looked at it, he notice that the number showing on the display was only one digit off of the number printed on the attached sticker, which he assumed was the number of the phone he was holding. "Must have been talking to the boss," he thought. He pocketed the phone, tied Jim's horse to the fence, and mounted his own horse to catch up with the others. Wade, Jack noticed, limped over to the truck and climbed in the back seat. He slumped in the seat as if in pain. Jack just scowled, leaning over to gather the reins of the other loose horse. He tied it to the fence also and rode off after the others.

Out in the pasture Jack was pushing his horse hard. The cows with calves didn't want to move and some of the calves were having trouble keeping up. The pasture was rough and covered in sage. Jack came around a skinny, old Hereford cow with a small calf and realized that she needed to be taken back to the ranch. She had cancer-eye and would never make it through to wean the calf. His frustration was showing. He wanted to get this job done fast and get back to check on Jim. He should never have taken off without him. Jack tried to cut the cow and calf out but she ran into some brush next to a ravine. Jack tried to follow but Buck balked at the steep bank in front of him. Jack yelled at him and spurred him hard. The big buckskin still would not go. The horse moved sideways and Jack could see down into the ravine. The cow had jumped off the bank and fallen. She had evidently broken her front leg and was trying to get back up. The leg would crumple at the fracture and she would fall each time she tried to stand. "Well I'll be damned," said Jack in absolute frustration. Buck pranced and backed up as the calf bawled and ran out of the brush past them. Jack was ashamed of himself now. He patted the sweaty neck of the big horse and closed his own eyes for a moment. He had blown his cool completely and he knew it. "I'm sorry Buck. There're just too many things going wrong all at once," he said to the horse. Jack uncoiled his rope from the saddle and caught the calf. He tied its legs with a pigging string and left the calf where he could pick it up on the way back. He went on to help with the cows.

When Jack came up to the herd, Billy was the first person he saw. "You wouldn't happen to be packin' would you?" he asked Billy.

"What?"

"I got a cow needs shootin'," said Jack.

"What's her problem?" asked Charlie, overhearing the conversation.

"Cancer-eye for one and a broke leg for another," Jack said with a note of disgust.

"I bet she would be grateful for a quick demise, then," said Charlie. "There's a twenty two behind the seat in the truck."

"You guys got these then?" asked Jack, dipping his head toward the gather of cows and calves.

"We'll handle it from here," said Charlie.

"I guess I've got it to do then," said Jack with resignation. He rode off quickly to the pickup to get the gun.

When Jack got to the pickup, Wade Archer was asleep in the seat with his hat pulled over his eyes and his feet sticking out the open window. Jack dismounted and tied the reins loosely to the brush guard on the front of the truck. He moved to the back of the truck and opened the door. Archer had evidently heard his horse walk up. The man lifted his hat and looked at Jack upside down. "I need you to move so I can get something from behind the seat," said Jack. Wade, ever so slowly pulled his feet down, opened the door, put on his hat and stepped out of the truck. Jack flipped the latch and pulled the seat forward to access the area behind it. He found an old Marlin lever-action 22 rifle in a leather saddle scabbard. He pulled it out and checked the action. The gun was well oiled, as was the scabbard, and showed much sign of use. He could see that the chamber was empty. He started to open the tubular magazine. The spring inside pushed it open and he pushed it back in, feeling it click along a line of cartridges. The gun had plenty of shells. He walked back around to Buck and fitted the scabbard under the fender skirt of the saddle, strapping it on. Wade Archer just watched him through this whole process. Jack mounted up.

"You want me to come help?" asked Wade.

"No." said Jack. He thought about saying "You've done enough", but he didn't. "We're pretty well finished," he said instead.

"What's the gun for?" Wade asked.

"Gotta put a cow down."

"I could do that," said Wade. A grin spread across the man's face.

"I'll handle it," said Jack and he turned and rode away. He thought about Archer. Offering to kill the cow was the only time Jack could think of that Wade had wanted to do anything close to work. The grin on the cowboy's face had been almost evil, as if he would really enjoy killing an old cow.

When he got back to the ravine, the cow was lying sternally. Her head jerked around and she made a few more feeble attempts at getting up when she heard Jack's horse. He dismounted and pulled the gun from its sheath. He tangled Buck's reins in the small branches of a nearby willow and he slid down the bank, keeping the gun up out of the dirt. The cow made one more attempt to get up. She finally made it and stood quivering on the good front leg. She tried to put some weight on the broken one, but each time she did, she nearly fell. Jack walked around to the front of her, staying back so that she would not get too excited. The cow watched him with her muscles twitching and bobbed her head at him. She wanted to charge him, but she didn't for fear of falling. Jack squared up with the cow as she faced him. He ran the action of the gun and watched through the side port to see that a shell went into the chamber.

"Well, old girl," he said. "I'll try to make this as painless as possible." The cow snorted at him and bobbed

55

her head again. He raised the gun to his shoulder and made an imaginary "X" between her ears and eyes. He aimed the rifle at the middle of the "X" and fired. The little gun seemed unnaturally loud in the bottom of the ravine. The cow froze for a moment, stunned, and then she fell over on her side. Her back legs kicked a couple of times and with a grunt she went still. Jack methodically released the spring pressure on the magazine and ejected the spent casing. He closed the action on the empty chamber and pushed the rod back up in the magazine. Even though Jack knew that he had done what was best, he still disliked having to shoot cows.

He walked back up out of the ravine and sheathed the rifle. The calf was still lying there with three legs tied together. It struggled to get up when Jack approached. He picked it up, still tied and walked up to Buck. The horse snorted and shied away at first, but Jack talked to him and finally he settled down. Jack pushed the calf up onto the saddle, hooking its legs over the saddle horn. He climbed up behind it.

"We're going to have to find you a new mother little fella'," Jack said to the calf. He spoke to the horse and touched his sides. The calf was small due to lack of milk from the cancer-eyed cow, so he wasn't that much extra weight. Buck walked all the way back to the pickup. Jack was wondering who was going to bottle feed this calf. Jim would know what to do with it. This wasn't likely the first orphan. Thinking of Jim, he urged the horse into a little faster walk.

As he got to the corral and pickup, Jack could see that the other cowboys were almost back also. He put the calf in the back of the truck still tied and they loaded the horses. Wade said nothing and no one spoke to him. Jack got into the driver's seat and the rest piled in. They all rode in silence back to the ranch. Once there, they all piled out and unloaded their horses.

"What the hell happened out there anyway," Jack asked Wade.

"I don't know," said Wade, "my horse started bucking and I fell into Jim."

That was all that was said. Jack, Charlie, and Billy piled into Charlie's pickup and headed for Pinedale.

They arrived at the Pinedale Clinic and inquired about Jim. No one seemed to know anything about the incident.

"What the hell?" said Charlie, "You reckon they hauled him to Jackson?"

"Can you check on that?" asked Jack of the nurse at the desk.

"Certainly," she said. They waited while she was on the phone. "The emergency room at Jackson says that they did receive a patient," she said, still listening on the phone. "Oh, my word," the girl said, "He was reported as DOA. Apparently he died before he got there," she interpreted.

"Couldn't be," the voice was Billy's, "He wasn't hurt that bad." The nurse was on the phone, double-checking the identity. Jack and Charlie just stood there waiting. Neither could think of any words to say.

"Yes, sir," the nurse explained, "Jim died at 10:34 a.m."

"He was way too good a fellow to die like that," said Charlie finally.

Jack couldn't even speak. He could not believe that such an accident could cause the death of a good man like Jim.

CHAPTER TEN

"What do we do now?" asked Billy. They were in the parking lot of the clinic.

"Let's go to the Stockman's," said Charlie. "A man's gotta eat."

Charlie was driving and he pulled into the parking lot at the Stockman's Bar and Restaurant. They went inside and ordered food. Jack walked through the poolroom on his way to the bathroom. Wade Archer was playing pool and drinking beer as if nothing had ever happened. His partner was John Kirby, the loud-mouthed outfitter that Jack had seen that first Sunday in the café at Big Piney. Jack just looked at him and then went into the bathroom. When Jack walked back through the poolroom, Wade said, "Hey, Wallace, I hear you been bangin' Larry Wilcox's old lady." He was leaning over for a shot. Jack walked up to him and, without a word, pulled back and swung a fist to Wade's nose. The crack of the punch was loud and all pool playing stopped as jaws dropped all around the room. Wade went down like a dropped marionette. Jack waited a moment for him to get up, which didn't look likely, then he walked out of the room. Kirby bent over Wade's limp form.

"You damned fool," said Kirby as Archer started to stir. A cigarette bounced in his lips as he spoke. "I don't know why you gotta run your mouth without lettin' your brain have time to catch up." He gathered the dazed figure up and half carried him out through the bar. They passed the table where Jack and the others sat. The waitress stood holding their plates, ready to set on the table. She was

58

staring at Kirby and Archer as they made their way past. Kirby didn't look at them and Archer seemed to be focusing on the floor in front of him.

"I'm not so sure I wanta' work for this outfit any more," said Charlie. The three cowboys ate in silence and then started back to the ranch.

Mick and Marion had followed the cowboys to the Hollis place and sat in there vehicle waiting. "Think he'll pull it off?" Mick asked.

"We will soon see," Marion replied, pulling out his cell phone and dialing. The phone began to ring. He watched as Jim Palmer fumbled for the cell phone Marion had given him only the day before. He finally answered.

"Palmer," he said, "Who's this?"

"Mr. Palmer, I want to take some photographs of you and your men and horses..." Marion was going on and on when he saw Wade lunge off of his horse and strike Jim with an elbow to the head. Jim hadn't seen it coming at all and fell hard into the fence as Wade caught himself across Jim's saddle and slid on down to the ground. Marion stopped talking, closed the phone and waited. He watched Palmer's form lying against the fence. The other cowboys were coming back now.

"That was better than I thought, Mary," said Mick. "None of the other blokes saw it at all."

"Let's go," said Marion, "and wipe that idiotic smile off your face. The man's just had an accident." They got out of the car and watched as Wallace, the new guy, kind of took over. Mick shut him down when he tried to ride to the hospital with them. Marion had to suppress a smile when this was happening. He knew that Mick already hated Jack. They convinced the others that they could haul Jim to the clinic. After loading the injured foreman, they drove back to the county road and turned towards the highway. Out of sight of the cowboys, Mick turned the Cherokee down a little-used ranch road and stopped where the road was partially hidden by an outcropping of rock. Both men got out and Marion opened the door to the back where Jim lay across the seat. Mick had retrieved a long handled shovel from the back of the vehicle. Marion gently pulled Jim's semi-conscious form from the backseat and leaned him against the side of the Cherokee. He then stepped away and said, "Mr. Palmer, you should not put your nose in other people's business." Mick swung the shovel in a wide arc like a baseball bat. It struck Jim squarely in the back of the head with a loud ring. The old foreman dropped to the ground in a heap.

"What was that?" said Mick. Both men had heard what sounded like a gasp and some rocks rolled from the outcropping above them.

"Go see," said Marion. "I'll tend to this."

Mick ran down the road far enough to see around the rocky burm. He heard the pounding of hooves and saw a black and white pinto pony and its small rider disappearing into an arroyo. "Shit!" he exclaimed.

Mick was panting from having run back up the road when he returned to the Jeep. Marion was holding a leather glove over Jim's mouth and nose to insure that the man had breathed his last. His fingers were blanched white at the tips where he held pressure on the glove. "Some kid on a pony," said Mick between breaths.

"That's not good," Marion stated. "Where does this road go?"

"It swings around by a couple of small ranches and then back out to the highway."

"Let's go," said Marion, pulling his hand away from the foreman's face. He tossed the glove into the back of the jeep. Together they picked up the lifeless form and shoved Jim into the backseat. Marion got in on the driver's side this time. He turned the vehicle around in the middle of the gravel road and went back out to the main road. "I'll take this man to the ER in Jackson. That might make it easier to deal with than if we take him into Pinedale where he is well known." He paused for a moment, thinking. "We will have to find out who the kid was. I'll drop you at the ranch. You get your car and check this road out. If you can do it without getting caught, find where the kid lives and watch to see if he goes anywhere."

"Want me to grab the kid?" asked Mick.

"Only if he's alone." Marion swung around in the drive by the guesthouse near the big ranch house. He let Mick out and sped back down the drive and turned toward the highway.

Once on the highway Marion turned on the radio. He pressed the search button and let it look for a channel. He wasn't listening anyway so it didn't really matter. He just wanted a little noise so he could think. The whole plan had gone so well until the thing with the kid. He looked at the cell-phone that he had laid in the seat. He thought about calling the boss, but then thought better of it. You didn't discuss stuff like that on a cellular phone. It wasn't the boss's problem anyway; it was his. In fact, the boss need never know if he played his cards right. The kid could have an accident too. The town of Pinedale could mourn two accidental deaths as easily as one. He smiled, but the smile quickly faded. They had work to do. He hoped Mick could handle his end. The Aussie was devious but he wasn't all that smart sometimes.

Reid Wilcox drove his rusty Jeep into the yard and climbed out. His new job had started early that morning, sorting parts that came in on a truck after midnight. That allowed him to get off early in the afternoon. He was surprised to find Bud home alone, watching TV. "What do you think you're doing, Bud?" Reid scolded. "If you didn't show up to Mrs. Brewster's again, Mom's gonna' skin you alive."

"Shut up!" said Bud, "Leave me alone!" He ran out of the house and to the barn.

"Wonder what's eatin' him?" Reid said to himself

61

opening the refrigerator.

Bud was supposed to go to the neighbors with Jesse while Kate was at work. Kate left early and had dropped Jesse off. Bud often rode over on his bicycle after doing morning feeding. Sometimes he hung around the house and watched TV, delaying going over to Mrs. Brewster's. Bud considered the neighbor's place to be pretty boring. The old lady was nice and doted on the kids, but she didn't have a satellite receiver. The kids had to entertain themselves with games and feeding the big trout in the pond behind the house. The pond was pretty neat. It had irrigation water diverted through it and had been stocked with trout, which were fed regularly and had grown to enormous size. The moving water and the little spillway provided some enter- tainment, but that only went so far.

Bud had been watching the "Western Channel" on the dish at home lately. It didn't take much imagination out here to pretend you were back in the Old West. On this day he had saddled his pony and ridden over on Circle "A" land. He had been pretending to "injun up" on an imaginary foe when he had witnessed the murder of Jim Palmer. Bud had not been able to see who got hit with the shovel and he didn't know either of the other two men. He had run his pony all the way home, stripped the saddle off the sweat-lathered horse, and had been staring out the windows of the house the remainder of the morning. He wasn't sure what he had seen, now, but it scared him. He had wanted to tell Reid, but he thought Reid would think he was making up an excuse for ditching the babysitter. He had ditched before and worried everyone and gotten in big trouble. He had tried to lie his way out of it, which didn't work at all; in fact, it had just ruined his credibility and right now, he didn't know what to do. He doubted that anyone would believe him. He cringed each time he thought about the ringing sound the shovel had made when it hit the man in the head.

Bud started back for the house. He could hear Reid on the phone when he got closer.

"Mrs. Brewster?" Reid inquired into the handset. "Bud's at home, so don't worry about him. He'll get his backside warmed when Mom gets home. She'll ground him for the rest of the summer." He paused listening. "Okay then. Mom will be home shortly and she'll pick Jesse up." He put down the phone.

Bud didn't go in. He went back out and curried the dried sweat off his pony and turned him out into the front pasture. He decided to avoid Reid for now.

CHAPTER ELEVEN

Back at the Circle "A" several cars were parked at the old ranch headquarters. A solemn-faced preacher and his wife and another older couple were offering their sympathy and prayers for Nadine, Jim's wife. Word had made it to the bunkhouse that the cowboys were to take the rest of the week off and that the funeral would be on Friday. Some out of state relatives were flying in to attend the service. Charlie had gone on home and Billy was going into town to buy some clothes for the funeral. Jack decided to take one of the ranch pickups and go over to Ethan's to get the rest of his clothes. He chose an older Ford that was only used to feed with, but was licensed. He headed for town.

Ethan was already aware of the tragedy and lamented the passing of a good man. Jack found the excitement of all the girls at the ranch was more than he needed at the moment, so he didn't stay long. He was coming back toward the Circle "A" when he turned down the road to the Wilcox place. He felt the blood rise in his face when he thought of the remarks Wade had made at the Stockman's.

Jack realized that it was right at suppertime when he pulled up to the Wilcox home. He decided that he couldn't just back out and leave, so he went to the door. He was invited in and offered supper which he declined, saying he had already eaten. The mood was somber and Bud had not touched his food at all. Reid had explained that Bud was in the doghouse. Bud stood up and left the room without saying a word.

"I don't know what's wrong with that boy," said

Kate. "When he heard about Jim Palmer's accident he cried and cried. We really didn't know Jim and Nadine well, but Jim is the one who Bud got his pony from."

"I didn't know Jim that well either," said Jack, "but I really liked him, too." Jack thought of the repair manual and went to the pickup to get it for Reid. Reid excused himself from the table and followed Jack outside.

"What are you boys doing the next couple days, Reid?" Jack asked.

"I've got to work and Bud will hang out at Brewster's I guess."

"I think I'm going to hike up into the mountains for a couple of days. I could do with some solitude. I thought you guys might be able to go with me," said Jack.

"You can ask Mom," said Reid, "she might be glad to get rid of Bud for a day or two."

Jack went back in to where Kate was cleaning up the dishes. He explained what he had in mind. She thought that it sounded like a good idea and agreed that Bud should go. Perhaps it would do Bud some good to hear someone else talk about responsibility and integrity. Jack promised that he would try to counsel the boy.

"I don't have to work tomorrow," she said. "We'll go to town in the morning and get a few things for your hike." Jack told her not to overdo it, that it was only overnight, and that he and Bud would have to carry it all on their backs. He said that he would have to ask for the use of the Circle "A" truck to drive up to the trailhead, but Kate offered to let them use the old pickup from their ranch. He said good-bye and headed back to the Circle "A".

Mick had spotted the little pinto pony, still showing wet saddle marks, in the front pasture of a small ranch soon after he had been let off to get his car. An old rusty jeep had been the only vehicle that he had seen until an old blue Suburban had come up the drive late in the afternoon. A woman had left the vehicle and gone into the house. Mick

65

had waited, expecting cop cars to show up, or the family to take a trip to town to the sheriff's office. Neither happened. Maybe the kid didn't see anything after all.

The Australian had given up after a while and went into town to grab a bite to eat. He pulled into the gas station/convenience store and was loading his arms with packaged honey buns and potato chips when he heard the clerk talking to a customer about the "accident". At first Mick began to put the food back and was considering slinking back out of the store. He thought that the kid must have told what happened. It was too quick for anyone to have heard the news from Jackson. Another customer came in and was confronted with the news.

"I already heard," said the patron. "I was in Stockman's when Charlie and them boys come in with the news."

"So it was Wade Archer's horse that threw a fit?" asked the clerk.

"Way I heard it," said the man, "just a freak accident." The guy pointed to some cigarettes behind the counter and the clerk, familiar with his preference, pulled down two hard packs of Marlboros and handed them to him. "That one rider," continued the man, "must have thought it was Archer's fault. He decked Wade in the pool room at Stockman's."

Mick had heard enough to reassure him that the plan was working on this end. He laid his goods on the counter and said nothing as the clerk rang it up. He decided to get back out to where the kid lived and watch a while longer.

Mick had fallen asleep after his snack and was awakened when an old Ford came chugging up the lane to the house and a man got out. The sun was getting low and Mick could not see what the man looked like. He didn't recognize the pickup as belonging to the Circle "A"; he hadn't paid much attention to the ranching end of things. "Must be Daddy coming home," he mused to himself. He waited a while longer and then decided to drive by one time. It was about an eighth of a mile up the driveway, but with the lights on in the house, Mick could see them sitting around the supper table. Suddenly, he heard a screen door slam; the sound was crisp in the clear evening air. A kid came running out from the house and went to the barn. Mick had stopped in the road. "What's the matter little lad?" he said to himself. "Mommy and Daddy don't believe your story?" He went on to the highway and made the circuit once more. As he came again to his earlier surveillance point, he saw the old Ford leaving with only the driver in it. "What's this?" he asked himself, "Daddy going to talk with the sheriff?" But much to his relief he saw the truck turn to the right when it got to the highway. "I believe we may be home free," he said. He watched a little while longer and then went back to the ranch to report to Marion.

Jack walked out to the barn to see if he could find Bud. He could see light leaking out through the cracks between the boards on the old shed. He swung the door open enough to enter and saw Bud sitting on the seat of the old Panhead. His eyes were wet with tearstains and Jack immediately felt sorry for him.

"You okay?" he asked.

"Fine." Bud turned his face away as he gave the short reply. He was trying to wipe the tears away, not wanting this man, whom he looked up to, to know he had been crying.

"I'm feeling kind of down in the dumps, myself," said Jack. "I was thinking that maybe you and I could go for a little hike. Maybe stay up in the mountains for a night." He paused to let that soak in and then he continued. "We could take some fly rods and maybe do a little real fishing." Bud was staring at the gas tank on the old bike. Jack could hear the occasional sniff. "Would you be interested in going?"

"Yes, sir." He answered politely but without enthusiasm.

"Okay. I talked to your mother and she said it would

be all right. She's going to get us some food in the morning and then we'll go to the trailhead. You'll need your best walking shoes. Something that's well broken-in 'cause if your feet get sore, it can get pretty miserable." Bud simply nodded and climbed off the bike. Jack patted him on the shoulder and pulled the cord on the light as they went outside.

CHAPTER TWELVE

"Maybe the kid didn't see anything," said Mick, fixing himself an egg sandwich in the kitchen of the guesthouse.

"We need to find out," said Marion. "We can't leave that kind of loose end."

"Okay then, let's drive over there and ask the kid if he saw us kill a man," said Mick sarcastically, his mouth was full of sandwich and bits of runny, yellow yolk hung in his mustache.

"Maybe we will," said Marion. At this Mick stopped chewing and stared at him.

The two men got into Mick's car and drove over to the Wilcox place. Mick stopped in the same spot where he had watched from the day before. "Now what?" asked Mick.

"Is that the pony?" Marion asked. He pointed at the pinto grazing close to the entryway.

"That's it alright. Hey, there's a kid out there." He indicated a blonde-haired little girl feeding another small gelding out of a bucket.

"Drive on up there. Let's talk to the little girl," Marion motioned with his hand as he spoke. Mick pulled into the driveway and stopped. Jesse looked at him through the fence. He started to get out, but Freckles, the blueheeler, came bounding up snarling and barking. Mick quickly pulled his leg back in, shut the door, and rolled down the window.

"What's your horse's name Missy?" he asked.

"Jack," she said.

"Ask her if she wants to sell the pinto pony," Marion prompted.

"Is the pinto yours, too?" Mick asked.

"No," she said, "that's my brother's horse." Freckles was growling and patrolling the ditch between the fence and the vehicle.

"Where is your brother? I'd like to buy that pony from him," Mick pressed.

"He won't sell Patches. Besides, he's going on a hiking trip. He went to town with Mom to get the food."

"Is he leaving real soon?" Mick asked.

"Yes, but they're camping out. He won't be back until tomorrow night."

"Okay then, we'll come by when he gets back maybe," Mick started to back up.

"Ask her where the kid's going. We still need the kid," said Marion. Mick stopped the car again and rolled the window back down.

"Where's your brother hiking to, by the way?" Mick asked.

"Wally's taking him to Glimpse Lake to go fishing," said Jesse.

"Oh, that's nice down there. Good day now." Mick backed the car out and drove off.

"Get a map and find out where Glimpse Lake is," said Marion. "I think we may take a hike ourselves."

Later, at the guesthouse, a late eighties Chevy pickup was parked in the small circle drive. It had been some shade of green at one time, but now it was mostly primer gray with rust bleeding through the poorly done bodywork. The truck had already leaked a puddle of oil on the surface of the drive. Mick pulled up behind it and got out. He was looking at a hiking map of the Wind River Range as he opened the front door and walked in. "Hey Mary, that bloody lake is in the mountains..." he stopped talking when he looked up. Wade Archer was standing just inside the small foyer where Marion was counting out a sizable amount of cash into his

70

hand. Archer looked up nervously and was relieved to see that it was Mick.

"I been needin' this," said Archer.

"Just remember," said Marion in his oily voice, "this buys your silence as well. If you talk to anybody about any of this, I'll personally silence you for good." He paused for effect and stared at Archer. "Besides, you're the one that killed Palmer when you knocked him off his horse." Marion was not sure that Archer was smart enough to comprehend the threat he had just issued.

"I ain't talkin'," said Archer with a nervous laugh. He turned to Mick, "What lake you lookin' for?"

"Glimpse Lake," said Mick. "We're thinkin' about takin' a little hike."

"You better be horseback if you're goin' up there," said Wade.

"Maybe we'll take four-wheelers then," said Mick.

"Ha!...You can't take four-wheelers in there, that's wilderness area. The rangers would lock you up!" said Wade, again with a nervous laugh.

"What would it take for you to guide us in?" asked Marion.

"When do you want to go?" asked Wade.

"Right now would be good," said Marion. He looked at Mick with a questioning glance. He was wondering if they might have their opportunity to silence this redneck yet.

"Hell, I got me a woman waitin'. I ain't gonna' do it," said Wade. He was lying about the woman. He was simply too lazy to put out any effort. "I know somebody who will though."

"Can he be discreet?" asked Marion.

"He'll be anything you want him to be for money, and he's got his own horses," Wade added.

Upon Wade Archer's recommendation Marion hired John Kirby to pack them in to Glimpse Lake. Marion had insisted that they leave that very afternoon, but Kirby refused to start so late in the day. He used the excuse of not having

71

horses caught and ready, but if the truth were known, he was still hung over from the night before.

Kirby had stayed in the bar after the crowd left the previous evening. He had seen a girl that he had gone to high school with looking lonesome and he started buying her drinks. He had figured he could get her drunk and take advantage of her. He stayed with her drink for drink, but she just held on. He was drinking beer and had to hit the bathroom frequently. The girl would take these opportunities to pour her drinks into the potted plant next to her table. She was getting a kick out of watching Kirby waste his money and get really ripped trying to pick her up. She finally got up, slapped him on the back, said "Thanks for the drinks, Big John" and left. John hadn't even tried to follow. He was just hoping he had enough reflexes left to herd his pickup home.

John Kirby was just beginning to take solid food again when Marion called. He really didn't want the job, but he needed the money and thought he could tough it out. They finally agreed to be at a pack corral at Spring Creek Park, mounted and moving by daylight the next day. On the way back to the guesthouse Mick asked Marion, "Are we gonna' have to wax this guy when we're done with 'im? 'E doesn't seem like the type to keep his mouth shut."

"We'll let him get us there. Then maybe we'll send him back before he sees the kid. He won't see anything to talk about," said Marion.

"What's Mr. Alexander say about all this?" queried Mick.

"For all he knows you took up fishing. So we went fishing. Or would you rather tell him we let the kid see us finish off Palmer?"

"I like fishing. It's a great pastime, quite relaxing." Mick grinned broadly.

"Yes, quite."

When Jack and Bud finally had everything together and sorted, they climbed in an old Dodge four by four and

72

left the ranch. Jack was a minimalist when it came to backpacking. He just didn't like carrying any more than he had to, especially in the mountains. He had talked with Ethan about how to go up with a nine-year-old kid in tow. Ethan had suggested leaving from Spring Creek Park and going up to Glimpse Lake. The trail wasn't as steep and full of switchbacks as starting at Elkhart Park. He also knew that this early in the season they would see almost nobody and that was what Jack wanted. "Glimpse might have some big trout up in the shallows right now," Ethan had said, "I'm sure you've already thought of that." He was right.

The four-wheel-drive trail that went up to the trail-head at Spring Creek Park was every bit as rough as what Jack remembered. He wasn't too sure the old Dodge would make it, but it finally did. Jack was pleased to find that theirs was the only vehicle in the grassy glade that served as a parking lot. The corrals were empty and there was not a sign of anyone else at all. Bud had said very little on the way up. He seemed a different boy than the one Jack had come to know. He had a small pack without a frame that Jack knew would be uncomfortable with any weight in it, so he didn't put anything in it that was heavy. His own pack was probably weighing in at about fifty pounds, but they weren't really going that far if they stopped at Glimpse. He hoped Bud would last that long.

"Well, we had better get moving or it will be dark before we get to the lake," said Jack. "Are you up to this, Bud?"

"Yeah," said Bud with a definite lack of enthusiasm. "Let's go."

Jack took the lead, afraid that Bud would not set a fast enough pace in his present mood. He tried to start some conversations but didn't get much reaction from the boy. "Nothin' wrong with quiet," Jack said, thinking of the movie Jeremiah Johnson. The trail started out along a two-track road and went past a cabin that had a small corral. There was still a fence next to the trail with some cows on the other side. The trail became a single track at this point and roughly followed a meandering stream through a picturesque valley. Jack stopped at the stream and pointed out a few trout, some of them good sized, languishing lazily in the mild current. A startled cow moose and her long-legged calf splashed through the stream and disappeared into the trees. This seemed to perk Bud up a little. They began to talk about fishing and Jack related several tales of trips he had been on and fish he had caught or missed. Talking about fishing made Jack think of his father. He felt like he had been extremely fortunate to have a dad that would take time to go on vacations and take his son fishing. Bud had missed all that through no fault of his own.

As they passed out of the little valley, they began to climb. The trail was rocky here and there. Jack was afraid that Bud was beginning to tire, so he stopped them on a high spot where they could look back the way they had come. Bud sat down on a big granite boulder and took off his pack. It was almost two o'clock so Jack suggested they lighten Bud's pack by eating their PB and J sandwiches, which Bud had been carrying. After eating, Bud slid a bright red poncho out from under the ties on his pack. He left it in a roll and used it as a pillow and he stretched out in the sunshine on the big gray rock. Jack followed his lead and stretched out himself, thinking it best not to push too hard. He didn't know what was bothering Bud, but the kid seemed to have a black cloud hanging over him.

Jack's eyes were closed and a cool breeze had come up. This made it just chilly enough that he would not fall asleep. He lay there thinking how perfect it would be if not for the circumstances. Jack had always found solace in the mountains. Just lying on a big rock and listening to the wind in the pines was one of the most relaxing things he had ever done. He concentrated on nothing, trying to let his mind have a rest as well as his body. Bud sat up and looked over at Jack's resting form. He broke the silence. "Jack?" he asked.

"Yes, Bud," Jack sat up, wrapping his arms around his legs.

"I think I saw something I wasn't supposed to see," said Bud. The boy didn't look at Jack now, he stared off over the valley. Jack waited, not saying anything. Finally Bud went on, "I was riding Patches yesterday after I fed the calves...I was supposed to go to Brewster's..." He hesitated. "Patches spooks at cars sometimes, and I was supposed to ride my bike...but I thought if I cut through the pasture, I'd be okay," Bud's voice was faltering.

"Everybody bends the rules, now and then," said Jack. "Sounds like you had good reasoning."

"I know, but, I was pretending to be an Indian," Bud went on, "and I climbed the little hill by the road cut. Then I heard a car pull up on the road and stop." Bud stopped again, his feet were moving nervously back and forth on the rock, and his body was rocking back and forth. Jack was thinking he had seen some teenagers necking or something. Bud continued, "Two men got out. Then one of them pulled a man out of the backseat..." Bud was starting to cry. "One of them hit the guy with a shovel...hit him real hard!" The boy buried his face between his knees and his body shook as he sobbed.

"Bud, it's gonna' be alright. You didn't do anything wrong. Why don't you tell me what you saw and we'll see if we can make some sense of it," said Jack. He rubbed his hand on the boy's shoulder.

"I know I should have told somebody, but I was afraid no one would believe me," said Bud as he sniffed back the tears.

"I believe you, Bud." Jack had begun to put two and two together. The confession had taken a very serious turn. This surely had to be Jim Palmer that Bud was talking about. Jack knew he would have to suppress his growing anger and concentrate on Bud for the moment.

"Thanks," said Bud.

"What kind of car was it, Bud?" asked Jack wanting to confirm his suspicions.

"It was black," said Bud between sobs, "I think it was a Cherokee." Jack was beginning to understand Bud's

75

morose mood of the last two days. A secret like this was too much for anyone to bear, especially a young boy.

"What happened after that?" Jack asked.

"One of them hit the guy with a shovel...as hard as he could..." Bud repeated. He was crying hard again. Jack put an arm around the boy's shoulders. "After I heard about Mr. Palmer...I just couldn't..."

"Don't say anymore, Bud," Jack said in a quiet voice. "We'll take care of this."

"But...I think they heard me...some rocks fell..." Bud was talking fast. "I ran to where I tied Patches and we ran home..." Bud had a desperate look in his eyes. "One of them came running down the road and he saw me..." Bud buried his face in Jack's fleece. "I was so scared," he sobbed.

"It's going to be all right," Jack consoled. "Everything's going to be all right." He hoped that what he was saying was true.

Jack pondered what to do. This information had to go to the authorities right away, but he could hardly expect Bud to make it all the way back to the trailhead now. They were practically at the lake. Those men had killed Jim and then they had hauled him all the way to Jackson. It was looking as if Jim's suspicions about his employer were warranted. "We better go," he said finally. He helped Bud up and pulled on his own pack. "Put that stuff out of your mind for now, Bud," he said. "Let's enjoy the walk. We're almost there." As they struck out down the trail, the red poncho still lay on the rock. Bud had neglected to pick it up. It slowly unrolled itself in the wind and clung to the boulder in the sunshine.

CHAPTER THIRTEEN

After a few more switchbacks and steep climbs, a lake appeared in a basin ahead of the hikers. A stream poured out of the lower end of the lake and gurgled over the rocks. "This is it, Bud, Glimpse Lake." Jack turned to look at the boy. Bud's eyes were on the lake as it glimmered in the late afternoon sun. Jack led the way across the stream, picking his way from rock to rock to avoid going over his boot tops. The old Vasque hiking boots he was wearing were, surprisingly, still waterproof. Bud's boots were of the sport shoe variety and, although they weighed almost nothing, they would let in water at every opportunity. Bud had made this discovery before lunch and was now finding out what wet cotton socks could do to your feet on a hike. Jack picked a spot to set up camp not far from the outlet to the lake, but away from the soggy ground that surrounded it.

"My feet are so sore," said Bud as he flopped down on a rock next to the water's edge. Jack had suspected as much, but had not said anything. He hadn't wanted the boy to feel sorry for himself and give up. He had wanted to make camp at Glimpse and not along the trail somewhere.

"Go ahead and take your shoes and socks off, Bud," said Jack, unrolling a Thermarest pad. He blew the pad up slightly before closing the valve. Jack then unrolled Bud's sleeping bag and put it on top of the pad. Bud had his shoes off by now, and was surveying a couple of blisters that had formed on his heels. "Why don't you wash your feet off in the lake," Jack suggested. "The cold water will soothe them, and I doubt if it will kill too many fish." Bud chuckled for the first time since the day before.

"Wow! This water's freezing!" Bud exclaimed, jerking his bare feet back out of the lake.

"Just swish your feet around a little bit in the water. We'll dry them off and get some dry socks on you and they'll feel all toasty again," said Jack. Bud did as he was told, and Jack picked him up around the ribs and swung him over to a big rock where a towel was waiting. Soon Bud was in dry socks and his shoes and socks from the hike were catching the last few rays of the setting sun on a large rock.

"It's getting cold," said Bud with a shiver. The breeze had picked up again and the warmth of the sun was rapidly leaving the mountains behind. The boy crawled into his sleeping bag while Jack started a fire.

"Where did you find all that wood?" asked Bud, looking around. Among the rocks there had seemed to be no firewood to be had.

"It's there. You just have to look around," replied Jack. "Even if the ground is wet, you can find dry sticks like these."

"Where?" asked Bud.

"You see all that stuff sticking out on the bottoms of those big spruce trees?"

"Yeah. Those little limbs look pretty dry," Bud admitted.

"I guess Indian squaws would break off those lower branches when they gathered the wood for their cook fires. The man who taught me about such things called it squaw wood. It worked for them; it'll work for you."

Soon a crackling fire of spruce and pine boughs was shedding light and warmth on the chill evening. Jack found several larger pieces of wood that had drifted up on the shore when the water was higher during spring runoff. They had plenty of fuel for the night. A slight breeze off the lake took the smoke away from them and up between a crack in the big boulders.

"It'll get pretty cold up here before morning, but I think you're pretty well dressed for it. The ground hasn't warmed up yet and can really sap the heat out of your body. A good sleeping pad is really important, but if you don't have one, you can insulate yourself with pine boughs or whatever you can find to get you off the ground. Some people will bury rocks from the fire to sleep on. Those fleece britches your mother packed for you are going to be your best friends tonight," said Jack. He was cooking up a small pot of pasta and sauce in the only pan they had with them. Jack kept talking to Bud, hoping he could get some food in him before he fell asleep. He had encouraged the boy to drink a lot of water as they walked, and warned him of the risk of dehydration. They had used some iodine tablets when they refilled their bottles, and added a little Gatorade powder to mask the metallic taste. Bud ate his share of the pasta and then some. Jack was glad to see him acting a bit more like himself. The kid had probably not slept well the night before with such a weight as he carried. Before the last of the light had faded from the sky, Bud was sound asleep.

Jack cleaned up what few dishes and utensils they had used and took Bud's shoes down off the rock. He walked over and set the shoes beside the sleeping form next to the fire and then dug out his own bag and pad. He laid the pad against the slope of a rock near the fire and reclined against it. He sipped coffee, which he had made in the same pan as the pasta, and chewed on the grounds that floated to his lips. Sleep would not come quickly tonight; Jack simply had too much on his mind. The thought of the two thugs killing Jim raised such anger within him that he contemplated taking revenge himself. But no, he couldn't do that. He had too much respect for the law to do that. Bud could be in danger as a witness and would need police protection. This whole affair was going to turn into a huge mess and was definitely not what he had in mind when he came into Pinedale a little over a week before. A mouse appeared, skirting the fire, looking for morsels that had fallen. Jack felt a bit of envy for a creature whose only thought of humans was as a source of food. He watched the mouse and made no attempt to shoo it away.

Jack had not been aware of having fallen asleep, but when he awakened, it was in the cold part of the morning just before dawn. He poked a few sticks into the embers that still glowed in the stone fire ring he had made. He didn't want to disturb Bud, so he walked back away from the camp and pulled his fly rod out of its tube. He assembled the rod and attached the reel. As he pulled line off to string through the eyes of the rod, the ratcheting of the reel seemed unnaturally loud in the gray semi-darkness of morning. He hadn't had time to find out about the fishing before they left town, so, not seeing any rises on the water, he tied on a small nymph. The fluorescent green color of the line looked strange arcing back and forth in the dim light. While stripping in line on the third cast, he felt a hit and landed an eight-inch trout. He laid the fish out in the grass since he didn't bring a creel with him and went back for another. Jack stopped with three and took them back to the camp. He had brought along some bacon to fry to get a little grease in the pan and a small bag of salt and corn meal. A breakfast of fresh rainbow trout would lift anyone's spirits and Jack hoped it would be like medicine to Bud.

The night before, Jack had put what little foodstuffs they had in the stuff sack of Bud's sleeping bag and had hoisted it over a limb high in the air with a small rope. He had been thinking of mice as much as bears, but either was a possibility. Seeing Bud still sleeping, Jack put the fish down and poured coffee out of the pan sitting near the fire. It was hot and strong, for the wind had changed and it had boiled a little too long while he was fishing. He refilled the cup and walked back down to the outlet and crossed the little stream; again he carried his fly rod. Jack had seen a couple of lazy rises near the outlet and thought he would tie on a dry fly and see what happened. He didn't care one way or another if he caught the fish. He was just killing time until Bud got up. Jack was feeling the need to move, to get on with it. He was finding it difficult not to force Bud beyond his physical limits. It would be tough on the boy, but they would have to start back right away.

Mick and Marion had met Kirby at the edge of town in the predawn darkness and followed him up the gravel that would take them to Spring Creek Park trailhead. The road was so incredibly rough that Marion wondered aloud if the county even owned a road grader. The dust raised by the stock trailer, which Kirby was pulling behind his truck, was so thick that it was all Mick could do to keep track of the taillights. After what seemed like an eternity, the truck finally stopped and Kirby got out and swung wide the rear door on the old trailer.

"I'm surprised that rig made it up here as many times as we bottomed out," said Mick as Kirby unloaded three already saddled horses.

"We ain't there yet," said Kirby, "You can follow while I lead these two up to the trailhead." Kirby tightened his cinch and wondered to himself why he had even considered this job. He mounted his own horse and led the other two, starting up the trail to the pack corral.

The Cherokee bounced and drug its way up the rough track, while the cowboy cut across country, leading the horses. They soon reached the pack corral. Kirby tightened the cinches on each animal and helped the two men tie on their fishing gear. Kirby doubted that the fish were in much danger of being caught by these two. They had a big tackle box like the kind you would see used by a tournament bass fisherman. These morons didn't have a clue.

"Now I know why we started so damned early," said Marion staring around in the darkness. "It's a long way up here on a road like that."

"You said you wanted to start early," said Kirby, lighting another cigarette. "I got you all a couple a' broke horses, but this little dun horse here is pretty green."

"Whot's that mean?" asked the Aussie.

"Means he's barely broke to ride. I figure he'll learn a lot today," said Kirby. He thought the little horse was ready for a pack trip and he might as well get some experi-

81

ence on this fiasco.

They mounted up and began at a brisk pace on the insistence of Marion, who looked like he was going to pull the saddle horn off. Mick was decked out in khaki bush pants and shirt and Marion was dressed in a pair of camo pants and an old olive drab jacket. "I got Mr. Greenjeans and the Crocodile Hunter," Kirby said to himself. They covered the ground quickly in the darkness and only slowed when they got to the steeper sections of the trail. Marion was definitely just a passenger on his horse, but Mick at least, looked to be at home on his mount. As they climbed up the switchbacks that led out of the small valley, Mick found a spot and passed Kirby. He wasn't liking the uneven pace the green horse was requiring him to make. It was beginning to get light and Mick was becoming impatient.

They were walking their horses up a steep switchback when Mick spotted the red poncho that Bud had left laying on the rock. "What's this?" he yelled, as he leaned in his saddle and grabbed the poncho. He waved it in the air for the others to see.

John Kirby had been leaning forward to light a cigarette. When Mick waved the poncho, the little dun horse spooked and reared, throwing his head back, catching Kirby square in the face with the bony poll of the horse's head. This knocked Kirby back at the same time the horse reared up. His pull on the reins to regain his balance caused the young horse to topple over backwards, and horse and rider both fell down the steep mountainside. The accompanying sounds were sickening. A leg bone on the horse made a sound like a rifle shot, followed shortly by a dull crunch as the horse landed squarely on top of Kirby driving the saddle horn into the man's chest. Mick's horse had bolted up the trail and Marion had dropped his reins completely as both hands were clinched around the saddle horn. Marion's horse pranced and snorted before it too bolted on up the trail.

Mick dismounted and secured his horse quickly to a tree and he ran back down the trail. Soon Marion managed to get off as well and joined Mick, surveying the carnage ten yards below them. John Kirby lay motionless. His unseeing eyes stared up at the two men while blood drizzled out of his mouth and nose. There was no question that John Kirby was dead. The horse lay against a tree where it had come to a stop. With a loud grunt, it struggled to get up but could not. "Now what do we do?" asked Mick, still staring at the dead man.

"We go on," said Marion. "He said we were almost there. Accidents occur all the time out here in the wilderness." He was thinking of the boy as well as Kirby.

"Guess we don't have to worry about him talkin' anymore," said Mick jerking a thumb toward Kirby. They went back to their horses and mounted up. Mick took the lead as they hurried on up the trail.

CHAPTER FOURTEEN

Sam Davidson wasn't his real name. His mother had been from a stodgy, old family of wealth in London, while his father was from Saudi Arabia. It had been a strange mixture of cultures for Sam as a boy growing up mostly in the United Kingdom. He had decided that he was called to follow his father's side of the family while still in grammar school. His mother was not pleased, but his father was a domineering sort and Sam's mother feared crossing the man. Sam went to Saudi Arabia with his father while in his early teens and had come back to England a quite different young man. He studied the Qur'an and assimilated himself into the Muslim culture. Upon his return to England he was presented with a visa, British no less, and came to the United States to Boise State University, presumably to get an education. He had blended in well with the college freshmen that first year. He had lighter features than most Arabs, not that it mattered, for college campuses in the states seemed to crave diversity over academic prowess. In fact, it was impossible to guess where his sympathies might lie by his lifestyle or his looks.

Sam had begun to wonder after graduation, just what his purpose was. Perhaps he was supposed to drop a virus in Simplot's potatoes, so that it would be distributed in McDonald's French fries throughout the country. "You want Ebola with that?" he imagined a pimple-faced kid saying at a drive-up window. He was now in his fifth year of college and had taken a job at a pawnshop close to a warehouse district on the outskirts of Boise. Next door was a seedy looking video store that had a separate room marked "Adults Only". Sam often frequented this room and rented X-rated videos. He dreamed of the day when he would be surrounded by virgins because he had done Allah's bidding. At least that's what he told himself as he sat in his apartment and the television flickered its glow in the darkened room.

At last he had been contacted. It was as simple as a phone call late one night. "This is your cousin, Fahad," the voice had said.

"It is good to hear from you Fahad bin Rahman," he had answered. A meeting was set up and Sam was given instructions. He was disappointed to learn that his part was not earth shattering, as had been the part of the martyrs of last year. But, after all, he was not in any hurry to take that final step himself. He could wait.

Allen Avery had walked into the shop where, outside, a large sign read: Idaho Family Gun and Pawn. He had received a call the day before and could not wait to get in on such a good deal.

"Ah, Mr. Avery," said Sam, "I believe this is what you came for." He reached under the counter and hefted up a large green ammo box.

"Hey man," said Avery, "I'm glad you called. A guy's gotta' look for deals on this stuff." He leaned on the glass top of the counter, resting his elbow on a hand lettered sign saying Don't Lean On Glass!. "Full auto can really go through shells in a hurry," he said confidentially. He had a devilish, just-between-you-and-me, smirk on his face.

Sam carried the 7.62 X 39 ammunition around the side of the counter and sat it on the floor. Avery paid cash, picked up his prize and went out to his vehicle. Sam walked to the bars of the glass door and watched the man climb into a late 70's Ford pickup done up in crude camouflage paint with rust holes around the fender wells. Sam's eyes scanned across the street to the black Jaguar. Although he couldn't see the faces of the two men inside, he nodded and the car started and drove off. Sam's job was done. He hoped that his research had been accurate.

Fahad bin Rahman and Hamad Al-Busaid followed the camo Ford at a distance. They passed several Mexican establishments and stopped in front of a small market as the Ford pulled up at a liquor store. The men did not talk but patiently waited until Allen Avery emerged carrying a thirty pack of Natural Light and a bottle-shaped brown paper bag. Avery slammed the door twice before the latch caught, and he pulled the truck back out onto the pavement. The old Ford ambled its way out of town and had gone less than two miles when the first empty can hit the pavement of the deserted highway. The Jaguar followed the old pickup onto a narrow dirt road that wound back behind some trees and then skirted a barley field. An old mobile home surrounded by trash and old appliances materialized near a line of scrubby trees.

Hamad stopped the car and the two men conversed in Arabic as they watched Avery park the pickup in the yard and go inside. They got out and approached the trailer. Fahad jumped when a hound hit the end of his chain and began barking loudly at the intruders. The ground was bare all around the staked out dog. The dog wrapped its chain around an old wringer washing machine whose legs were half buried in the dirt. Most of the appliances abandoned in the yard were riddled with bullet holes of various diameters. The pickup, it appeared, was the only vehicle in working order; there were others in various stages of disassembly and decay adorning what was probably once the yard of a farmstead, the house long gone.

Fahad walked up the rickety wooden stairs and rapped on the aluminum storm door before backing down a couple of steps to give the door room to open. A face appeared in the small, square window of the unpainted wooden door on the inside. The wooden door opened and Allen Avery looked out through the missing panes of the storm door at the two well-dressed men, both wearing dark glasses. He was dressed in ragged jeans and a black Harley T-shirt stretched tightly over his ample belly. His right elbow was bent in front of him, holding a can of beer.

"It's for you Maude," Avery yelled toward the bedroom. "Goddamn Mormons again." He didn't see the small muzzle flash of the pistol. He didn't feel the spray of cold beer that spattered his shirt as the 22 hollow point bullet exited the can, already beginning to expand. Allen Avery only sensed that something was wrong when he tried to speak again and nothing came out. The small caliber bullet had shattered his larynx on the way to the base of his skull. It was followed by two more shots, which also punctured the beer can on the way to their target. Avery fell to his knees before hitting the storm door, pushing it outward and rolling down the steps to the bare dirt at Fahad's feet.

Hamad mounted the steps quickly, going past Fahad and over the body at the foot of the stairs, and stepped inside the house. An overweight, bug-eyed woman in gray sweatpants and sweatshirt stared at him from the end of a short hallway. Her mouth moved slightly and a wail came out of her that became a scream. The report of another small caliber gun echoed through the mobile home. The screaming stopped and the woman slumped to the floor of the hall. The hound outside was barking and baying. Every other bark was distorted by the collar the dog wore as it hit the limit of its chain. One more report and the dog too lay silent. When the barking and gunfire stopped, Hamad stiffened as noises emitted from the back bedroom. He relaxed as he realized it was just a television game show blaring from a TV at the foot of an unmade bed.

The two men ransacked the trailer and had begun to think that Sam had led them on a wild goose chase. All they had found was an older SKS rifle, made in China with a bayonet attached, hanging above the very door where Allen had taken his last breath. They decided to search the grounds. When Fahad opened the back door, he found what he was looking for. Butted up to a shabby deck attached to the trailer was an old delivery van. The floor of the van was level with the deck. Fahad removed the padlock, which hung, unlocked, through the latch, and swung open one of the double doors. Exposed wiring led up the wall of the van to a porcelain fixture and a pull chain. A kerosene heater sat in the middle of the floor. He stepped in and pulled the chain on the light. Fahad smiled and called to Hamad. Along the left side of the van was a bench with various tools and reloading equipment. Across the far end was a rack made of notched two-by-fours. It held an assortment of rifles, most of them Chinese versions of various military arms. The whole van smelled of gun oil and kerosene. The two men looked at each other and smiled.

CHAPTER FIFTEEN

Jack wasn't fishing now. He was only watching the big trout feeding on something just below the surface of the water. It would have been a difficult cast from here anyway. He was standing in a couple of inches of water between two huge boulders. The constant gurgle of the outlet nearby echoed off the two rocks making it seam louder than it was. He had heard nothing but the rush of the water, when Marion stepped around the rock to his right and faced him straight on.

Marion wore a triumphant grin and said nothing as Jack started to back up. "Well now, what have we here," a voice with a thick Australian accent spoke, directly behind him. Jack recognized the voice immediately. A chill went up his spine. "Let's not get excited here, we're all among friends aren't we?" Jack felt a jab in his back that was unmistakably a gun. He looked over his shoulder confirming what he already knew. He instinctively looked over toward the camp where he could see Bud still curled up in his down sleeping bag. Marion's eyes followed Jack's and a satisfied smile crept over his face.

Marion spoke, "Hello, Mr. Wallace, fancy meeting you here. Or is it Wally as the girl said?" Jack started to lunge toward Marion, wondering what they had done to Jesse, but a sharp pain in the middle of his back brought him up short. Mick had jabbed the gun hard into Jack's spine.

"Easy there, mate," said Mick. "Let's keep those hands where we can see 'em. Drop the fishin' pole, now." Jack let his rod fall to the water as he raised both hands

89

slightly above waist high.

"You know Mick," said Marion in a conversational tone, "I believe this is some sort of child molestation thing. Wally here took the kid camping, molested and killed him, then, in a fit of despair flung himself off a cliff. What do you think?"

"By God, I believe you've nailed it Mary!" said Mick feigning astonishment. "This bloke is a real sicko, 'e is."

Jack knew that he must act suddenly and violently, just as he had been taught in his self-defense classes so many years ago. He concentrated on the gun in Mick's right hand directly behind him. "Don't shoot me..." he spoke to distract the man and immediately twisted hard to his right. His right elbow struck Mick's arm, knocking the gun out of line with his body. The gun blasted and Jack felt the sting of powder on his forearm as the bullet missed him. He continued to turn and grabbed the outstretched arm of the Aussie, pulling the man off balance. Jack slammed his left forearm into the upper arm bone and threw his entire body weight on it. He was hoping to feel the bone break, but the man's strong muscles prevented it. Both men fell on the rocks in the shallow water. Jack was concentrating on the gun. He tried to reach it with his left hand. He had no intention of letting go with his right. He could feel the Aussie struggling under him, trying to free his arm. The man's left hand was free, but it was underneath him and he couldn't strike Jack, much as he tried. Mick had landed face down and water was dripping from his mustache as he gasped for his breath. Jack raised his body slightly, groping for the gun with his left hand and finally felt it. He grabbed it and twisted hard, feeling the finger in the trigger guard snap. Mick screamed and with a sudden effort got a leg underneath and knocked Jack over backwards. The gun fell into the lake. Both men struggled to get up, splashing wildly in the water. Jack regained his footing when Mick swung at him with his uninjured left hand. Throwing up a hand to block the punch, Jack was a little too slow and took the blow square on his cheek bone. He saw stars and his eyes teared up. He felt another blow slide past him. It struck his shoulder knocking him sideways. Instinctively Jack swung back with his own left hand and struck Mick under the chin with a palm heel. Jack felt the man's jaws clack together and his head snap back as he continued the drive of his blow. Mick flew over backwards and, with a loud pop, his head hit squarely on a partially submerged rock. Mick's body went suddenly rigid, then it shuddered and twitched in the shallow water. The thickset body of the Aussie convulsed a few more times and finally stopped moving.

Jack almost relaxed until he realized he had neglected the other man. He spun around, staring at the spot where Marion had been. There, lying face down in the shallow water was the inert form of Marion. The olive coat was dark with water as were the fatigue pants he wore. Jack walked over and rolled the body over. Blood had turned the water dark and now trickled down Marion's lifeless face from a neat, dark hole in the middle of his forehead. Mick's stray round had killed the man with a single shot, like the cancer-eyed cow that Jack had put down only a few days before.

Jack drug Marion's body back between the rocks and went over to Mick. He knelt down and felt for a pulse in the man's neck. There was none. He picked up the fly rod and hurried across the outlet stream and to the camp. Bud was sitting up in his sleeping bag cowering. He had seen the men fighting after being awakened by the shot. "We've got to go, Bud," Jack said, helping the boy with his shoes. "Those men you saw followed us." He paused, seeing fear on the boy's face. "They won't bother you any more." Bud said nothing, but, feeling the urgency of moment, he began quickly stuffing his sleeping bag in the stuff-sack, which Jack had retrieved from the tree. It took them less than five minutes to break camp. Jack dug out some band-aids and put them in an outside pocket on his pack. He figured they could apply them to Bud's feet later. Right now they had to get moving.

The going was easier heading back down the trail and Bud hadn't complained at all yet. Jack explained to him that they would have to go to the sheriff's office and tell about

91

what Bud had seen on Monday. Bud didn't ask what had happened back at the lake, and for that, Jack was grateful. They reached the rock where they had stopped the day before. The red poncho lay on the ground to the side of the trail. "Hey, that's my poncho," said Bud, reaching for it. Jack heard something in the trees below them.

"Hop up on this rock, Bud," he said. "Pull your shoes off and see what you can do about those blisters." He shucked off his own pack and pulled out the band-aids, giving them to Bud. "I'll be right back," he said and Jack walked on down the trail and came to the switchback. A horse's head came up and the horse nickered at him. It was saddled and had short, broken reins hanging from the bridle bit. Just to the left of this horse, Jack could see the dun's distended abdomen as the dead horse had rolled on its side before it died. He picked his way down the rocks as he left the trail. He froze when he saw the dead man. The piercing blue eyes of John Kirby now stared into nothingness. A shudder went through Jack's body and he had gooseflesh. The rude man from the café in Big Piney, that Jack had seen that first morning in Wyoming, now laid in a crumpled heap before him. Jack had seen the tracks of shod horses going both directions on the trail. It had puzzled him, but now it started to fit. He could see that the dead horse had a broken leg and he surmised from the brokenness of Kirby's body that the horse probably fell on him. The other horse had most likely been tied up at the lake and just came back down the trail after getting loose; perhaps it spooked and broke free when the gun went off.

Jack walked down to the loose horse and took hold of the broken reins. Leading the horse, he made his way back up to where Bud was putting his shoes back on. "There's been an accident," he said. "Get on this horse and we'll bypass this section of the trail." Bud complied and Jack adjusted the stirrups as high as they would go. He pulled a small rope from his pack and made a lead for the horse.

By carefully picking his way down the other side of the rocks, Jack managed to avoid the area where Kirby's body was. He didn't think Bud needed to see that at all. When they again reached the trail, Jack looped the small rope on around the horse's neck to form a continuous rein and tied it back to the other side of the bit. Now Bud could handle the horse on his own. When they reached the little valley with the stream, they heard a nicker and the pounding of hooves. Another horse, saddle empty and trailing reins, came galloping back up the trail. The horse held its head to one side to avoid stepping on the trailing reins. Bud's mount whinnied back at it. Jack caught the horse and tightened the cinch before climbing aboard. They rode on down the trail to the pack corrals. The day was beautiful and the weather was clear, but just about everything else was screwed up, Jack thought.

They stripped the saddles off the horses and turned them into the corral. Jack figured the authorities could take care of them later. He and Bud threw their gear in the old Dodge and started for Pinedale. Jack was glad that they met no one else. It would not have been an easy thing to explain to someone why they might not want to go hiking to Glimpse Lake right then.

CHAPTER SIXTEEN

When they reached town, Jack stopped at a pay phone near the Laundromat and called Kate's number. Jesse answered. "Jesse," said Jack with relief. "Are you okay? Is everything alright?"

"Sure," said Jesse. "Who's this?"

"Oh, I'm sorry," he said. "This is Jack. Just tell your mom that we'll be home soon."

"Okay," she said, unconcerned.

"We'll see you a little later then, bye." He hung up the phone. Jack was relieved that nothing had happened to Jesse. He got back in the truck, where Bud was waiting, and started to pull out of the parking lot. A pickup loaded with bagged feed pulled in and stopped. Jack saw that it was Abe Cain and he was stopping to talk.

"Been fishing Jack?" asked Abe.

"Yeah...a little," said Jack, "Not much luck." He wanted to be on his way.

"You need to stop at Mrs. Palmer's. She's needin' some information from you. Friday's payday and she doesn't even have your full name.

"I'll do it," said Jack. "Thanks Abe."

Jack pulled out onto Pine Street and then pulled off on Tyler when he saw the courthouse. He was betting the sheriff's office was close by. He found the building in the same block and parked on the street. "Alright partner," Jack said to Bud. "Let's get this done." Bud just nodded. They got out and Jack led the way inside the small office. A pleasant looking woman with rimless glasses and a grandmotherly smile looked up from a computer screen at them.

"Hello," she said.

"Is the sheriff in?" asked Jack.

"Yes, he is, but he has..." she paused, leaned back, and looked down a short hall, "Oh, I think they're just finishing." Voices became apparent in the hallway as a door opened to a windowed office with its blinds closed. Two men came out exchanging pleasantries. One was dressed in traditional khakis and the other was older and dressed more casually, the second man looked strangely familiar to Jack. The older man walked past them, eyeing Jack carefully and glancing at Bud. He left the office through the front door. The sheriff walked up to the desk where the lady sat at the computer and stood beside it.

"What can I do for you gentlemen today?" he asked.

Jack glanced back to the office as he said; "We'd like a word with you, if that's possible."

"Sure, come on back," he said turning to walk back down the hall. Jack and Bud followed. They sat down in front of the sheriff's gray metal desk in straight-backed cushioned chairs.

"My name is Jack Wallace," Jack began, "and this is Bud Wilcox. His mother is Kate..."

"I know who Bud is," the sheriff interrupted. He smiled at the boy, "How is everyone out at the Wilcox ranch?"

"Fine," said Bud, looking nervous.

"I've been working at the Circle "A"," Jack continued. "What we wanted to talk to you about has to do with Jim Palmer's death and something Bud witnessed." The sheriff's look became one of concern and he reached for a pair of reading glasses.

"You're telling me...what?"

"That Jim Palmer's death was not an accident," replied Jack.

"Hang on just a minute, fellas," said the officer, flipping through his Rolodex. "I want someone else to hear this." He picked up the phone and dialed. "Joe," he spoke into the phone, "Come back here a minute. Something you need to hear." He put down the receiver and looked back at Jack and Bud. "How long have you worked at Circle "A"?" he asked Jack.

"Barely over a week," said Jack. Jack heard someone come in the office and soon the door behind him opened. The same older man who had just left the office was back. Once again Jack had the odd feeling that he should know this man. The sheriff stood up and introduced him.

"Jack Wallace, this is Joe Riley," he said as the two men shook hands. Riley looked to Jack like a church deacon more than a law officer. "And this is Bud Wilcox." The man shook Bud's hand. "And I'm Ben Tate, by the way," said the sheriff to Jack. The older man pulled a chair to the side of the desk and faced Jack and Bud. "All right now, let's hear what you were going to tell me," said Sheriff Tate.

Jack had Bud tell of what he had seen two days before. Bud got a little choked up, but got his story out with reassurances from Sheriff Tate that everything would be fine now. The sheriff and Joe Riley gave each other knowing glances as Bud finished. "I'm glad you came to us with this information, Bud," said sheriff Tate. "I think we can take it from here." He buzzed the lady in the outer office. "Mary Ann, do you think you can find a soda for this young man."

"I'll do better than that," came the woman's voice back over the intercom. In a moment the door opened and Mary Ann, the receptionist, came in and took Bud with her.

"There's a lot more to tell," said Jack, when the boy was out of the office. "The two men who did this are lying dead up at Glimpse Lake."

"What?" Sheriff Tate looked astonished. He shot a glance over at Riley.

"I think you better start at the beginning," said the older man. He pulled a badge from his pocket. "I'm with the FBI. You were probably wondering." Jack began his story of the Palmer "accident" and the backpacking trip. When he got to the part where he fought with Mick, the two men were giving each other looks again.

"It all happened pretty fast," said Jack.

"We had better be sending some people up there right away," said the sheriff. Jack told them about finding Kirby on the way back.

"This just keeps getting a little worse, it would seem," the officer said.

"Ben," spoke Riley, "I need this to be kept quiet." He had a very stern look on his face.

"I know," said Tate. "I know two good men in Fish and Game whom I can trust to keep a lid on it. They were both in town this morning. I had better see if I can catch them." Tate left the office to get something going up in the wilderness area before anyone stumbled upon the dead men. The weather wasn't warm enough or reliable enough this early to draw a lot of backpackers to the high country yet, but it seemed that they were coming earlier every year.

The FBI agent turned his attention back to Jack when the sheriff was gone. "Sounds to me like you handled yourself very well up there, Jack," he said.

"I didn't have much choice," said Jack.

"Look, Jack," said Riley, "We're going to have to keep a lid on all this for now." He paused, thinking. "It appears as if you and the boy are the only ones who know anything about it. I'm assuming you've told no one since you got to town."

"That's right," said Jack.

"Good," the agent said, "It's going to have to stay that way for awhile. What you have seen is only a small part of a much bigger picture. Everything you've told us today can go no farther than this office. We have an ongoing investigation and any leakage of this information would damage that investigation."

"I can keep my mouth shut," said Jack, "but I think you need to get some protection on the boy."

"Oh, we will, we will," said Riley. "I agree with you on that."

"I think if I explain it in the right way to Bud, he won't say anything either."

"That would be good," said Riley. "We'll have to do at least that."

"What do you mean?" asked Jack.

"I mean it would be best to get him out of here for now."

"Well, yeah...I suppose..." said Jack.

"It's entirely possible that the lid will blow off when they start packing bodies out of the mountains," said Riley. "Let's go over this in a little more detail. Tell me exactly how you left things up there." He settled in behind Tate's desk and picked up a pen. Riley was going to have to do some damage control or his investigation would be wasted. As Jack talked, Joe asked questions and took notes.

The interview took about half an hour. By the time it was over, Bud was back. Mary Ann had taken him out to get a hamburger and he was in much better spirits. With Joe's help, Jack explained to Bud that everything was taken care of and that he needed to keep quiet about it. He convinced Bud that it was better that way for now and that he was not in any danger anymore. Bud seemed to be somewhat relieved to know that he didn't have to talk about it anymore. Jack told him that he couldn't even tell Kate for now. The boy appeared to relax even more. He was not looking forward to explaining any of this to his mother right away.

Bud went out to the truck and Jack was about to follow him, when Joe Riley held him up. "We were suspicious about Jim Palmer's death," the agent confided. "We had an autopsy done in Jackson and found some things that didn't add up. Actual cause of death was probably suffocation," said the agent.

Jack looked at the ground. He felt an involuntary clenching of his fists and his jaws tightened. "I have no remorse for the deaths of those two bastards," said Jack. He relaxed a little bit and looked up at Joe. "I was kind of hoping the bears would eat them."

"I don't blame you at all for feeling that way," said Riley. He paused and said, "I'm going to want to talk to you tomorrow."

"I'll be at the ranch. I've got to turn in my social security number to get my first paycheck," said Jack.

Riley thought for a moment and said, "Hold off on that until you've talked to me. Meet me at the parking lot at Faler's at, say, 10 am tomorrow. Remember: don't talk to anybody about any of this. Got it?"

"Got it," said Jack.

Jack and Bud got to the Wilcox home only to find a note on the door. Kate had been called in to work for the afternoon. Jesse was at Brewster's and Jack was to take Bud by there. Jack was somewhat relieved not to have to explain anything to Kate. He figured that Bud might deal with keeping secrets from his mother better than Jack could. He felt pretty guilty about the whole thing, thinking Kate had a right to know what her son was going through. Jack reiterated with the boy about the need for confidentiality on the matter as he dropped Bud off at the Brewster's.

Jack went back to the now deserted Wilcox ranch and parked the old Dodge truck next to the creaky, weathered barn where Bud had shown him the old Panhead not so long ago. He placed the key in the ashtray where he had found it two days ago and thought about the things that had happened in that time period. Jack got out and walked around to the back of the truck and leaned against it. The wind was beginning to pick up and a low moan came from the roof of the shed as the breeze found its voice in the overlapping of sheet metal and a loose nail. Other than a calf pushing an empty plastic bucket around looking for a morsel of grain, no sound competed with the wind's mournful tone. Jack paused for a moment to take stock of his very soul. He had killed a man. He told Riley that he held no remorse, which was true, but that didn't change the fact that he had taken a life.

Jack walked over to the Sportster and tied his backpack and rod tube onto the bike. He needed to do some thinking and he knew of no better place than on the old bike where he had spent many a lonesome hour asking himself the questions that seemed to have no answers. He pulled out the choke and started the motor in a routine that never varied. Even with the loud exhaust sound he could hear the moan of the wind through the tin, as if the devil himself were sending Jack salutations for returning one of his own to him. "I'll tell you what old son," said Jack aloud, "I don't work your side of the fence. If I did you any favors, it was purely by accident, and you didn't get much in those two." With that he pulled the bike out onto the drive and started back for the ranch.

CHAPTER SEVENTEEN

"You have all the account numbers and you know what to do," Yuri was saying. He was staring at an account page of some kind on a computer screen as he spoke to the person on the other end of the phone line. "Check all of the orders to make sure that they are not duplicated. You can call Geneva if you have any questions."

"As you wish Mr. Aleksandrov," replied the businesslike voice coming from the speakerphone. "I will send confirmation by phone and email as soon as the orders are filled. Do you require anything else at this time?"

"That is all," said Yuri. He pressed the speaker button on the phone and the connection was terminated. He sat back in his chair and took one more look at the account information before him. This was all going quite well. It was perhaps better than he could have hoped. Soon he would be relieved of some 'difficult to market' merchandise and he would be very much wealthier for his troubles. Yuri's financial situation had suffered greatly with the stock market devaluation in recent years. He had become accustomed to a certain amount of opulence in his lifestyle and the falling markets had begun to cramp his style. Soon that would change. His foresight and planning would pay off handsomely in this turbulent time for America. When opportunities presented themselves, Yuri had always been ready to take advantage of them. He thought it fortunate that he did not choose sides. That sort of thing could cut your business opportunities in half quickly.

Yuri's cellular phone warbled. "Yes?" He answered.

"No, I had completely forgotten about it." His exuberant mood of only minutes before changed quickly as he listened to a secretary on the other end of the line. "It is not possible at this time. Perhaps she could...Damn it! We will have to make other arrangements. Damn! Alright then." He hung up the phone. He was upset with himself for having cursed at the secretary. He forced himself to regain his composure. This could be handled. It would only be a minor inconvenience. He stood up from his desk and turned to walk out of the study. Anna stood in the doorway.

"Something wrong?" she asked.

"My niece is coming to visit," he said.

"Surely not now," she was astonished. "Tell her not to come." Anna had been setting up some of the trades that were to take place. She knew that, for whatever reason, Yuri had taken some very risky positions in the stock market recently. These trades would have to be monitored closely or they could quickly become disasters if the market were to have even a minor rally.

"Her flight is due in Jackson this afternoon," said Yuri, some irritation coming back in his voice. "She's on her way, now."

"Should I go to pick her up then?" Anna asked.

"No, I need you here. There is too much to do and time is short," said Yuri. "We'll have Marion pick her up."

"He's not here," said Anna. She could see by the look on Yuri's face that he was not at all pleased with this bit of news. "I thought you knew," she said. "He and Mick went fishing."

"Fishing!" Yuri said with astonishment, "You must be joking."

"No. That is what they said when they left. They said that they would be gone all day, maybe two days."

"How can he leave now? He knows that we have important dealings right now," Yuri fumed. "Get him on his cell phone. Tell him to come back here immediately."

Anna walked to the computer desk near the door and picked up a phone. She punched in the number and waited.

Yuri began to pace as Anna waited. After what seemed like an inordinate amount of time to Yuri, she said, "I'm getting voice-mail." She held her hand over the phone as if someone would hear her on the other end. "Marion, call in as soon as you get this," she said into the phone and hung up.

"Call Mick's number. I don't believe they went fishing. They must have found some women or something," said Yuri. He sat down at a computer on his own desk and brought up some sort of spreadsheet, which he began to pore over.

Anna dialed again. "I don't even get voice-mail on his," she said. "It just says that the customer can't be reached."

"Then get someone else to pick her up," he said testily, referring again to his niece coming in at the airport.

"Tino?" she offered dubiously.

"Not Tino. Get one of the cowboys. At least they can talk."

"They are all gone. You let them go until we could find someone to run things," she said as she walked to the window and looked down toward the bunkhouse. She didn't want to look at Yuri, she knew that he was getting angrier by the minute. Yuri did not take it well when unknown factors forced him to modify his plans. He did not like surprises.

As she looked out the window Jack was just pulling up in front of the bunkhouse. This gave Anna some hope. "The cowboy who rides the motorcycle just came back. Perhaps he would be available to go to Jackson." She looked back at Yuri, hoping that this would be suitable.

"Then go tell him he has a new job," said Yuri, not looking up. "Go!" Anna left the study.

Back at the bunkhouse Jack was considering what to do with himself. He decided to go for a run since the weather was nice. Running always seemed to help him to figure things out and the ride from Wilcox's had not been long enough to suit him. He was undressing to get into his running clothes when he heard a car drive up. He looked out the window, expecting to see one of the hands, hoping it wouldn't be Wade Archer. He was surprised to see the white T-bird outside with the top off this time. Getting out was a lanky, dark-haired lady who could easily have stepped out of a Victoria's Secret catalog. She was dressed in a black body shirt with long sleeves and white Capri pants that had an expensive look and fit to them. Jack quickly pulled on his running shorts as she came to the door.

"Is someone here?" she said with a slight accent that Jack did not recognize.

"Yeah," said Jack appearing at the screen door. He opened it and stepped out into the sunshine. The woman looked Jack over approvingly. He suddenly became self-conscious, standing there in his running shorts and nothing else.

"You work for Mr. Aleksandrov, do you not?"

"Yes, I guess I do," said Jack. He slid a T-shirt over his head.

"I have a job for you," she said. "What is your name?"

"Jack," he held out his hand, "Jack Wallace." She shook the offered hand with a surprisingly strong grip.

"I'm Anna Petrenko, I am a personal assistant to Mr. Alexander."

"I see," said Jack, wondering what a personal assistant did. "Nice to meet you."

"Mr. Alexander's niece is arriving at the airport in Jackson this afternoon and we find ourselves to be short on drivers. Would it be possible for you to go to Jackson for us Mr. Wallace?"

Jack thought about it a moment then said, "I guess I can do that. What happened to your regular driver?"

"He and his companion went fishing," she said.

"I'll have to ask them how they did. What's the guy's name, the driver?"

"Marion," she hesitated, "Marion Rossi."

"I met him on the road, I think," said Jack. "What do you want me to drive? I'm a little short on luggage room." He turned his head to indicate the motorcycle, which still had the backpack strapped to the sissy bar.

"I see that," she said smiling. "You can take this car." She waved toward the T-bird. "You'll have to leave soon," she said.

"Guess that means I don't have time for a run. Do I have time for a shower?" he asked.

"Of course," she said. "The plane will arrive at 4:30. The girl's name is Elena." She pronounced it 'Eh lay' nah'. "She is dark complexioned and she's a dancer. I'll get you a photograph." Anna walked toward the car. "I'll return with the car in about 20 minutes. You will be ready by then?"

"Sure," said Jack. He stood transfixed as she walked back to the T-bird and got in. She gave him a smile and a slight wave as she drove off, the wind blowing her dark hair. She was beautiful.

Jack showered and shaved. He put on a clean pair of jeans and a KU sweatshirt. He was looking in the mirror, wondering why he was doing this. Jack thought of Joe Riley. He liked the old FBI guy for some reason and he thought maybe he could pick up something to help the investigation. Jack heard the car again and he looked out, surprised to see two cars this time. A black Mercedes driven by Yuri Aleksandrov himself followed the T-bird. Both drivers got out of their vehicles as Jack came out of the bunkhouse. The three of them met in front of the cars.

"Here is everything you will need to pick up Elena," said Anna, handing Jack a manila envelope. "The airport has been notified that you will be the one to receive her."

Jack popped the clasp on the envelope and pulled out a 5X7 black and white photo of a beautiful, smiling young lady striking a pose in ballet tights. "How old is Elena?" he asked.

"She is fifteen," offered Yuri. "Take care of my niece Mr. Wallace. She comes at an inopportune time or I would pick her up myself." He started to walk back to the car when he turned back toward Jack. He reached in his pocket and tossed something to Jack. "You may have expenses. Get yourself some clothes before the plane comes. I don't want my Elena to think I sent a farmer to pick her up," he said smiling. "And take a phone with you." He nodded to Anna, who handed Jack a cellular phone. Anna got in on the other side and the Mercedes pulled away.

Jack looked at the wad of bills in his hand. There must have been a dozen hundred dollar bills in a silver money clip. "Now I've got to go shopping, too," he said to himself. Jack had always looked forward to shopping like a trip to the dentist for a root canal. He looked towards the white car. The top had been put back in place. Jack put the money clip in his pocket and double-checked to make sure he had his billfold. He got in and started the car. The engine sounded powerful. Perhaps this would not be such a chore at all.

The highway felt good to Jack. The little white car was quite responsive and he was enjoying the drive. He had always enjoyed the drive. It gave him time to ponder things. He hadn't even thought of turning on the radio or putting in a CD. He didn't have those options on the old Sportster and he hadn't missed them. He thought now about Anna. Had the circumstances been different, he would have been excited about meeting her. She was mysterious, very beautiful, and she possessed a quality that kind of drew a man in. But she was one of *them*, one of the Aleksandrov crowd which was responsible for Jim Palmer's death. He could feel his face flush with anger when he thought about that. He couldn't believe that those two cretins had come after Bud. Maybe Marion and Mick had acted on their own, but it was difficult for Jack to believe that.

His thoughts went to Kate. He found himself comparing her to Anna. Kate was a few years older than Anna, but hard work and kids made the age difference even more obvious. Kate was pretty where Anna was beautiful. Jack hadn't really had any romantic feelings for Kate. Wade Archer's comment had infuriated him because the man had disparaged a decent woman. Thinking of Archer again brought his anger back. Jack felt like he was awfully close

106

to some sort of edge, the way he kept getting mad about things. His original intent was to come out here and go fishing. He hadn't done much of that either, but there would be time. He would make sure of that.

The Thunderbird wound through the picturesque valley heading for Hoback Junction. The Hoback River meandered back and forth across the valley, crossing underneath the highway several times. The water looked a little high for fishing. At one point near the junction, Jack pulled off and walked down to the river. He had done this several times at this spot. A big hole of blue water swirled directly under a sizeable overhang of the bank. He looked down over the bank to see several big trout languishing in the eddy currents. The big trout were nearly always there. Jack looked at his watch and sighed as he walked back up to the car and got back in.

The Hoback finally met up with the Snake River at Hoback Junction. Highway 191 joined 89 from the south here also. Jack saw the familiar orange pylons of the road crews. It seemed that this highway section had been under construction for years now. Jack recalled getting his shoes and footpegs sticky with tar the last time he rode his bike through this stretch of road. Having traveled this way several times, Jack knew that he was getting close to Jackson. It was hard to imagine that this area was ever wild. It was touted as having been a haven for lawless types in the old days, then came the dude ranches and the National Parks, and now this. The Jackson Hole area was getting built up, especially to the south of the town of Jackson. With Teton National Park to the north and rough mountain country on the west and east, there was nowhere else to go. This explained why land values had skyrocketed around Pinedale as the billionaires pushed the millionaires out of Jackson. Celebrities and other high rollers had bought many of the old ranches. Some of the ranchers relocated to where the land was cheaper. Others just took the money and retired to warmer climates. Jack hated to see the old west disappearing.

CHAPTER EIGHTEEN

As he pulled into the bustling town of Jackson, Jack smelled barbecue. The heavenly aroma of ribs and smoked brisket made his mouth water. He realized that he hadn't eaten all day, but he looked at the clock on the dashboard and decided that he had better go shopping first. He drove on downtown and found a parking spot on a side street. He got out of the car and began walking past shops by the dozens. Many sold souvenirs and T-shirts, while some appeared to be actual art galleries with sculptures and paintings in dramatic displays.

The smell of coffee reached out to the sidewalk like a pheromone to Jack. He heard the cough of an espresso machine and could see a small coffee bar down a few steps. "What the heck," he said to himself, "I've surely got time for a coffee." He went down the short flight of stairs to a kind of mall area and stepped up to the counter. A girl behind the counter looked him over as he read the menu on the wall behind her.

"Get you something?" she finally asked without emotion.

"How about a café au lait," said Jack thinking of New Orleans.

"'Kay," clipped the girl. Jack looked her over as she worked the machine and poured steamed milk. She would have been pretty, in Jack's estimation, but she had apparently gone for the shock value of eyebrow and lip rings rather than compete in the beauty arena. She wore a tanktop, which revealed a tattoo of barbed wire around her flaccid bicep.

Her slim figure was undoubtedly due to diet rather than exercise. Looking at the tattoo, Jack couldn't help but think of all the times he had helped his father try to salvage the feet of cows and horses that had become entangled in wire. The foot would swell and further cut off the circulation, then it would start to rot.

The girl set the steaming cup in front of Jack. "Three fifty," she said. Jack handed her a five and took an exploratory sip of the brew. The girl turned to the register to make change and Jack suddenly thought of an old Far Side cartoon. A crusty, old cowboy walks up to the fire where another squats on his heels. "Latte' Jed?" the one at the fire asks, holding out a cup. Jack smiled involuntarily.

"What?" the girl asked, turning back around.

"Nothing," said Jack. She probably thought he was laughing at her. She grimaced at him as he picked up the coffee and walked off. He had just paid the price of a meal for a cup of coffee. Again he silently lamented the passing of the old west.

He found an upscale fly-fishing shop right in the middle of town that had pricey looking men's casual clothes on mannequins in the window. It was not the sort of place Jack would normally have shopped, but he gathered from Yuri that he was to look sharp when he picked up Elena. There had been a time when he had kept up with fashion, but that seemed a long time ago now. He went in and began to look through the racks for the slacks and shirt he had seen on the mannequin. A girlfriend had told him years ago that he had the fashion sense of a street bum, so he was wary of picking out something that he liked. It took him less than ten minutes to find what he needed. He explained to a clerk that he would wear the clothes now, and she picked him out some shoes while he went to the changing room.

"There now," said the clerk, "You look like you could model for Orvis." Jack laughed at the thought. Looking at himself in the full-length mirror, he thought that he looked like the attorney Jack Wallace. He gathered his old clothes in a bag, thanked the saleslady, and walked back to the car.

He looked at the clock; it was after 4. "I'd better get to the airport," he said to himself. The airport was north of town and it would take a few minutes to get there. He left the busy sidewalks and studios of downtown Jackson behind and drove north. To the right of the highway was an elk refuge, an open grassy area broken by low shrubs and meandering creeks. It went on seemingly for miles. No elk were visible; perhaps it was the wrong time of year.

Jack reached the airport and found a parking spot. Jackson Hole Airport was small as far as airports go. He didn't even have to ride a shuttle; he simply walked over to the single terminal building and walked in. He looked across the small waiting area out the windows and could see several small jets and turboprops parked along the tarmac. A single Airbus 319 dominated the space near the terminal. A ramp had been pulled up to it and passengers were unloading. Jack had seen this plane landing as he approached the airport. He remembered thinking that the backdrop of the Tetons made the jet look like a child's toy. He waited as passengers began to file into the building. At last he saw a stewardess get off the plane talking and laughing with a teenage girl. He knew immediately that the young lady was Elena. They came into the terminal building and Jack walked up to them and introduced himself. The stewardess politely asked Jack for identification and checked his driver's license against the name on the papers she held.

"You're from Kansas," the stewardess said, "My grandmother lives in Wichita."

"That's not far from where I come from," said Jack.

"I hope you had a nice flight," the stewardess said to Elena as she handed Jack's ID back. "Your luggage will be out soon. Please fly with us again."

"How was your flight?" Jack asked.

"Long!" she exclaimed. "I'm worn out and all I've done is sit."

"Here comes the luggage," said Jack. "You'll have to show me which bags." A jumbled lineup of suitcases and duffels had begun to emerge from the wall and began snaking its way around on the belt. Children jostled for position to be the first to get their bags. Jack smiled at a few adults who seemed to have the same idea.

"I have two," Elena said. Jack had expected more from a teenager. "There," she pointed, "The green trunk." Jack saw a solid trunk, slightly larger than the largest suitcase he had ever seen. He pulled it off the belt, guessing its weight at about 70 pounds. She pointed out another duffel, which probably weighed two-thirds as much and sported more outside pockets then a paratroopers vest. Jack was hoping the Thunderbird had a big enough trunk as he hoisted the heavy bags and began to waddle toward the exit.

Jack sent Elena ahead of him through the doors leading to the parking lot. He watched her as he struggled to carry the bags. She was gazing around with a rather awe-struck look on her face. She wore low-cut jeans of the 70's-look variety that seemed to be so popular now days. Her top was close-fitting in narrow horizontal stripes and ended just above her navel. Jack couldn't see any tattoos, just a couple of bracelets on her left arm. He was not a big fan of tattoos, especially on a girl Elena's age. At first glance Jack thought they usually looked like bruises rather than body art. A tattoo on a beautiful girl was like graffiti on a fine sculpture as far as Jack was concerned.

"Where is your car?" asked Elena.

"The white one right over there," Jack pointed with his chin.

"Oh, neat! I just love the new Thunderbirds," she said excitedly.

"It belongs to your uncle," said Jack, not wanting her to think it was his.

They reached the car and Jack popped the trunk. He lifted the large case in and pushed it around to make room for the other bag. He had unlocked the doors with the remote and Elena was already sitting in the passenger seat. He dropped into the driver's seat. "Where did you fly from?" he asked as he started the car and pulled from the parking lot.

"Boston," she said, "then Philadelphia, then Denver, then here."

"That was a lot flying," he said. "You must be worn out."

"Yes, and starved!" she said. "Can we get something to eat?"

"Sure," said Jack, "What do you feel like?"

"I don't know. Something western. What is there?" she asked excitedly.

"There's a place that has buffalo and steaks and stuff like that," said Jack.

"I don't know. That might be a little too western. What else is there?"

"I smelled barbecue when I came into town," he said. "It didn't look very fancy though."

"That sounds perfect," she said, clapping her hands together. Jack was liking this girl. She was full of energy and seemed to genuinely enjoy everything she experienced. Jack could sense her stopping her gaze upon him occasionally. He wondered what she was thinking.

"Can you see the sleeping Indian?" Jack asked, looking out his window.

"What?"

"Look at the top of the ridge to our left." He gave her a moment. "See it?" The top of the mountainous ridge across the valley had the silhouette of an Indian lying down if you looked at it just right.

"Oh, Now I see it. That is so cool! It's like a chief or something, with the headdress."

"That's it alright," said Jack. He drove through the downtown area with its shops and the town square adorned with archways made of intertwined antlers from elk and deer.

"Oh, man!" she said looking at all the antlers, "Did someone kill all those deer to make that?"

"I don't think so," said Jack. "Elk and deer shed their antlers each year. So do moose. You can pick them up out

112

in the mountains sometimes."

"Oh, so they didn't have to kill them then?" she asked.

"Well, they do hunt them out here. Some of them may have been shot. But the hunting helps keep the population in check. People are predators too, you know." Jack was starting to feel like he was preaching. He changed the subject. "So, have you been out west before?" he asked.

"No, not out here. I've been to California, but that's different," she replied.

"Yes, that's definitely different. Especially if you're talking about the cities," he added. He tended to think of California as the "left coast".

"I can't believe these mountains!"

"Pretty incredible," agreed Jack. "So I guess you see your uncle...Yuri isn't it?" She nodded. "I guess you see him when he is back east." Jack was wondering how close she was to the man who may have conspired to commit murder.

"I've only seen him once. He was in New York when we were there. He contacted my mother and wanted to have dinner with us. We met him at a really fancy restaurant. He was very gracious. He ordered caviar, which I didn't like," she said. "He told us about Wyoming and invited me out. So here I am!"

"Is he your mother's brother?" Jack inquired.

"No, he was married to my mother's sister. Her name was Elena, too. My mother lived in Russia before I was born. My aunt Elena died there. I never knew her at all," she said. "But she was very pretty. She and my mother were very close."

"I'm sorry," said Jack.

"That's alright. I would have liked her, I think. She was in the ballet in Moscow. That's where they met. Uncle Yuri and Elena." She pointed to a sign that read: Jackson Hole Ski Area. "They have ski slopes here? I would love to ski in these mountains."

"The Rockies are about as good as it gets, I think,"

said Jack.

"Have you skied here?" she asked.

"No. My uncle used to ski Jackson Hole, so I know it's good," he said. "I've skied Colorado, though, I can vouch for Vail and Copper Mountain." Jack thought the girl looked a little fragile to be a skier. "So you ski back east?"

"Yeah, some, my mother thinks I'm going to break something though," she said, annoyed. "I'm in ballet, you know."

"So I hear," said Jack.

"I guess she thinks that I'll come back from the slopes in a body cast or something."

"Sounds like a mom," said Jack.

"Is that the place you were talking about?" asked Elena, pointing at a sign for the Gun Barrel Steak and Game House. "The one with real buffalo?"

"Yeah, that's the one."

They were coming to a traffic light, which had just turned green, so Jack didn't have to stop. Suddenly, Elena put her hands out and screamed as Jack saw a black car in the intersection in front of him. He slammed on the brakes and the car, a black Jaguar XJ, jerked sideways in front of him, catching his front bumper with its own. The car didn't even slow down as Jack looked at the occupants. The driver was on a cell phone and the passenger was looking directly at them. Both appeared to be middle-eastern, they wore the head-cloth thing. "You son-of-a-bitch!" said Jack, involuntarily. He gunned the Ford and caught up with the Jag. It began accelerating and pulling away.

"Please, don't chase them," screamed the girl, "You're scaring me!" Jack slowed down. He had reacted without thinking about his passenger. He could see that she looked a little shaken.

"Rag heads!" he said under his breath. He looked at Elena. He was afraid that she was going to cry. "I'm sorry," he said, "people like that just sort of ...tick me off." She looked at him. She smiled, and then began to giggle.

"Mr. Wallace," she said, "you are such a nice guy.

Then all at once you are like a wild man. Like a cop on TV!" She was laughing now. "I'm sorry, but it strikes me funny somehow."

"Call me Jack." He said it with a smile. "Mr. Wallace is my dad."

"Okay," she said, regaining her composure, "but you must call me Elle." She pronounced it like the letter of the alphabet.

"I can do that," he said. They had been driving with the windows down and now the smell of smoked meat wafted in through the open windows. "This is the barbecue place. What do you think?" He indicated a rough cedar building with a big sign that read: Billy's BarBQ.

"I think it will be wonderful," she said.

As they got out of the car, the smell of barbecue was overpowering. Jack was glad that this girl had not turned out to be a vegetarian, as seemed to be a popular fad. They went inside and sat down at a table made of thick wood with benches instead of chairs. They ordered and were soon swamped with more food than they could eat. The sliced meats were piled high on the buns. Jack wondered if his mouth would open wide enough to take the first bite. To Jack's surprise the girl ate more than he did. He thought she must have been famished.

"This is so good," she said, squirting on more barbecue sauce from the bottle marked "HOT". "I could have eaten a horse!"

"Well...," said Jack with a deadpan look, "that's what you're eating. It's a big deal out here," he continued. "Horsemeat is a delicacy."

She stopped chewing. "No!" she said, a worried look on her face. It took her a moment to realize that they had ordered beef, ham, and turkey. Jack couldn't keep a straight face and let a smile slip. "YOU!" She was grinning, but mad at the same time. "You're ornery!" She was laughing again.

"I had you going there for a minute," he said.

"You are quite the comedian, I think," she said with a

broad smile. Jack thought that the girl's smile made her look like someone from the movies. She had raised, dark eyebrows that were not painted on, and her mouth was wide when she smiled, showing a perfect set of teeth. She looked at Jack and giggled again, then she took a napkin and dabbed it in her water. She reached over the table and wiped some sauce off of Jack's chin.

"Thanks," he said.

"Do I have any?" she asked.

"No, you look great," he said. She grinned again and met his eyes. Jack didn't know why he had said that. It was just that she *was* a very pretty girl.

CHAPTER NINETEEN

They finished their food and Jack paid the bill. When they got to the car, Jack checked out a black smudge on the corner of the white integrated bumper on the T-bird. It could probably be easily fixed. He was glad that the air bags hadn't deployed when the other car bumped them. They continued south alongside the Snake River, with Elle continually asking questions and talking excitedly. "Are we going to ride horses while I'm here?" she asked.

"I'm sure you can," said Jack. The "we" part of her question was not lost on him. "Have you ridden before?"

"I rode dressage until last year when my mother made me quit," she said.

"Why did she make you quit?"

"She wanted me to concentrate on the ballet," she said with resignation. "She is right though, both things take a lot of time. I had to choose one or the other."

"We have plenty of horses at the ranch," said Jack, "but there may not be anyone to ride with."

"You could ride with me, Jack," she said with a smile.

"I'd like nothing better," he said, "but I have to work sometime. I ride for a living...for Mr. Alexander."

"Are you kidding?" she asked. "You ride a horse for a living?"

"Well, yeah," said Jack, "for the time being anyway."

"So you're like a cowboy?"

"Like, yeah," said Jack, teasing her.

"That is so cool!" she said. "You don't dress like a

cowboy."

"Well, not today maybe," he said.

"I'll talk Uncle into letting you off," she said.

Jack smiled. "I'll bet you could," he said. He thought for a minute. "I know some really nice people with a dude ranch that have a girl's camp going on right now. Most of the girl's are a little younger than you, but you might like it."

"That could be fun," she said.

"Many of the girls are from places like Atlanta, Charlotte, maybe even Boston," he said. "We'll have to ask your uncle if he'll let me take you over there. It's just on the other side of Pinedale." Jack thought the girl was going to get bored out on the Circle "A".

Jack tried to give Elena the windshield tour without sounding like it. He stopped along the Hoback and showed her the trout in the big blue hole where he had stopped earlier. When they came out into the high rolling hills towards Pinedale, Elle had him stop twice more so that she could look at the antelope alongside the highway. The antelope walked quickly away but would turn back and stand there to look at the intruders. The creatures fascinated the girl from Boston.

They came to the Green River and Jack explained how it started up high in the mountains from glaciers and snowmelt. He had always been fascinated by the fact that so much water could just keep pouring out of the mountains. It was almost impossible to comprehend.

They were nearing the turnoff for the ranch when Elena said, "Those mountains are incredible! They are so much more rugged than what I expected." She was pointing toward the high peaks of the Wind River Range, which dominated the horizon to the northeast. A few lazy clouds hung around the taller peaks, but the day was clear and the sun was bright, putting the mountains in dramatic relief. Snow capped several of the taller peaks and the late afternoon light gave a rich orange glow to the jagged rocks. This contrasted with the deepening shadows of the valleys giving the whole scene a surreal appearance.

"Those are the Winds," said Jack. "That one right there," he tried to point out a single peak, "is Fremont Peak. I climbed that once on a fishing trip. It's the second highest peak in Wyoming. I think it's around thirteen seven or something like that."

"Was it hard to climb?"

"Not really. It's like climbing a giant rock pile. You don't need ropes or anything like that. The weather has to be good though. When you reach the top ridge it just takes your breath away. It's a sheer drop into a huge glacier way down below on the other side."

"That sounds wild," she said. She looked around once again, trying to take it all in. "I can't believe how big it is out here!"

Jack pulled into the ranch entry and took the right fork to the big house. Elle was impressed with the enormity of Yuri's villa and its view of the mountain range behind it. They pulled up in front of the house on the circle drive and Jack shut off the car. He assumed Elena would be staying in the main house. The front door opened and Yuri Aleksandrov stepped out.

"My dear Elena," he said, giving her a hug. When Yuri pronounced her name it sounded as if it started with a "Y"; it sounded very Russian, Jack thought. "You are more beautiful than ever. And so mature." He stepped back and looked at her. "You look so much like your mother," he said. "How is she?"

"Momma is fine. She sends her love," said the girl, smiling. Anna came out of the open door.

"Anna," said Yuri, turning, "I want you to meet my niece, Elena. Elena, this is Anna." The two embraced cordially.

"Welcome, Elena, how was your flight?" asked Anna.

"It was okay. Just kind of long," she said.

"Are you hungry? Did they have dinner on the plane?" Anna asked.

"We ate in Jackson," Elena said. "Jack took me to a

119

wonderful barbecue place. I'm stuffed." Jack was bringing the bags up now. Anna gave him a look that he did not know how to interpret, but she seemed to be somewhat amused.

"Can I carry these inside?" Jack asked holding the heavy trunk and duffel.

"No, just put them down. Tino will get them," said Anna. Just then a small man in a white coat and black pants came out. He smiled at them and picked up the bags. Jack wondered if he would even be able to carry the trunk, but the little man seemed to be managing. He appeared to be of Asian decent and dressed like a butler. Anna did not introduce him and he said nothing, he just smiled and nodded, carrying and half-dragging the bags inside.

Yuri spoke to Elena, "Come, come in my dear. Let me show you where you will stay."

"I'll take you back down the hill," Anna said to Jack. She walked toward the car and got in on the driver's side.

"Oh, Jack, thanks for everything. You've been a great tour guide," Elena had approached Jack and now gave him a hug. "We'll go riding soon," she whispered.

"The pleasure was all mine," he said, "Bye, Elle." He walked to the car then turned to Yuri. "I have some change for you," he said, feeling his pockets for the money clip.

"No, No," said Yuri, "You keep whatever was left. A small bonus for helping us out."

"Oh, no," said Jack, "That's way too much. I..."

Yuri interrupted him. "I insist," he said, holding up a hand. Jack tried to protest again but Yuri would not listen. Jack got in the car with Anna; he waved once more to Elle.

Anna drove slowly back out the drive. She turned to Jack. "So, it's 'Elle' is it?" said Anna with a smile.

"That's what she asked me to call her," said Jack. "What?" He turned to look at Anna, wondering what she was getting at.

"The girl is smitten with you," she said. "Can't you tell?" Jack had to smile.

"She wants me to take her riding," he said.

"And what did you say?" asked Anna.

"I told her I had to work."

"Nonsense," said Anna with a laugh, "Of course you'll take her riding. That will be part of your work. We mustn't let the poor girl get bored." Anna seemed to find this all very funny. Jack didn't respond. They were at the bunkhouse now. He got out, grabbing his boots and the sack of his old clothes, which had spilled out behind the seat. He left the cell phone on the seat in the car.

"Goodbye, Jack," said Anna, "and thanks for everything." She said it with a breathless voice, mimicking Elena. Jack had to laugh. Anna was enjoying this at Jack's expense, yet she seemed maybe just a little jealous. "I'll call you when we need you," she said and drove off. Jack stood there for a moment, wondering again what he was getting himself into.

"I think I need that run, now," he said to himself, looking at the retreating sun.

He changed quickly into his running clothes and took off down the drive. He ran very slowly at first since he hadn't taken the time to warm up. He looked over toward the big house as he headed out the driveway. He thought about Elle. She was innocent enough. If Yuri was everything Joe Riley thought he was, this was no place for the girl. His thoughts kept drifting back to Anna. She was stunningly beautiful, and she seemed very intelligent. Letting his thoughts go where they would, he couldn't stop thinking about her. He felt as if he was doing something dangerous just entertaining thoughts of her. He knew she was on the wrong side, but something told him that she wasn't a criminal, or maybe he was just hoping that was the case. Jack kept telling himself that he had to stick with the facts. He could not operate from emotions in this or he would screw everything up. Now he was sounding like a lawyer again. That was part of what had made him leave that all behind, the fact that he could never separate his innate sense of right and wrong from the cold hard facts and the law. Sometimes these things conflicted and Jack was immensely troubled when they did. Nothing was ever that simple. His watch beeped and he turned around.

CHAPTER TWENTY

The next morning Jack was at the parts store early. He picked up the oil filter that the man had ordered for him earlier and bought some oil. Reid was in the backroom stocking parts on the shelves and Jack talked with him for a little while. He apparently didn't know anything of what had happened the day before and Jack didn't prod him at all on the subject. The store's owner had graciously offered Jack the bay in the back of the parts store to change his oil. Jack had decided to take him up on the offer and performed the much-needed maintenance. Reid watched with interest and Jack explained things as he went. "Oil is the lifeblood of any motor, even more so with an air-cooled one like a motorcycle," Jack explained, trying to sound like his old shop teacher in high school. He checked a few other things and oiled and tightened his chain, while he had the use of the facilities. Customers were coming in steadily now and Reid was needed up front. Jack wished the boy luck and thought to himself that he might need it as he looked at the line of characters at the counter in the front of the store. All kinds of people with all kinds of problems stood there waiting with greasy parts in their hands.

Jack pushed the motorcycle out the back and closed the door. He thought of all the times that he had waited at the counter at a parts store with some one-off custom contraption of his own, only to be waited on by some kid with no idea what he was talking about. They would always ask for model numbers and years so that they could look up the parts on the computer or in some huge parts book. Jack

122

would have to explain that it was a fifty-seven Chevy motor but it was in a sixty-one Chris Craft ski boat and that the part in his hand wasn't the original. The kid behind the counter would get this dazed look in his eyes and Jack would politely ask if the owner was around. It would be the same with Reid. It took a real motor-head geek-type to be good behind a parts counter. Jack swung his leg over the bike and gave the starter a kick.

The Wrangler Cafe looked like the main breakfast and coffee spot for the little ranching community, so that's where Jack went next. He had some time to kill before he needed to meet with Joe Riley. He went in and sat at the counter. He drank coffee while waiting on some breakfast and listened to the babble of the café crowd.

"Did you here what happened up at Glimpse Lake?" said a man in a giveaway, feed-store cap to another who had just walked in.

"What?" asked the second man. He had just driven up in a cement truck coming back from an early morning pour.

"Couple a' imports from out ta' Circle "A" went fishin' and killed each other," said the first man.

"Are you kiddin' me?" asked the second.

"That ain't all," said the first, "Ol' John Kirby took them up there and he's dead too."

"No shit!" the man exclaimed. "They killed him too?"

"Naw, the rangers think he was comin' out fast ta' report the deaths and his horse fell and killed him," the first man explained. "Looks that way anyhow."

Jack was taking all this in and trying not to choke on his coffee. He began to hear others talking about the news, also. The comments ran more toward Kirby than the other two. "He was kinda' worthless but he didn't deserve that," and "He was sure good with horses. He started my old bay, best horse I ever had..." were some of the jewels of wisdom imparted over the incident. John Kirby would probably be a

123

hero before the day was over. It would be even more dramatic when the bars opened in the afternoon. The waitress brought his food. "That's really horrible what happened up there," she said to Jack.

"Sure is," he said, declining further comment. He finished his breakfast quickly, hoping to avoid anyone recognizing him as a Circle "A" employee. It was nearing 10 o'clock so he went on across town to Faler's. He parked his bike in front of the hardware store side of the complex and, not seeing Riley, he went inside. He picked up a free paper with vacation-type ads in it and went back out front looking for a place to sit down. Just as he came out, a beige, official-looking car pulled up and he recognized the driver as Joe Riley. Jack walked on out to the car and the agent indicated that he should get in.

"Hello, Jack," said Riley, as the younger man entered the passenger side of the car.

"Morning," said Jack. "Heard the latest gossip?"

"No, but I have a pretty good idea what it might be," said Riley. He put the car in gear and left the parking lot as Jack recounted what he had heard in the Wrangler. Riley began to drive on a road that went past the Museum of the Mountain Man, a memorial to the trappers who used to rendezvous on the Green River, and on up to Freemont Lake. The paved road was nice and headed northeast towards the mountains on a slow gentle climb. The Lake itself was good sized and served to provide irrigation water for the area as well as recreation. The lake had a small marina on the south end and was a popular place for boating and even swimming and skiing if you could stand the cold water. Riley pulled off toward the lake and stopped at a little beach area with a parking lot. The place was deserted as usual this early in the year; it took a pretty warm day to bring anyone out to the beach up here. "So what's happening out at the ranch?" the agent asked.

"I had to drive to Jackson to pick up Alexander's niece yesterday. Seems they were short on drivers," said Jack.

"Really," said Riley.

"It seems as if the regular driver went fishing and hadn't come back yet."

"And he won't," said the agent. "I think the story we put out is going to work just fine."

"From what I heard at the coffee shop, I'd say it already has."

"That's good," said Riley. He was silent for a moment, then began, "Look, Jack, I can't tell you much about our investigation right now. I can tell you that it is vitally important. It may be a lot bigger than just the killing of one man." He stopped talking for a moment and then added. "I don't mean that Jim Palmer is unimportant, but there are bigger considerations."

"What is it that you're investigating Aleksandrov for?" asked Jack.

"First let me ask you something, Jack," said Riley. "You're in a position to help us...that is...if you're willing."

"How could I be of any help?" asked Jack. He had already surmised that they wanted him to get information.

"Your close proximity, right there on the ranch, gives you a lot of room to maneuver. I've checked you out thoroughly, Jack, and I feel like you can help us a lot," said Riley.

"So you've investigated me?" asked Jack.

"We've checked out everyone going in or out of that place for the past few weeks. But I did better than that on you," said Riley, smiling.

"What does that mean?" asked Jack.

"Once I found out who you were, I called an old friend about you."

"And who might that be?" asked Jack warily.

"An old vice-cop-turned-private-detective from Kansas City," said Riley with a grin. It was beginning to dawn on Jack where he had seen Riley before.

"I've met you before, haven't I?" asked Jack, looking hard at Riley.

"Twenty years ago, at least," said Joe.

125

"You're Uncle Jack's old ski buddy. You came to Thanksgiving dinner at our house when I was a kid," Jack recalled aloud. It all came back to him now. His Uncle Jack was a cop on the K. C. Metro Squad back then. Uncle Jack was now a P. I., still working the Kansas City area. Jack knew that he still worked with the FBI occasionally and had a lot of respect for them. "You guys talked a lot about skiing Jackson Hole back then. Do you still ski?"

"No," said Riley, "bad knees. We used to hit the slopes pretty hard though. Jack Hayes is pretty competitive. He doesn't like to be beat."

"That's Uncle Jack alright."

They talked on for a while about Jack's namesake uncle who had always been a practical joker as well as a loyal friend to both the agent and Jack. When old home week was over, they got back to the business at hand. "Anyway," said Riley, "your uncle has a lot of confidence in you. He claims that if anyone can pull this off, it's you."

"I think maybe you better tell me what it is that we're pulling off," said Jack.

"Fair enough," said Riley. He paused for a moment watching a small catamaran cruising up the lake, its sail billowing in the wind as it turned on a new tack. "U.S. intelligence monitors everything they can nowadays, Jack, we have a lot of technological goodies that we never dreamed of in the past. The problem is, the bad guys know about most of them and they know how to get around them. Our best sources of information are still people on the ground." He paused again and glanced at Jack, then looked back up the lake to find the sailboat again. "There has been some talk about tactical nuclear devices missing from the old Soviet arsenal. You may have heard something about it on the talk shows. Some ex-general named Lebed and others throw out numbers and claim that munitions are missing, but none of it can be verified and some of these guys just like to get on the talk shows. Most of that talk has been discounted, but we do think that some of these smaller weapons existed and may not have ever been on the military lists."

126

"You're talking about what? A suitcase bomb?" asked Jack.

"Well, sort of," Joe went on, "It's not your basic Samsonite case, the things will probably weigh close to 100 pounds. The thing is; they don't require a president to press a big red button somewhere. They can be activated by whoever is in possession of them."

"So you think Aleksandrov may have one of these devices?" asked Jack.

"Let me finish my story," said Joe with a patient smile. "These devices were made for the KGB. They're small compared to most nukes, maybe a kiloton. That's like 1000 tons of TNT." He paused again to let that soak in. "They could easily wipe out Capitol Hill or the Kremlin. You get the picture. And, then there's the fallout."

"Not the sort of thing that you would want in the hands of terrorists," said Jack.

"Exactly," said Joe. "Recent information from the Middle East has alerted us to the possibility of one of these things coming on the market. Just rumblings mainly, the information coming out of there is generally not too reliable, but there's enough this time to take it seriously."

"What makes you think it's Aleksandrov?" asked Jack.

"He's former KGB, for one thing, high enough up the ladder to have known where and how to get hold of one of the weapons," replied Joe. "He's also an opportunist. He's sold or stolen just about anything else you can think of to make a buck since the Soviet Union broke up."

"So can't you just tap his E-mail or something and find out?" asked Jack.

"NSA has been doing something like that. So far, we've got nothing on him. In fact the only thing he's done in the last several years is lose a lot of money on tech stocks. We can't cover everything, but we can cover a lot. Cell phone intercepts, wire taps, those are all well and good. We can do more now than at anytime since the Church Committee hearings, but I think Yuri knows that. He's not going to tip his hand to us like that."

"You can't just storm the place with federal agents and bring him in?" asked Jack.

"It doesn't work that way, Jack. You know that. Believe it or not this guy is a naturalized U.S. citizen as of about six years ago," said Joe. He looked at Jack's reaction. "Our borders were a sieve back then...and still are as far as that goes."

"How can I help?" asked Jack finally.

"Just be there," replied Joe. "Keep your eyes and ears open. We'll know more as things unfold."

"I wasn't planning on staying here forever," said Jack.

"You won't have to," said Riley. "If this is a real threat, and I think it is, something will happen soon. Aleksandrov is going short on the markets in a big way. He's looking for a major crash. I can't help but think that he knows that something big is coming down and he's a part of it." Riley looked down at his hands gripped on the steering wheel. "Not everybody in the Bureau thinks this is real," he said somewhat wistfully. "We're strung out pretty thin, if the truth were known." He reached in an envelope on the seat and produced some papers. "Here's your new ID."

Jack looked at the attached driver's license and social security card. He was surprised at first that Riley had been so confident. But then again, he was surprised at himself also, for in his mind he had already accepted the assignment. "It doesn't look any different from..." he started to say, and then he realized that the numbers were different and it had a Topeka address.

"If they do any background on you, they can't trace you back to any of your relatives," said Riley. He was not smiling now. "These people are dangerous, Jack. I think you already know that."

"What about the Wilcox family?" asked Jack. "Aren't they in danger?"

"Kate and the two younger kids are going on vacation for a couple of weeks," said Joe. "We are fairly certain,

128

from cell phone intercepts, that the only people who knew about what Bud saw are dead. They probably didn't want their boss to know they screwed up. Reid is not going with the family. He will stay with the neighbors and work at his summer job. We'll keep monitoring things. We can protect him."

"Was Jim Palmer under your protection?" asked Jack seriously.

"No," said Joe, "we had no reason to believe he knew anything or was in any kind of danger."

"Who is *we* by the way?" Jack interrupted. "Is this just an FBI investigation?"

"Homeland Security, Jack," said Joe. "That's all of us. I'm with a special task force out of Denver dealing with organized crime in the Rocky Mountain States, but since the nine eleven thing, we're all in this together. We're getting help from Langley and the NSA. We even have an FBI office in Moscow now, believe it or not. When the president asked for cooperation after nine eleven, he got it. But homeland security is you too Jack. Every citizen has to be vigilant."

"Okay, Okay!" said Jack chuckling. "I believe."

"I know," said Joe. "Your uncle assured me you would rise to the task."

"How am I going to keep in touch with you?" asked Jack.

"For now, if you keep up your evening runs, I'll meet you when you're out of sight of the ranch," said Joe. He started the car and pulled away from the beach area. "I really appreciate this, Jack," said Riley. He pulled out onto the pavement and headed back for town.

As they went back down the drive from the lake, Jack was thinking about a lot of things. It was dawning on him just what a disaster one of these tactical nuclear devices would be in the wrong hands. He thought about airports and security checks, how they were searching grannies and children. What would you do just check your nuke and walk on the plane? He suddenly felt the hair on the back of his neck stand up. Suitcases! One hundred pounds!

"Joe!" he said, startling Riley out of a reverie of his own. "Alexander's niece had a big suitcase." His mouth was suddenly dry, when he thought of what he might have been carrying.

"We checked it," said Riley, "the girl has lots of clothes."

"How did you know?"

"Like I said, we have phone taps. We checked her bags when she changed planes in Denver." Riley gave Jack a smile. "But you're thinking. That's what I want you to do." Jack felt a little foolish for having gotten excited, but it was too late now. He hoped Riley didn't think he was stupid.

Back at the parking lot at Faler's, Joe Riley handed Jack a pair of binoculars in a nylon case. "You might need these," he said. Jack took the case and strapped it on the bike. "I'll be in touch," said Riley as he drove away.

As Jack started the bike and pulled out onto Pine Street, a dark figure in a primer-gray and green Chevy pickup watched him leave. The man struck a match to light a cigarette and, if Jack had been looking, he would have recognized the face of Wade Archer behind the flare of the match.

CHAPTER TWENTY-ONE

After leaving Jack, Riley went back to his motel and pulled into the parking lot. He shut off the car and sat there for a moment; his talking with Jack had him thinking about when he was a young man. He liked Jack Wallace and could see a lot of his old friend in the younger man. He had actually known Jack Hayes since their fraternity days at a small state college in Kansas. The memories came flooding back of all the crazy things that they had done together. He remembered the ingenious ways that Jack used to come up with to torture the pledges and he had to laugh. One time they set up an old commode in a closet of the annex to the fraternity house. After having washed it out really well at the car wash, they poured in water and tossed in some peeled bananas. After blindfolding the pledges and scaring them to death with threats, they would take them one at a time to the closet. On hands and knees they would have to fish a banana out of the stool and eat it. Some would flat refuse, but most were so harried they would dip in eagerly. Joe laughed at the thought. Most of the pledges could tell that it was a banana and would try to eat it, but it was hard to get around the fact that it came out of a stool. To think that those young men that they had harassed all those years ago were now old men just like him. The thought made Joe laugh out loud.

Riley got out his pipe and began to methodically tamp in the tobacco one thin layer at a time with a golf tee. Packing his pipe had become a ritual. If he didn't have time to pack it right, then he didn't have time to enjoy it and, therefore, he wouldn't even bother to get it out. As he struck a large kitchen match, he let the sulfur burn off before lighting the pipe; his mind was still on Jack Hayes and the good times they had together, and how long ago that all seemed. He pledged to himself that, when this was over, he was going to go visit Jack back in Kansas City. He grabbed the crank and rolled the window down a few inches, letting the fragrant, blue tobacco smoke roll out of the car. A rapping on the passenger side window arrested his thoughts and he looked over at an aging black man standing there looking in at him. The government-issue, civil service sedan did not have power windows or power anything else for that matter, so Riley simply motioned for the man to get in the car with him.

"Good thing you don't smoke that thing in the motel. You'd set off the smoke detector." The black man smiled as he spoke. He rolled down the window on the passenger side as he took a seat in the car. He pulled the door shut. "Smells kinda good though. Makes me wanta have a cigarette." Leroy had quit smoking cigarettes years ago and knew that his wife would kill him if she ever found out he had had one, and she *would* find out.

"Hello, Leroy," said Riley.

"How'd the recruiting go?"

"I think it went very well."

"Glad to hear it. Maybe we can get this gig over-with in a hurry, now," said Leroy, shaking his head.

"You don't think there's anything here, do you?" asked Riley.

"Let's say I'm hoping." The man grinned and looked at Riley. "You still think there is, though. Lord knows you got a nose for this stuff. You been acting like a pointer pup with his first scent of a covey, nosin' all around, sure that there's something here, but just haven't seen the birds yet."

"I can feel the heat off their bed ground."

"I hope you're wrong this time."

"So do I my friend. So do I."

The two men got out of the car and Riley tapped out his pipe on his heel in the parking lot. They went into the motel, and Riley got out a government-issue, topographical map of the area that had been made during a U. S. Geological Survey, probably back in the sixties. Leroy slipped on a pair of reading glasses as he watched Riley run his finger over the little lines indicating elevation and relief.

"There," said Riley, pointing at a small cross on the map. "That's a cemetery up on the hill behind the house."

"Yeah, so?" asked Leroy.

"I was thinking of putting one of us up there with the long lens. We might get something...catch a glimpse of them packing assault rifles...I don't know. We need some evidence of something going down here, if we ever want to convince the Denver office to get us some more help." He moved his finger along a dashed line winding around the back of the big hill and stopping at the summit. "This must be the road up to cemetery," said Riley.

"Yep," said Leroy, "the gate to that trail is just across the creek. It's got a 'no trespassing' sign on the gatepost." Leroy thought a minute. "Trouble is if that big jet comes in, we'd be standing out like a neon sign from up there."

"That's true," said Riley, "but we need to get around behind the house for a good look."

"I think I can do that," said Leroy. "This might work right in here." He pointed to an area where the irrigation ditch came close to the runway. "This area's all grown up in willows now. It just don't show up on this antique map you got here."

"Alright, you be the judge. Be sure to take that digital camera with the big lens whenever you're out there. If we could get an idea who else is involved...maybe catch them flying in somebody on the list..." Riley stopped short, knowing that as short on manpower as he was it was going to be tough.

"If we get something, some pictures maybe, that'll wake some people up. That might be just what it takes to convince the brass that we got a live one out here," said Leroy, looking up at Riley. He was trying to give the man some hope, but his eyes betrayed the fact that he didn't put

133

much faith in what he was saying. Riley just looked at him and smiled.

"You might be right. I hope you are and that we get something to send up the line and start a bureaucratic brushfire." He grinned again at Leroy and went back to the map.

The two agents discussed the surveillance of the ranch and how they were going to try to get closer than the drive-bys they had been doing up to this point. A car would easily be seen from the air as out-of-place and that jet would have a bird's-eye view every time it made a pass, which seemed to be every few days.

"You need to camouflage yourself, Leroy."

"I'm a duck hunter from way back. I'll have myself a make-shift blind in no time...comfortable too."

The real problem was that they didn't have enough manpower to do the surveillance right. All they had were a few agents that were all either approaching retirement age or past it. That was proof that some pencil-headed bureaucrat up the ladder had already decided that this was a wild goose chase, but Riley had decided that it might just be for real. In fact it had better be for real, because he had already called in a chit from another should-already-be-retired desk jockey in the Denver office in order to bring Jack in as a free-lance. Riley had even stretched the truth a little on Jack's credentials in order to convince the man. He had sort of given the guy a resume of a young Jack Hayes instead of telling him that Jack Wallace was a lawyer who got tired of his job and took off on a motorcycle to go on a walkabout out west for a couple of years. Again Riley was going with his instinct rather than just sticking with the documented facts. He just felt that there was not enough time to get an agent to infiltrate even if he had one available.

"Where's Cecil?" asked Riley.

"He went down to Provo. His brother-in-law died and he had to go to the funeral," said Leroy. "Gonna' leave us even more short-handed for the next couple of days."

That was another problem with using the older agents

in the field, you could spur them or whip them all you wanted, but they would never go any faster than they wanted to. It was like an old horse that refused to get out of a trot. Younger agents you could push pretty hard, kind of like the pledges in a fraternity; their job and reputation were at stake. Cecil Albertson wasn't going to be pushed and Riley certainly couldn't blame him. Family is still the most important thing to most people or at least it should be.

Cecil had been the night man for this operation. He claimed that he couldn't sleep more than an hour at a time without getting up to go pee anyway, so he might as well be working. Riley knew that to be partially true. Cecil did have prostate trouble, but he had always taken the night jobs. The guy seemed to sleep fine during the day.

Riley himself wouldn't have been here if things had worked out as he had planned. He always thought that he would put in his thirty years with the bureau and retire back toward Kansas City where his wife's family was. They would play bridge and socialize, and he would finally have time to fix up that fifty-five Nomad that he'd had in storage for the last fifteen years. He had imagined cruising around to the car shows and going on Caribbean cruise ship vacations, the whole nine yards. He hadn't counted on Evelyn getting breast cancer. She hadn't lasted even a year. Maybe Jack Wallace had it right. Live your life in the present for tomorrow may never come.

"You and I are going to have to cover while he's gone," said Riley. "Now that we've got a man on the inside, it should be a little easier, but he's green as a gourd and we have to protect him."

"He looks an awful lot like Jack Hayes," said Leroy. "If he's as tough as that old scoundrel, he will take care of himself and then some."

"He's tough," said Riley. "I can feel it."

"You and your feelings. Sometimes I think that you're as bad as my wife about running on your intuition," Leroy said with a smile. "Trouble is, most of the time you and her are both right."

"Yeah, well I got a feeling you better get some sleep, Leroy. You may have to take the night shift tonight."

"What are you gonna' do?"

"Right now I'm going to go back and talk to Ben Tate and make sure our cover story is working out right. I may have to give him a little more of the real story, let him know about Jack. I've been thinking about letting him pick a deputy he can trust to help us out, but it will have to be someone who can keep his mouth shut."

"Wouldn't be the first time local law enforcement spooked the game on us."

"Tate won't let that happen. I'll make sure of that. He's sure been good so far with the ranger thing. From what Jack heard at the coffee shop, these folks took the bait... hook, line, and sinker." Riley thought to himself that they were extremely lucky on that standpoint. He just hoped that their luck would hold out until this thing was over.

CHAPTER TWENTY-TWO

When Jack got back to the ranch after his talk with Riley, he went up to the old headquarters house and gave Nadine Palmer his "new" social security number and other information. He offered his condolences and asked if he could help with anything around the house.

"That's good of you, but no," she said. "Miss Anna is going to take over paying you boys. I plan to move into town with my sister." The woman paused, finding it hard to speak. "This has been home for quite a while. I've enjoyed cookin' for you boys. I suppose someone else will be livin' here soon."

Jack walked back down to the bunkhouse. He began looking through his box of clothes, trying to find something to wear for the funeral the next day. He heard a vehicle pull up outside and looked out the window to see who it was. It was Charlie.

"Howdy Jack," Charlie said coming in the bunkhouse.

"What's new?" asked Jack.

"Nadine says they want my wife and I to move in here and run this place," said Charlie. He looked at Jack expectantly.

"You gonna' do it?" asked Jack.

"Maybe," said Charlie, "maybe not."

"Things will be kind of slow for awhile now," said Jack.

"Yeah, I know," said Charlie. "I wouldn't mind the pay raise. My wife could quit her job and cook for the hands. It seems like a good idea."

"You hear what happened to the two goons?" said Jack, meaning Marion and Mick.

"Couldn't have happened to two nicer guys," said Charlie without smiling. He changed the subject back to the ranch. "I know of a couple of hands who would work. They're on the rodeo circuit right now, but will probably wash out by the time we need them this fall. I guess you're not staying around?" he asked, thinking he already knew the answer.

"Not that long," said Jack.

"First thing I'd do is fire that fool Archer," said Charlie. "Jim would have done that a long time ago, if he had been the one that hired him."

"Who did hire Archer?" asked Jack.

"The dead guy, Marion," said Charlie. "Kind of pushed him down Jim's throat. Jim went to Alexander, but that didn't seem to help." He looked out across the meadow at the lush green hayfield with seed-heads waving in the breeze like ripples on water. "Jim already had Homer Goodall lined up to do the hay this year. I reckon there ain't much goin' on here for awhile." He looked at Jack. "Abe's quittin' if I don't take the foreman job."

"When do they want to know?" asked Jack.

"Next week."

"I'll hang around if I've got a job," said Jack. "For a few weeks anyway."

"You got one as long as you want one, Jack," said Charlie. It sounded as if Charlie had made a decision about the job.

"Thanks," said Jack. Charlie walked to the door, hesitated as if he had something else to say, then he put his head down and walked out. Jack knew that he was feeling bad about jumping into Jim Palmer's shoes so quickly, but it couldn't be helped. He heard Charlie's pickup leave.

Jack decided to take a walk up the hill behind the bunkhouse and try to survey the layout of the big house from a higher vantage point. He put on his old felt hat and took the binoculars that Joe Riley had given him. When he got to the top of the hill, he circled back behind a small clump of spruce trees. He crawled up under one of the trees and pulled out the glasses in the shade where he figured they wouldn't make a reflection. He scanned around the area of the villa where it was perched on the end of a flat where the runway had been constructed. The day was perfect; sunshine flooded the entire area, taking away all the shadows. A large irrigation ditch and the hayfield separated the old ranch headquarters and bunkhouse from Alexander's personal spread. Jack could see the big house and pool from here quite well.

Some movement by the pool caught his eye. Two women were toweling off after a swim. He could see, with the aid of the binoculars, that it was Anna and Elle. He felt a twinge of guilt at spying on the ladies, yet he also felt a bit of an adrenaline rush like he was looking into the girls' locker room or something. He could tell that Elle was laughing and Anna was smiling as well. The two women looked so relaxed and happy that it was hard to imagine that something sinister was happening here. Jack wondered if all the suspicions were just paranoia from the spy community. It was entirely possible that they were wrong about Yuri. Then he thought again about what Jim Palmer had said, and of Marion and Mick. Maybe he just wanted to believe that Anna was innocent. Just thinking about her was exciting. Again he looked through the glasses and focused on Anna. She had put an arm around Elle, giving her a hug, and the two walked toward the house.

As the women disappeared Jack put down the glasses. Out of the corner of his eye, he thought he saw a flash from the big knob that stretched out beyond the runway on the other side of the little valley. He picked up the glasses and focused, scanning along the crest of the big hill. At the top was a small fenced area containing a small cemetery. It was probably from some family who had homesteaded here or the family that had established the ranch anyway. A large, gnarled old juniper was the only tree; and several big granite rocks, stranded by a melting glacier eons ago, surrounded the old tree near the headstones. He saw a movement, then a slight flash of reflection once again. As he looked he could just make out a man, standing behind a large stone cross that evidently marked a grave. The man was leaning on the cross and looking through something. Jack's body tensed involuntarily, as he realized that the position was as if the man were aiming a rifle. But it wasn't a rifle. It was a spotting scope on a tripod. Just then, the man folded the tripod and picked up the scope. Jack watched as the man turned and walked away from the cross, away from the cemetery. The man put something white on his head just as he ducked down out of sight over the crest of the knob. A slight puff of dust appeared and as Jack watched, he thought he saw the black, shiny top of a vehicle appear and then disappear just over the brow of the hill.

So he wasn't the only one surveying the Circle "A". Perhaps it was some of Riley's people. He would have to find out.

Jack walked on down the back of the hill and came around it from the west, just below the bunkhouse. He doubted that anyone had seen him go walking at all, but he wanted to make it look good, just in case. As he came to the empty bunkhouse, he suddenly thought of the black Jag that had bumped him when he had picked up Elle. He had not reported the damage and had forgotten to tell Anna or Yuri. He thought about it for a moment and then decided that it might look good for him to tell someone now. He would also get another look at the house if he just showed up at the door.

Jack had forgotten about lunch and realized that it was after noon. He microwaved a prepackaged hamburger from the freezer as he looked around the phone for a number to the main house. He found nothing other than the number to Palmer's house, which was written on a sticky note that was now bleached out by sunlight coming in the window. He bit into the sandwich and felt the roof of his mouth erupt in flames as some hot cheese scorched it. He shook his head, as if that would help, and groaned until the pain subsided. He chose the next bite out of the middle of the burger and found it to be partially frozen. At least that felt good after the first bite. He let the sandwich cool while he put on a clean shirt and looked at himself in the mirror. He wasn't sure why, but he wanted to look good when he knocked on the door of the villa.

Jack walked out the door of the bunkhouse and down the lane to the small bridge that crossed the irrigation ditch. He then cut across the hay meadow toward the sprawling house on the plateau above him. He reached the drive and walked across the paved circle to the large porch, which covered the front entryway. Neatly laid paving bricks lined the entire circle drive and gently curved into the porch and covered its floor. Two large multi-paneled doors stood before him. They were made of beautifully varnished mahogany and Jack was admiring them when he noticed the camera. It was concealed to some extent by some foliage tied to a brass lamp by a ribbon. He thought that he had better ring the bell if he was being watched so he reached for the button. He did not hear a chime but soon he heard the deadbolt moving and the left-side door opened. The smiling face of the butler, Tino, appeared in the doorway.

"Is Miss Petrenko available?" Jack asked the neatly dressed man. He was asking for Anna in order not to bother Yuri with such details as a fender bender. That's what he told himself, anyway. Tino was still smiling, but did not speak. He merely gestured with his hand toward the interior and Jack walked in.

"Jack, what brings you up here?" came the accented voice of Anna as she appeared around a large, dark granite pillar. She leaned against the pillar wearing a white, silken robe drawn tightly around her slim waist. The robe gaped open at the bottom just enough to allow Jack a glimpse of a bronze-colored, shapely leg underneath. Jack thought she looked like she was ready to do a shampoo commercial or something. Her hair was still damp, from showering after

141

her swim he guessed. "Well aren't you going to talk to me?" she asked, breaking in on his silence. He blushed realizing that he had been staring.

"Oh, yeah," he stammered, "I forgot to tell you that somebody hit us in your car. You know, when I picked up Elena." He felt like an absolute hick. Anna's face showed concern.

"No one was hurt?" she asked.

"No," he said, "just a little scratch on the bumper. I can take it to the body shop and have it repaired.

"Don't worry," she said, smiling again, "I have seen the scratch. I thought that perhaps the car had been struck in a parking lot. It is nothing."

Jack started to protest when Elle entered the greatroom from a hallway to the right. "It's Jack," she said with a giggle. "I thought I heard you out here. When are you going to take me horseback riding?" She realized that Jack was looking at her sweatshirt, which hung down to her bare thighs. He was grinning. "This is your shirt, isn't it?" she asked. She pulled at the front of the shirt where a large "K. U." with a Jayhawks logo stood out in bright blue and red. Jack realized that he must have left it in the T-bird. He was relieved to see that she had a pair of short, cutoff jeans on underneath, which the large sweatshirt had been concealing.

"You can have it Elle," he said. "It looks better on you than it does on me." He could see that Anna was finding this very amusing.

"Thank you, Jack, I love this shirt," she said reaching an arm around his neck and drawing him down for a hug. "Now, when are we going riding?" she persisted as Jack blushed; he was not really a hugger.

"Well I..." Jack started to give an excuse when Yuri's voice interrupted him.

"Why don't you go now?" said Yuri, smiling broadly. "All this chatter is making it hard for me to get anything done. Take both of these noisy women. They need to get out for a while."

"Well, okay, sure Mr. Alexand..."

"Please, call me Yuri," he interrupted with a wave of his hand. "Now I must get back to work." Yuri disappeared into a dark paneled room. Jack could see the glow of a computer screen in the background and another computer near the door.

"Then it is settled," said Anna. "You will get the horses ready?"

"Should take fifteen or twenty minutes," replied Jack. "You might want to put on some jeans," he said, giving her bare legs a look.

She laughed, then smiled, mostly with her eyes, and turned down the hallway. "We'll be at the corral in fifteen minutes," she said over her shoulder.

"Bye," said Elena following quickly behind Anna. "Isn't he a doll!" Jack overheard the girl say as the two rushed down the hallway.

This left Jack with Tino, who merely smiled and ushered him out the front door. Jack thanked him, receiving a slight bow in return. Tino still had not uttered a sound.

Jack walked briskly back down the hill going straight to the corral, where he whistled up the horses from the small pasture and closed the gate. He caught Buck and saddled him, then he caught two more mounts that he knew to be reliable. He had no idea what kind of rider Anna might be, but he figured Elle would not be a problem if she had ridden dressage. He looked up toward the house and could see Anna and Elle coming around from the back. They were both dressed in jeans and nearly matching, white, long-sleeved casual shirts. He thought how much the two women resembled each other; they could have passed for sisters, although he believed Anna to be almost old enough to be Elena's mother. The thought struck him that none of the Alexander bunch seemed to be affected by the fact that they had lost two of their own in a violent episode recently. It seemed impossible that they didn't know.

"I hope you did not give me a mean horse," said Anna. "I don't ride often."

"You'll like this one," said Jack. "He's a saint."

"Oh! They're beautiful!" exclaimed Elle, looking at the three saddled horses. Jack had given them each a quick currying, but this time of year they were pretty well slicked off anyway.

The three riders mounted up and started down the dirt track behind the corrals that led to a pair of gates where three pastures met. Jack suggested that they ride up on the big knob directly above the valley. Both women thought that to be an excellent idea, as neither had been anywhere on the ranch except the grounds around the main house. They walked their horses and talked as they approached the hill from the southeast. The girls' horses were breathing hard with the steepness of the grade and trying to keep up with the fast walk of the big buckskin that Jack was riding. The ladies' mounts had to trot occasionally to keep up. Jack looked back to make sure his riders were comfortable with this. Anna caught his gaze and she smiled, showing even white teeth. She looked to be at ease, as did Elle. The younger girl was pointing out different wildflowers and asking the names of each. Jack only knew a few of them, but answered when he could. Just past the irrigation ditch he spotted some pink flowers that he identified as Elephant Heads, which he pointed out to Elle and Anna.

"Look at these, Anna," said Elle jumping off her horse, "each flower looks like a little trumpeting pink elephant. Isn't that cool?"

"Yes, that is quite extraordinary," said Anna, staying on her horse. "Don't pick them. Let them grow so that we can enjoy them another day," she said quickly as Elle was about to pick one to hand to her. Elle remounted her horse with ease and they moved on up the hillside again. Jack was feeling successful as a guide, having noticed the flowers and actually coming up with the correct name for them.

Upon reaching the top of the broad hill, Jack was impressed with the sight below. The entire backside of the big ranchhouse was in full view with its great glass windows and alluring pool. He realized that whoever had been scouting from up here had done their homework; with a good scope you could probably read the sports page of Yuri's paper from here.

"Oh my gosh! It's a graveyard!" Elle exclaimed. Jack looked around at the girl to see that she was getting off her horse. Anna followed suit, so Jack dismounted as well and opened an old gate with the name "Fowler" on the wrought-iron header bowing skyward between its posts. A gentle breeze moved the heads of a few wild flowers growing close to the headstones. Jack led the horses inside and pulled their bridles off, allowing them to graze among the dozen or so graves scattered inside the fence. He walked over to the large cross in the middle of the cemetery and looked around its base. He could see that the grass had been trampled where the watcher had been standing. Jack then looked toward the backside of the hill and could discern a faint double-track road, a trail really, skirting the hill down to its base and disappearing through an old gate on the backside of the property. He surmised that it would meet up with the county road where it turned about a half mile further.

"I had no idea that there was a cemetery up here," said Anna, interrupting Jack's thoughts.

"Lot's of these old ranches have their own family plots," said Jack. He looked at Elle who was kneeling beside each headstone in turn trying to read the weathered inscriptions and dates.

"Oh, that is so sad," said Elle. "These two little girls died a week apart and they were only a year old."

"Probably cholera," offered Jack. He could see that she was really moved by this discovery. Anna walked back to the spot where Elle knelt.

"This must have been the mother and father," said Anna, indicating two nearby graves with the Fowler name repeated. "They must have faced incredible hardship back then." The dates were all from the latter nineteenth and early twentieth centuries.

"I'm sure it was tough," said Jack. "They were pretty

145

much on their own, I suppose." He sat down on a big granite rock half-buried near the base of the old juniper, the only tree on the entire hill. The wind whistled through its branches adding an eerie but soothing aura to the place. The sun was getting low on the horizon, which was dominated in the west by the Wyoming Range. Jack lay back on the rock and was almost asleep when he felt something brush his chest. He instinctively reached for whatever it was and found himself grasping a strong but feminine hand. Anna did not pull her hand away, but let it rest on Jack's chest, clutched within his. He sat up, dropping her hand as he did so, but wanting to hold on to it. She was smiling at him.

"Thank you, Jack," she said.

"For what?"

"For bringing us up here. I think I needed this much worse than Elle did."

"It is peaceful here," said Jack. He looked over to see Elle, trying to feed a handful of grass to her horse. "She's a sweet girl, isn't she," said Jack looking at Elle.

"She's a breath of fresh air," said Anna.

"It's refreshing to see a girl that seems so innocent and carefree."

"I couldn't agree more," said Anna looking into Jack's eyes. Jack held her gaze for a moment and looked away.

"Would you like for me to take Elle to meet some people her own age out here?" asked Jack.

"Why yes, I think she would like that. She mentioned that you knew someone with a dude ranch." Anna paused for a moment, watching Elle. "I love having her here though. She's like the..." She didn't finish her thought and seemed relieved when Elle led her horse up to them.

"This is so huge!" she said. "You can see everything from up here! I didn't know that runway was so big. It just seems to go on forever." Jack looked where the girl was pointing. It looked as though the runway had been extended from an older airstrip. The lower portion had required quite a bit of fill in order to attain the runway's present length.

Like everything else around here, Jack thought, it must have cost a fortune.

Jack caught Anna's horse and replaced the bridles on all three horses. The three riders mounted and rode out under the archway. Jack closed the gate without dismounting and they rode slowly in the fading light back toward the ranch. The slight breeze that picked up was cool and Jack imagined that the women were getting chilly.

As they arrived at the corral, Jack mentioned that he would like to use a ranch pickup to attend the funeral the next day.

"Oh, I almost forgot," said Anna. "Yuri wanted me to ask you if you would mind coming with us to the funeral...and driving the car." She hesitated then continued, "He likes to have a driver sometimes."

"I thought he had a driver," said Jack, baiting her.

"Marion can't be reached. Yuri said they weren't coming back. I think he may have fired them for disappearing when he needed them." She looked up at Jack. "Actually I am glad. I did not like either of those two men," said Anna.

Jack looked behind Anna to see Elle making friends with a few more of the horses in the corral. She was out of hearing distance so he said, "Didn't he tell you what happened to them?"

"What do you mean?" she asked, puzzled.

"I heard this morning at the coffee shop that they got in a fight on a fishing trip and killed each other," said Jack.

"Oh!" she gasped, putting a hand to her mouth. Anna turned quickly to look at Elle, who was not paying any attention to them. "Now I see," she said, as if suddenly understanding. "We met the sheriff's car coming out on the road this morning. Elle and I went into town for some things. I guess Yuri didn't want to say anything in front of her."

"You don't seem too upset about it," Jack blurted out, realizing he shouldn't have said anything, but Anna didn't seem bothered at all by the statement.

"Believe me," she said calmly, "I am not. I have

wished those two men gone many times. Yuri does not need men like that out here." She stopped talking as if she had said too much. After a short silence she explained, "They were employees of a business partner from Chicago. It seemed that they needed to get out of the city for awhile."

"But they killed each other!" Jack pressed, wanting a reaction.

"That's not so unusual," she said with sadness in her voice, "not where I come from." She did not look at Jack, but fixed her eyes on Elle playing with the horses. She was silent for a moment then called to Elle. "We must go," she said, turning to Jack. "Thank you," she said. The carefree smile was gone from her face now.

"I'm sorry," said Jack, feeling he had pushed a little too hard.

"It is nothing," she said. "Will you drive us then?"

"What? Oh...yes," he said, fumbling. They agreed upon a time for the next day and the two women walked back up to the house.

CHAPTER TWENTY-THREE

Jack pulled the wet saddle blankets off the fence to put them in the stable. He then spent some time cleaning saddles and oiling some dry bridles. He was just in a contemplative mood after spending the afternoon with two beautiful women.

When he closed the shed up and walked towards the bunkhouse, he saw that Wade Archer's old Chevy was parked out front. He let out an oath. He had hoped that Wade would not come back at all and now here he was, like a bad penny. Jack walked on down to the bunkhouse to find Wade sprawled out on his bunk with his greasy hat pulled down over his eyes and his hands clasped behind his head. As Jack closed the door, Wade cocked the hat slightly, looking out from underneath.

"What ya' been doin' Wallace?" said Wade. "Hittin' on the boss's girl now?" Wade didn't seem to have learned much from his last run-in with Jack.

"Just babysittin'," Jack replied, refusing to be rattled. Archer grinned a wicked grin and rolled over to reach under his bunk. Jack heard the now familiar slosh of the bottle.

It was dark outside now, and a little early to turn in, so Jack read in his bunk, until Wade was snoring loudly, before he turned out the light. He had been asleep for a few hours when he was awakened by talking. Jack sat up in his bunk. Wade was babbling incoherently in his sleep and grinding his teeth. Jack rolled over and was about to doze off again when Wade's words caught his attention.

"Get that kid...," Wade mumbled, "Kirby'll do

it...Wallace knows...cops..."

Jack was wide-awake now. He listened as Archer babbled on. Wade Archer was definitely a problem. "Damn!" Jack swore under his breath. He had to get rid of Archer, but how? He reached up and turned the small reading lamp attached to the bunk sideways, so that it pointed directly into the wall, and turned it on. The light seemed incredibly bright and he squinted, letting his eyes adjust. He finally looked over at Wade. A tattooed arm hung over the side of the bunk. Wade lay on his stomach, his face half buried in the pillow facing away from Jack. He was snoring again. Jack had an idea. He quietly got up and went over to the closet where his leather jacket hung. The bi-fold doors were noisy, but luckily they were already open slightly and he reached in and unzipped a pocket and pulled out the two bottles of ketamine mixture given him by the vet at Ethan's. Jack contemplated for a moment on what he was about to do; he knew that they used ketamine in human medicine and that some used it to spike drinks of unsuspecting women. He thought about the bottle under the bed, but decided he needed something much quicker. He walked over to the sink where a pair of pistol-grip, stainless-steel syringes lay in pieces after having been washed. The syringes were normally used on cattle and calves and they had been sitting on a drying tray since they had finished the calf working. Jack had taken them apart and cleaned them, just like he had done so many times for his dad. Quietly he put a syringe together and attached a 16 gauge by one inch needle that had also been washed. He carefully drew out the contents of both bottles of anesthetic. The syringe was a 50 cc capacity and had no trouble holding all the liquid. He set the dosage ring to the maximum 5cc mark.

"Well, here goes," Jack said to himself as he stood beside the bunk where Wade slept. He could smell the stench of unwashed sheets as he leaned over the sleeping figure. With a suddenness born of commitment, he jumped in the middle of Wade's back. His right knee landed across the sleeping man's lower back while his left knee drove Wade's head deep into the pillow. Steadying himself with his left hand on the upper bunk, Jack stabbed the needle deep into Wade's right buttock. As the pillow absorbed the man's muffled screams, Jack pumped the contents of the syringe deep into the muscle. Wade thrashed, but was in no position to resist. When the syringe was empty, Jack stepped on over the bunk and moved quickly to his own. He sat down and turned to look at Wade. The man pulled himself upright and stood. He almost fell and was holding his hip. Wade's wide eyes tried to focus on Jack.

"What's the matter, Wade? Bad dreams?" Jack asked. He reached up and pushed the light a little closer to the wall, reducing the amount of light that leaked out and he waited. "I think you had a nightmare," said Jack coldly. "You better just sit down and take it easy." Wade stood there unsteadily, the alcohol was probably as much to blame as the ketamine at this point. Jack waited for what seemed like an eternity.

"Huh?...Wha..." Wade's body fell stiffly against the bunk and then to the floor. Jack moved over to the man. Had he killed him? He had no idea what the dosage of ketamine was for humans. He touched a finger to the inside "V" of the man's eyelid. Wade's eye blinked, satisfying Jack that the man wasn't dead, at least not yet anyway. Jack tried to pick him up. The man's body was not limp, like he expected, but fairly rigid. He threw Wade's arm over his shoulder and dragged him out the door and into Archer's own pickup. Jack got in the driver's seat and felt for the keys in the ignition. Jack pressed the button on his watch, which lighted up the dial. It was just after midnight. He started the old truck and drove out the drive, looking up at the big house as he did so. No lights were showing other than the little accent lights along the circle drive, which were on every night.

He drove toward Pinedale and pulled in behind the convenience store near the motel. He hoped no one would see him in Wade's vehicle, but figured he could tell them Wade had some kind of seizure. It certainly looked like that was the case. Jack went around to a pay phone under the roof that extended over the gas pumps. He reached in his pocket, found a card with only a phone number, and dialed.

"Riley," a sleepy voice said on the other end of the line.

"It's Jack. I've got a problem."

"Where are you?" asked the FBI agent.

"At the quick shop next to the Pinedale Inn," replied Jack.

"That's just outside," said Joe, surprised. "I can see the store from here. I'm at the motel." Jack looked over and saw a curtain move in a dimly lighted motel room. He recognized the beige sedan parked in the lot next to the quick shop. "Hang on," said Joe. "I'll be right out."

Jack went back to the truck and waited. He looked over at Wade. The man's eyes were open staring straight ahead; his chest rose slightly as he took a breath. "At least you're not dead," Jack said aloud. He looked in the mirror of the truck and could see Riley coming out through the side door of the motel talking on a cell phone. He was trying to pull on a jacket without dropping the phone. Jack got out of the truck and walked around to the passenger side where he met the agent.

"Jeez!" exclaimed Riley, seeing the unresponsive figure in the passenger seat. "Is he dead?"

"No," said Jack, "just a little kitty anesthetic. I gave him enough to knock a horse down, but I don't know how long it's going to last." Joe Riley leaned in, examining the catatonic Archer. "He was talking in his sleep. He knows something... too much...I had to get him out of there."

"Okay," said Riley. "We'll take it from here. Is this his truck?" He looked at the cluttered cab with food wrappers and cigarette cartons covering all the flat surfaces.

"Yeah," replied Jack.

"Get back in it and follow me," said the agent. Archer stirred and twitched a little. Joe pulled a pair of handcuffs from his jacket pocket and reached in through the window. "Jeez!" said Riley, "He's stiff!" He opened the

152

door then and pulled the man's hands behind his back and cuffed him. He let go of Archer and slammed the door. "Let's go before anyone sees us," said Riley. Jack got back in the truck and followed as Joe Riley pulled his sedan out onto the highway heading back west, out of town. Jack could see that the agent was on his cell phone again. As he pulled out of the parking lot, Archer's inert form started to lean over toward Jack, who roughly shoved him back into the corner against the door.

Wade was making smacking noises with his mouth when they pulled in to a scenic overlook area just outside of town. The beige sedan stopped and Riley got out. The agent walked around the front of the pickup and came up to the driver's side where Jack rolled down the window. Archer's head followed Riley, but appeared to stare somewhere beyond.

"That's pretty bizarre," said Joe, looking at Archer. "What did he say that you heard?"

"From what I gathered, he was somehow in on the deal with Kirby to follow us into the mountains," said Jack. "I can't tell you much else, but he mentioned my name in conjunction with the cops."

"We'll question this one. We can hold him, no problem," said Joe. "You just be careful, Jack."

"I'm supposed to drive Yuri and Anna to the funeral tomorrow," Jack added.

"Oh?" The agent's eyebrows went up. He had pulled a pipe from his jacket pocket and was tamping in tobacco. He looked up at Jack. "They don't have a driver now. You may inherit that job." He pulled out a wooden match and struck it with his thumbnail while he was thinking. "That would be perfect."

"Did you have someone on top of the knob today with a spotting scope?" Jack asked. He looked at his watch and realized that it was yesterday.

"No, did you see something?" Joe looked serious.

"I walked up on the hill to the south and was scouting with the glasses and I saw a guy watching," Jack explained.

He told of the horseback ride and what he found up on the knob.

"That wasn't us Jack," said Joe, looking concerned. "Somebody else is scoping out the place."

"I looked at that trail leading up the hill. It isn't much. Somebody did their homework to find it. My guess is a platte book," Jack offered.

"That would have come from the county courthouse," said Joe. "I'll check on that. I can find out if any inquiries have been made recently. Trouble is, the topo maps are good nowadays. That's BLM land next door. For all I know, that trail may be on every hiking map in print. I'll check it out." He looked intently at Jack. A slight smile came across his face as he sucked his pipe to life. When the smoke was rolling and the embers flared with each puff, he looked at Jack and said, "You've got an investigator's mind, Jack. Old Hayes was right...you'll do."

Headlights appeared from the east. As a car pulled off the highway behind them, Jack could see that it was a sheriff's car. Two men got out and Jack recognized one as the county sheriff, Ben Tate. He didn't know the other guy, a black man, graying slightly at the temples, probably in his late fifties or early sixties.

"Jack this is Leroy Donovan," said Riley, indicating the black man. "He works out of Fort Collins." The man shook hands with Jack. Leroy had a firm handshake and moved smoothly as if this sort of night maneuver were routine to him.

"Heard of you, Jack," the man said with a toothy smile. "I know another Jack. Looks a lot like you."

"No time for old home week boys. Let's get this thing done," said Riley.

"I'll take the pickup," said Leroy. "Sheriff and I can handle this end." He was looking in at the tottering head of Wade Archer. "This guy is really screwed up," he said opening the door. He pulled Archer out by his shirt and the sheriff assisted in getting the drugged man into the back of the patrol car.

"Come on Jack," said Riley. "We better get you back to the ranch." He indicated that Jack should get in his car.

Riley let Jack off close to the ranch and Jack walked through the hay meadow to get back to the bunkhouse. All was quiet. Luckily, Mrs. Palmer let the dogs sleep inside on the porch. No lights were on inside the big house. Jack stepped up on the porch of the bunkhouse and silently slipped in. The reading light still shown into the wall and the place was empty. Jack pulled off his boots and lay silent, staring at the bottom of the bunk above him. He suddenly wanted to go away. He stared at the penciled artistry surrounding an old limerick written on the unpainted plywood. "There was an old man from Nantucket..." he read, and he fell asleep.

CHAPTER TWENTY-FOUR

Jack walked slowly down the drive, being careful not to stir up dust on his shoes. The shoes were a pair of Sperry Topsiders that he bought in Jackson when he went to the airport. He liked them because they flattened easily into a backpack, but they were a bit casual for a funeral. It was a choice between those, running shoes, or scuffed boots. As he approached the house, he felt a little trickle of sweat fall from his armpits and it wasn't due to heat or the walk up the drive. He rang the chime or at least he punched the button; he heard nothing. Tino appeared. A smile, a nod, a wave of the hand and Jack was back in the foyer, standing next to the immaculately dressed little butler.

"Jack." The voice was Yuri's. "The women will be with us shortly. May I offer you a drink?"

"No," said Jack, a little surprised, "but thanks." Yuri had what looked like a glass of wine in his hand. It was only about 9:30 in the morning, when most people were still enjoying coffee. Jack thought it a little odd that the man was drinking wine, especially on the way to a funeral, but he was, after all, Russian. Perhaps it was customary.

"Jack let me ask you something," said Yuri. "You seem to be a bit more than what you appear." He waited for a response. Jack waited too. He was a little confused by the statement. "You seem more than a farmer. You seem...educated...cultured..."

"I've been to college," said Jack as if it were an admission of guilt.

"Excellent," said Yuri, pleased with the answer.

"Your education shows."

Jack knew that he should be putting on a friendly attitude, but he was suddenly wary.

"Please," said Yuri, "this is foolish. Let me ask you my question. Would you like to drive for me, for my people." Jack must have given him a look of bewilderment. "Please, don't get me wrong. I am not asking you to be a servant like Tino here." He indicated the butler standing just behind Jack. Jack had forgotten the quiet man was anywhere near. "Tino loves his work. He is not displeased at all to be a servant. His family has been serving important people for generations." The man paused and looked at Tino, who merely smiled at him, but this time Tino's eyes did not smile. Jack noticed it, but apparently Yuri did not. "Tino cannot talk," Yuri continued, "for that reason he was not asked to take up where his father left off. Tino loves helping us and we all love Tino." Tino smiled broadly and bowed toward Yuri. "It is give and take," continued Yuri. Jack could not help but wonder where Yuri was going with this. What had Tino's father been? Yuri stopped talking as female voices echoed from the hallway.

"Hi, Jack!" bubbled Elle, as she and Anna appeared from the hallway.

"Good day, ladies," said Jack a little more eloquently than he felt. He almost removed his hat, when he realized that he wasn't wearing one.

"Elle met Nadine last night," said Anna. "She insisted on going to the funeral after hearing about Mr. Palmer." Both women wore black dresses, plain but stylish.

"Well then," said Yuri, setting down his glass. "We should be going. You don't mind driving us Jack?"

"Not at all," said Jack. He was going to the funeral anyway.

"Excellent," said Yuri, "this way." He led them down another short hallway past the kitchen. Jack could see state of the art appliances in stainless steel adorning the kitchen. It looked like something from the set of a cooking show on TV.

157

"Someone likes to cook?" asked Jack as they passed.

"Tino is a wonderful cook!" said Elle. Tino smiled once again and opened a door to a covered walkway leading to a large garage.

Jack was impressed at the showroom cleanliness of the garage. Inside were both the Ford Thunderbird and the black Mercedes, shining like new. Jack noticed that the front bumper had been repaired on the T-bird. The place was big; two more cars could easily have fit in the empty bays. Florescent lighting reflected off the spotless tiled floor, which lacked the usual road grit that came with cars that were actually driven on the road. Yuri walked to the black Mercedes and opened a rear door for Elle. Jack followed his lead and opened the other door for Anna. Yuri sat in the front passenger seat across from Jack. Jack looked up between the visors and punched a button on an integrated panel which had a small picture of a garage embossed on it. The garage door opened and he backed out.

As they drove to the small church where the funeral was to be held, Elle told her uncle of the ride to the old cemetery on the hill. She had obviously been moved by the history she had surmised from reading the headstones. Anna had been impressed as well. Yuri had known of the cemetery but had not seen it first hand and knew very little of the previous owners or history of the ranch. Jack gathered that Yuri was not a man to dwell on the past. Perhaps that was a necessity for a man like him to keep his sanity.

The church was crowded and Anna, Elle, and Jack took seats in the back row of pews, following Yuri's lead. The pews were old and made of oak with no cushions of any kind, but surprisingly quite comfortable, at least when they first sat down. Jack imagined the arguments of the church board members of whether or not people might fall asleep if they got cushions for the pews.

A spunky Baptist preacher gave an enthusiastic rendition of a sermon about the "many rooms" and the "mansion, which Jesus had prepared." The man literally bounced on the balls of his feet behind the podium as he delivered his message. Jack thought that he was a bit too happy about all this, but certainly agreed with his theology. Anna and Elle looked on in rapt attention, while Yuri constantly checked the Rolex on his wrist. Jack watched them out of the corner of his eye, wondering what each of them was thinking, especially Yuri.

The service ended and the closed casket was loaded aboard an early-eighties Cadillac hearse that was shining brightly with a fresh wax job. Charlie Silvers was a pall-bearer, and Jack recognized several other faces in the crowd as the church let out. He met Abe's wife, Rita, and Charlie's wife, Pam. He was surprised at first to see how many people introduced themselves to Yuri and Anna, but then Jack realized that no one else knew what he knew. Both Yuri and Anna were very gracious and acted as if Jim Palmer's death had been nothing but a tragic accident. Jack found it impossible to believe that Yuri, at least, did not know the truth.

Most of the crowd went out to the small cemetery near Daniel where Jim was to be buried. After the short graveside ceremony, people began to break up into small groups talking. Jack saw that Elle was inspecting several older headstones near the tented area. Ethan and Betty Grant were still there and he went over to talk with them. He called to Elle, who came over where Jack could introduce her. Elle immediately engaged the older couple in conversation about their girls' camp and bombarded them with questions. Anna joined them and seemed to find the Grants fascinating as well. Jack was listening to all this when Yuri caught his attention. He walked over to him.

"If you can pull the ladies away. I am afraid that I need to be going," said Yuri.

Jack did as he was told, and they headed back to the ranch. He pulled into the spacious garage and the two men opened the doors for the women. Yuri let them get into the house and then turned to Jack.

"I want my people to feel special," he said. "These ladies deserve respect." He paused looking at Jack. "Would you like to do this for a living? Or would you rather hit cattle?" he asked.

"Punch cows," said Jack correcting the mistake.

"Really?" Yuri was surprised.

"No, I mean... the phrase is 'punch cows' not 'hit cattle'." He felt silly correcting his boss. "If you're offering me a driving job," he added quickly, "I might be interested...for a while anyway."

"That is exactly what I am offering," said Yuri, pleased.

"Well, then I guess I accept," stammered Jack. This was happening a little too fast.

"Walking to the house is inconvenient for you. If you would care to move into the guest house, there is ample room." Yuri waved toward the matching small house near the garage. It was visible through the still-open garage door. "You may punch cows whenever I am not in need of your services."

"I guess that would work," said Jack. "Can I wash the dust off this car for you?" He ran a finger over the trunk lid of the Mercedes leaving a trail in the gravel dust.

"Tino will do it," said Yuri. Once again the silent man had materialized before Jack had noticed him.

"I'll help him," said Jack, looking at Tino, who smiled genuinely.

"If you wish," said Yuri. "Would you like to discuss the terms? The money?"

"Not really," said Jack, smiling, "I trust you.".

"You will not be sorry," said Yuri, obviously pleased. He started to walk away into the house when he turned. "I ask that you treat all my guests with much courtesy. I think you will do much better than the last." He paused and looked at the butler. "Tino will help you move to your new quarters." With a wave, he was gone. The reference of displeasure with his previous driver was not lost on Jack.

After helping Tino dust the car off with a ragmop-looking duster, Jack walked back down to the bunkhouse to gather his things. He was rummaging through the box in the closet when he heard the quiet rolling of wheels and faint whine of an electric motor just outside the door. Tino appeared in the doorway. Jack looked out to see a dark-green, EZ Go golf cart parked in front of the door. Behind it was a small, matching trailer with a canopy. "Just like at the airport, eh Tino?" said Jack. Tino nodded. The two men loaded Jack's meager belongings in the trailer, although they would have easily fit in the rear of the cart. Tino jumped in and nodded for Jack to get in. "I'll bring my bike up if it's alright," he said to the neatly dressed little man. Tino smiled and saluted, then gunned the electric motor and rolled down the driveway. Jack followed in a few minutes on the old Sportster.

The guesthouse was bigger than it looked. The main house simply made it appear small. A family of five would have had room to spare. Jack winced as Tino dropped his backpack on the wood floor with an audible clunk. The old Colt auto had apparently made it's way to the bottom of the pack. Tino showed Jack to a corner room and opened the maroon-colored drapes allowing light to flood in. This was a *real* guesthouse. Jack's room had nice furniture, a built-in desk and bookcases in walnut, and its own private bath. Jack looked out the window at the view of the mountains and a full-on view of the hangar across the tarmac.

"Am I the only one here?" he asked Tino, wondering where the butler slept. The small man shook his head. He pointed to the hangar and raised two fingers. "Ah, the pilots," said Jack. Tino nodded and pointed out the bedroom door to rooms across the hall. "I see," said Jack. "Are they here?" Tino shook his head then pointed to his watch and again held up two fingers. "Two hours?" asked Jack. Tino nodded and smiled. "Good," said Jack, "I won't get lonesome." Tino shook his head emphatically and snorted slightly. Jack didn't know what to make of that, but thanked Tino for his help and the smaller man left as silently as a spirit.

Left alone, Jack scouted around his new digs. He thought it would be wise to check for surveillance equipment. He saw no signs of anything, but he admitted to himself that he was an absolute novice at this spy thing. He laughed aloud for even thinking of himself as a spy, but then he sobered quickly when he considered the fate of spies who got caught.

He checked out the kitchen and realized that he was hungry. The cupboards were well stocked and a partially completed grocery list lay on an island. The kitchen was clean, but had the appearance of considerable use. The refrigerator was well stocked. It even had a couple of heads of lettuce: Iceberg and Romaine. They were fresh. Although the butler had already left, Jack continued to talk as if he were still there. "Tino, you're a domestic dynamo," Jack said to himself. "You'll make somebody a great wife someday. The fact that you can't talk makes you almost perfect." He shook his head. He couldn't believe he had actually said that.

Jack opened a door off the kitchen and was surprised to find a stairway. He felt for the switch and turned on the lights. He started down the stairs and stopped halfway, ducking to look into the room he was entering. "Wow," he thought. Lying before him was a full basement that was a recreational paradise. The light switch at the top of the stairs turned on all the lights in the huge room. The green felt of an old-fashioned billiard table shown underneath a stained glass light canopy with "Budweiser" in red and white. Beyond the pool table was a foosball table and a couple of old-style pinball machines. The marquis on the pinball machine facing Jack showed a busty brunette in leather chaps and vest and very little else, astride a panhead chopper. Above this it read "Biker Chick Holiday". The other machine had a racecar theme with a blue Shelby Cobra coming around a curve on two wheels.

An old horizontal Coke machine sat next to the pinball machines. Jack stepped on into the basement and walked up to the machine. "Have a Coke" it read. "Don't mind if I do," said Jack lifting the lid. Inside were several racks of bottles. Some were soft drinks, some were beers, but they all swam in ice and water. "You're a thorough little fellow," he said, thinking of Tino. Jack reached out into a box of dimes sitting on a table beside the machine, picked one up and dropped it in the slot. He slid a Coke along the slot through the icy water and pulled it through the gate. He heard the coin drop.

Jack opened the bottle on the side of the machine and turned to take in the rest of the room. A wet bar ran for a short length across one wall. It had a shiny brass gooseneck faucet over a black granite sink and the bar itself was highly polished wood, rather than formica. Everything was decorated in nostalgia of cars, motorcycles, and sports memorabilia mostly from the 50's and 60's. The décor reminded Jack of one of those chain restaurants where it looks like they cleaned out an antique mall and nailed the contents to every open space on the walls.

Taking his Coke, Jack ascended the stairs and decided not to investigate the other bedrooms until he was certain that no monitoring system was watching. He went back to the kitchen and opened a few drawers. He found a jar of peanut butter and some wheat bread that looked fresh. He made himself a sandwich, but before putting the top slice of bread on it, he went back to the refrigerator, opened it, and pulled out a jar of sweet gherkins that he had noticed earlier. He sliced up four of them and carefully placed them on the sandwich. He applied the second slice of bread and took a bite of his masterpiece. The peanut butter and pickle sandwich was probably Jack's own creation. He had been eating these for as long as he could remember and had never found another soul who was not revolted by the thought. He savored his delicacy and chased it down with a swallow of ice cold Coke. "I could enjoy this," he said to himself, "if the circumstances were different."

He sat down on a leather sofa and rested his Coke on a coaster. On the end table beside the coaster was a neat stack of magazines. He picked up the entire pile and began to sift through them. Rather than the usual suspects like Time and Newsweek that you often find in waiting rooms,

Jack saw <u>National Geographic Adventure</u>, half a year's worth of <u>American Iron</u> (a Harley magazine), some fly-fishing periodicals and a well-worn copy of a <u>Sports Illustrated</u> swimsuit edition. His curiosity was peaked about whom his roomies might be.

Jack finished his lunch and went back to his bedroom. He lay down on the bed and luxuriated for a moment on the pillow-top mattress. As he lay there, he heard the high-pitched whine of an approaching jet. He rolled off the bed and looked out the open curtains as a sleek Learjet made an approach on the runway outside. He saw a puff of blue-gray smoke and almost immediately heard the chirp as the tires protested their sudden impact with the runway. He could hear reverse thrusters howl and could visibly detect a slowing of forward movement. "That is one fancy flying machine," he said. It was indeed an impressive airplane.

The plane whisked past the hangar and turned around effortlessly at the widened end of the strip. It taxied back to the hangar and stopped in front of the structure. A hatch opened and, true to form, Tino had appeared with the golf cart as the hatch dropped down to become a set of stairs. A tall man ducked out of the opening and came down the stairway. He was smiling and talking to Tino, who was smiling and nodding his head in return. The man wore khaki pants and carried a leather jacket over his shoulder. He was considerably older than Jack and he was followed by another pilot of comparable age.

Jack decided that it wouldn't hurt to show some interest, so he walked to the door and stepped outside. He found himself on a patio, which joined a larger one that encompassed the pool directly behind the main house. He started to skirt the pool when he met Anna coming from the big house. Her eyes were on the plane. She glanced at Jack and smiled.

"I thought I might go out and meet my new roomies," said Jack.

"Yes," she said, "you will like these fellows, I think. Come, I'll introduce you."

Together they walked toward the Learjet. The two pilots stood together talking, while Tino came from the plane carrying a couple of duffels. As Anna and Jack approached, the men stopped their conversation and looked at them.

"What's this, Anna? New boyfriend?" asked the taller of the two men.

"Ah!" Anna said in mock astonishment at the tease. "Jack I want you to meet Will Smith." The tall man swept his aviator glasses off his face and shoved a hand out to Jack.

"A pleasure, Jack?" the man paused, waiting for a last name.

"Wallace, Jack Wallace."

"And this one is Harold Jones," said Anna, indicating the second pilot. Jack estimated them both to be in their mid to late fifties. Harold was almost totally gray headed, while Will was merely gray around the temples.

"Call me Hank," said the other pilot in a smooth southern drawl, "everybody does."

"Smith and Jones," said Jack grinning. "Your names sound like you made them up." Both men laughed.

"I'd have picked something more colorful," said Will, "maybe Bogart or Stallone."

"I think I would have picked something Italian," said Hank. "How does Hank Andretti sound?"

"Sounds like you made it up," said Will.

"Of course it does," said Hank, "I did."

"You look more like a Jones than an Andretti," said Will.

"Now how would you know?" The two men began arguing good-naturedly, more like two college kids than two adults. Anna was looking at Jack and smiling as if to gauge his reaction to this.

"Jack will be driving for us for a while," Anna broke in. "He has moved into the guesthouse with the two of you."

"That's great," said Hank. "Maybe we can have an intelligent conversation now." He looked at Will.

"Who's gonna' carry your end of it?" asked Will.

By this time Tino had climbed back behind the wheel

165

of the EZ Go and had the bags loaded. He looked at Jack, did his little snort and wheezy laugh again, and took off toward the house.

"Come on Jack," said Will, "let us show you the "O" club."   He slapped Jack's shoulder and began walking toward the house.

"I'll leave you boys alone, then," said Anna, excusing herself. Jack was beginning to think that he had just been invited to a fraternity party. The two pilots were actually a welcome break from the tenseness he had been feeling for the past two days.

The two men, once inside the house, excused themselves to get into some different clothes. Jack took the moment to assess the situation. He wondered where Sasha was. He had not seen him for a few days and had expected him to walk off the plane when it landed.

Hank was the first to come back into the living room. He invited Jack downstairs and began racking up the balls on the pool table. Jack immediately picked up a cue and started chalking the tip.

"Eight ball?" asked Hank.

"Sure."

They played a quick game, which Jack won. It was not much of a competition; Hank was obviously not too serious as a pool player.

"What brings you out to Pinedale, Wyoming?" asked Hank casually, racking the balls again.

"Kind of between real jobs," said Jack evasively.

"You could do worse than working for Yuri," said Hank. "Will and I consider it a sort of retirement plan. We both flew TWA for years."

"You've known each other for a while then?" asked Jack.

Hank laughed.   "Oh, yeah," he said, "Will's my brother-in-law."

"So who's married?" asked Jack.

"Will was," said Hank. Jack waited. He didn't think it would be right to pry. Hank continued, "My sister was

166

married to Will. She died in an auto accident a few years ago." He paused a moment.

"I'm sorry," said Jack.

"Mary was a good woman," said Hank. "She and Will were a fantastic couple."

"What about you?" Jack queried.

"You mean am I married?"

"Yeah." Jack wondered if he had hit a sore spot.

"I was," said Hank bending over for a difficult left-handed shot. He shot a little harder than was called-for. The ball hit both sides of the pocket without falling. "I guess you could say I wasn't married to the right woman." He looked at Jack smiling. "She ran off with a stock broker from St. Louis."

"I'm sorry again," said Jack, not knowing how to react.

"Don't be," said Hank. "It was as if a great weight had been lifted from my shoulders." Hank said dramatically. "I hope that near-sighted little weasel went down with the ship when the market tanked. He was my broker. I bailed out of the market as soon as I found out about the two of them. I was in cash when the market went down. Best thing that ever happened to me." Hank chalked up while Jack took a shot. "What about you, Jack?" he asked. "Not married?"

"Never close," Jack said.

"Smart man," said Hank.

Will came bounding down the stairs in a pair of sweats, still rubbing his wet hair with a towel. "Hey, there's an old Iron-Head outside my window," he said. "Is that yours, Jack?"

"That's my ride," said Jack.

"Looks to be in good shape," said Will. He and Hank had exchanged glances. "You ought to park it inside."

"I didn't want to drip oil on that nice garage floor," said Jack.

"Hey," said Will, "bring it on over to the hangar. You can put it in there."

"It would be nice to have a place to do a little work

167

on it," said Jack.

"Great," said Will, "we'll put it away when we go to tuck the plane in."

The three men played a few more games of pool and got acquainted. It seemed that both pilots had found it a convenient time to take early retirement when TWA had gone belly-up. Yuri had come to them through a friend of a friend and now they spent their time flying him around. It sounded as if he let them do about whatever they wanted with their free time.

"This is our golden parachute," Will explained. "Hank and I came out better than most of the airline execs."

"We can fly-fish our way through the mid-life crisis, as the book says," offered Hank.

"Plenty of good fishing out here," said Jack.

"You a fly-fisherman?" asked Will.

"I'm better at fishing than catching, but I try."

Hank looked at Will and said, "A man after my own heart."

The men went back upstairs and were preparing to go to the hangar. When Will went to the bedroom to get some shoes, he came back looking happy. "Hey, Hank," he said, "the goons are gone!" Hank rushed to the bedrooms on the opposite side of the hall from theirs and checked each of them out.

"By golly," said Hank, "I believe you're right."

"They're gone alright." It was Jack who had spoken. The men looked at him waiting for him to continue. Jack told the coffee shop version of the story. Both men looked more relieved than surprised.

"They were goons," said Will. "We avoided them and they avoided us."

"Hated 'em!" said Hank.

Upon Jack's asking, he found out that the "driver and his companion" had only moved in a couple of weeks before. Will and Hank had enjoyed the guesthouse all to themselves up to that point and had thoroughly resented the intrusion of a couple of "goombas" onto their turf.

168

"They were gay," stated Hank. It sounded more like an insult than an observation.

"Really?" asked Jack.

"We don't really know," said Will. "We like to think of them that way." He laughed. "Either way," he said, "I'm just glad they're gone."

"You better hope Tino changed the sheets, Jack," said Hank with a grin. Jack felt an involuntary shudder pass over him.

"Let's go put the plane away," said Will.

Once outside, Jack started the old Sportster while the other two watched in rapt attention. It took one kick to prime it and a couple more to start it. Will and Hank walked over to the hangar while Jack gave his motorcycle its head a bit on the runway. When the other two men had reached the hangar, he circled back and pulled up to the huge door outside the building. He shut the bike off.

"That thing sounds great," said Will.

"Bored and stroked?" asked Hank.

"Yeah," said Jack, "It's about 80 inches now."

Will looked at Hank with a triumphant grin. "Pay up," he said.

Hank reached for his billfold, brought out a 10-dollar bill, and handed it to Will. "Must have been the mufflers," he said.

Jack had surmised that these two guys were Harley aficionados. Will took out some keys and unlocked the personnel door while Hank stayed outside with Jack. Hank continued to admire the old Sportster. Jack heard the whine of an electric motor and the huge doors parted in the middle and began to slide in the tracks to reveal the pristine inside of the hangar. As the light from outside flooded in, Jack saw two shiny motorcycles parked, facing out, next to a lounge area. One was a black Harley-Davidson Electraglide Ultraclassic. Its fairing and fiberglass saddlebags were expertly detailed and spotless. Next to this was a patriot red over birch white Road King Classic. The regal bikes leaned

169

on their side-stands as if awaiting their masters' commands.

"I can't park my bike next to those," said Jack. "It would look like some inbred hillbilly cousin."

"Sure you can," said Will. "It's a Harley. Besides, we like the Sporties too. We're just too spoiled to ride one."

"Try one of them, Jack," said Hank. "The Road King's mine. Take it for a spin down the runway." The pilot walked over to the bike and turned on the key. He thumbed the starter and the big bike came to life.

"Fuel injected?" Jack asked.

"You bet." Hank motioned for Jack to get on. Jack obliged.

Jack let the bike warm up for a minute. He reached down and felt the rear cylinder head with his right hand. When it was warm, he looked up at Hank, and the older man motioned for him to go on out the hangar door.

Jack toed the gear lever down with his left foot. He was going to have to pay attention on this bike, as his old scoot was a right-foot shifter. He felt the clutch engage as he let it out slowly and maneuvered around the Learjet and out onto the tarmac. Jack put the bike through its paces cruising easily down the smooth surface of the runway. When he had first straddled it, the bike felt big and clumsy compared to the old Sporty. But once he cracked the throttle, Jack was impressed with how nimble the big cruiser felt. It was so smooth that Jack felt like he was coasting with the engine off. He moved his feet around on the big footboards. This was cool. Jack pulled the bike back into the hangar.

"What do ya' think?" asked Hank.

"I think I'm in love," said Jack. "This is one incredible machine." Jack took his hands from the handlebars and watched them vibrate slightly. It was nothing compared to what the Sportster would do. And you could talk easily with the bike running. Jack was impressed with how far Harley had come...finally.

Jack turned the key and the bike went from quiet to silent. He looked at Hank. "Would you like to ride that one?" Jack nodded toward the old Sportster.

"I was hoping you'd say that," replied Hank.

Jack started the Sportster and Hank climbed aboard. Jack gave him a little pep talk about the right-side shifter, but realized that it wasn't needed when Will told him that Hank had once owned a '72 iron head. Hank took off and the cackle of the pipes echoed off the hangar as he disappeared down the runway. He came back and idled in beside the other bikes. "You gotta' try this," he said to Will. "It sure brings back the old days."

Will took a turn on the older bike and came back with a huge grin on his face. He pulled his hands off and watched as the handlebars jumped around as the bike idled. He shut the key off and the motion died with the sound. "This thing shakes like a dog shittin' a peach pit," he said with a laugh.

"Spoken like a true hillbilly," said Hank. "He's from the Ozarks, you know. MU graduate. You just can't take him anywhere."

"What about you?" Jack asked. "Your accent isn't exactly Midwest."

"I'm from Texas, son," he said, adding a little more accent. "I'm an Aggie. We're all in the same conference now, so I reckon Will has gained some status at my expense."

"I'm a Jayhawk, myself," admitted Jack.

"I'm sorry to hear that, Jack," said Hank in mock concern.

"I always heard that all the trees in Missouri lean to the west because Kansas sucks," added Will.

"Nah, it's because Missouri blows," said Jack.

After a few more alma mater jabs, the three men decided that they might not have to kill each other. Will hopped aboard a small tractor, more like a forklift without the fork. Hank hooked up a tongue to the front landing gear of the Learjet and they maneuvered it into the hangar. Jack was walking backward, watching the big craft move into position, when he stumbled over a heavy iron ring sticking up out of the floor.

"Watch yourself," said Will. "I don't know why we

have tie-downs inside the hangar. Maybe it's just to give us something to trip over." He parked the tractor and got off. "We'll have to get it out again tomorrow, but the boss wants it in the hangar when it's home. You can't blame him, though, it's almost new."

"All the bells and whistles too," added Hank. "It's a pleasure to fly...and fast!"

"You have to fly somewhere tomorrow?" asked Jack.

"Las Vegas," said Will. He looked at Hank and said, "We should get our clubs out of there." He waved toward the plane.

"Leave them in," said Hank. "We'll have room. Besides, once you've lost a month's pay at the crap tables, we'll need something else to do."

Will shrugged, as if Hank was right. Jack marveled at the way the two got along.

"So the boss likes to gamble?" Jack asked. He hoped he wasn't prying too hard.

"Not really," said Hank. "I think he's just meeting someone there. We're only stayin' overnight."

"So you all get to stay at one of the big hotels?" Jack asked.

"I'm not sure," said Hank. "It'll be somethin' nice, though. Yuri doesn't do anything half-assed."

Jack thought he had gone as far as he could. It was getting late and he wanted to get in his run. He wanted it for himself as much as to pass some information to Joe Riley. He thought it was a safe bet, so he asked if either of the pilots would like to join him.

"No thanks," said Hank. "I'm just gonna' get cleaned up and turn in early."

"I've already showered," said Will. "At least that's my excuse." He grinned.

"Okay," said Jack. "I just thought I'd offer." They walked back toward the guesthouse.

On the patio outside the main house stood Elena as the three men walked up. "When do I get a ride?" she asked, pouting.

Jack was a little embarrassed. "Maybe tomorrow," he said, "if you're talking about the motorcycle." He introduced Elle to the pilots, who greeted her enthusiastically. "Are you going to Las Vegas too?" Jack asked Elle.

"No," she said. "I couldn't even get into the casinos. Anna said you might take me over to the Grants' place to meet some other girls."

"That will probably work," said Jack. He surmised then that he would not be needed in Las Vegas.

"Great!" she said. "Maybe you could take me on your motorcycle." She gave them all a big smile and turned to go back into the house.

"She's sure a cute little ole thing," said Hank.

"I reckon she's about got Jack wrapped around her little finger," offered Will, with a big grin at Jack.

"Come on guys," said Jack. "She's the boss's niece. It's not like I can tell her what to do." The two pilots just looked at each other with a grin.

"For crying out loud," said Jack, "she's fifteen."

"We're just funnin' you, Jack," said Hank.

"Yeah," said Will, "you go ahead and run. Then come in and take a cold shower."

"You guys never let up. Do you?"

"Get used to it friend," said Hank, giving Jack a pat on the shoulder. "We haven't even got warmed up yet."

CHAPTER TWENTY-FIVE

Jack changed into his running clothes and stepped outside the guesthouse. He was doing some stretches and thinking. He began his run slowly, but, feeling an urgent need to talk to Riley, he soon picked up the pace. It felt good to stretch his legs out, each step putting another few feet of the pavement behind him. He got to the ranch entrance and turned out onto the rough gravel of the county road. Some of the rocks were big enough to twist an ankle, so he kept his eyes scanning the surface of the road. The Wind River Mountains seemed close enough to run to and perhaps he could have done so on a good day. The gain in altitude would make it tough, but his body was acclimatizing well to Pinedale's thin air by now.

Jack looked over his shoulder. The ranch buildings were almost out of sight. He came to the intersection of the other county road. He decided that taking it would get him out of sight of the ranch more quickly. About a half mile down the road he saw an S.U.V. parked at the side of the road. A small stream went underneath the road at this point. At the rear of the vehicle was a man in waders putting a fly rod together. Jack slowed his pace and came to a stop near the man. "You know how to use that thing?" he asked, panting.

"It's my passion, Jack," said Joe Riley. He wore a vest with multiple pockets and various gadgets hanging off of it. "How's it going?"

Jack was leaning over with his hands on his knees. "Not bad," he said. "How did you know I would turn down this road?"

"Oh, call it a hunch, I guess," said Riley.

Jack walked around a little, trying to get his respiratory rate down where he could converse. "What did you do with Archer?" he asked finally.

"He's in jail. Outstanding warrant in Salt Lake. We've known about it for a while. Just couldn't grab him without tipping our hand until now." He paused, stringing up his rod. "We've been looking for that watcher from the hilltop. Nothing yet."

"Yuri and company are heading to Las Vegas tomorrow."

"Really. We'll have to get a tail on him there. Know where he's staying?" asked Riley.

"No," said Jack. "I've met the pilots. They're my roommates in the guesthouse. Their names are..."

"I know who they are," interrupted Joe. "We've checked them out. They're clean as far as we know."

"Yeah, I got that impression too."

"Any idea why the trip to Las Vegas?"

"May be meeting someone. Just an overnight deal," said Jack.

"So you're in the guesthouse?"

"Yeah, I'm the new chauffeur slash babysitter."

"The niece?" inquired Riley.

"Uh huh, I think I'm going to take her over to Ethan Grant's tomorrow."

"Maybe you could get her to stay over there for a week or so."

"That's a possibility. I think she'd like that," said Jack. "I'll see what I can do."

"If the rest go to Vegas, that would give you a chance to look around."

"I suppose it would," said Jack, "except for Tino."

"He goes shopping every Saturday in Jackson," said Riley. "Yuri has expensive tastes. Can't get that sort of stuff in Pinedale."

"Does he drive himself?" asked Jack.

"Yeah, usually takes the four door Mercedes," said the agent.

"I haven't seen the other guy," said Jack.

"Sasha?"

"Yeah, the ponytail guy," said Jack.

"He leaves every once in a while in a car. It would be nice to get a bug on that S500 Mercedes and track him. That reminds me." Joe dug around in the back of the S.U.V. "I think you better take this." He handed Jack a cell phone. "Don't let them get ahold of it. It won't ring, but it will vibrate if you have it on you. I want you to be able to call me if something's going down. My number's in the speed dial. Just punch one."

Jack slid the small phone into his pocket. "I hope it's sweat proof."

"It is," said Riley. "It's a satellite phone. It'll work if you need it." The sound of a vehicle brought the man's head up. A diesel pickup rumbled down the county road, its driver not even glancing at them as he passed the road they were on. "What's the security around the place?" he asked looking back at Jack.

"There's a camera by the front door. From what I can tell, they monitor it pretty closely. They seem to know when someone's at the door anyway."

"I'll check around. See if I can find out who installed it. There can't be too many of those type companies out here. Probably out of Jackson." Riley paused and thought for a moment. "You watch. If Tino leaves tomorrow, he'll probably go in the afternoon. You call me when that happens. If no one else is around I may be able to come in for a sneak and peek."

"If I can get rid of Elle first," said Jack.

"You can do it," Riley said confidently.

"Yeah, I think so."

"What about the hangar? Can you get in there?" asked Riley.

"I may be able to get a key. The pilots let me put my bike in there."

"Good. Let's check that out thoroughly."

"I better be getting back," said Jack. He put his foot up on the bumper of the vehicle and stretched his calf.

"Alright," said Riley, "Now that you've got that phone, you can call me when you're alone. Keep me informed." He shook Jack's hand. "Be careful."

"I will," said Jack as he jogged off down the gravel road.

"That's a fine young man," Riley said to himself as he stepped down to the water's edge. He thought about what kind of peril he might be putting Jack into. He hated it that it was necessary. If only Denver would take this thing a little more seriously. It was kind of hard to blame them though. They must get a dozen calls a day about some nutcase with a possible nuclear bomb nowadays. And to think he could be lying back enjoying a good government pension right now. But he couldn't walk away. Not now.

Jack got back to the house and showered. Hank was fixing some supper and he was, Jack found out, one heck of a good cook.

You'll need to keep up that running, Jack," said Will. "Hank will fatten you up."

"I sent a grocery list with Tino," said Hank.

"Did Tino go to town?" asked Jack.

"Yeah," said Hank, "he went to Jackson for groceries. You need something? He's got a cell phone."

"No, I guess not," said Jack. "Cell phone, huh. I've never heard the guy talk."

"Hell, I don't think he can," said Hank. "You can send him a message though. The phone's got that digital messaging or whatever the hell."

So Tino went tonight. "Is he coming back tonight?"

"Yeah," said Will, "he didn't want your little girl-friend to miss breakfast, I guess."

"Yeah, right," said Jack with sarcasm.

"I believe you have an admirer there, son," said Hank.

177

"If I was fifteen, I'd be interested," said Jack.

"I've got a daughter not too much older than her," said Hank.

"What about Anna?" asked Will with a grin. "You think you could handle her?"

"I have no idea," said Jack a little embarrassed. "I have to admit that she is a fine example."

Will and Hank both laughed. "She is *that*!" said Will. "I think maybe Sasha has laid claim to that one, though."

"I haven't officially met Sasha," said Jack. "What's he do around here?"

"By golly," said Hank, "that's a good question. I'm not even sure what Yuri does as far as that goes."

"I think he made his money when the Evil Empire collapsed and now he just trades stocks and enjoys the fruits of his labors," said Will.

"Yeah, I think that sums it up pretty well," agreed Hank.

"He works hard at this stock market stuff. Anna does too. She's a pretty smart gal I think," said Will.

"Sasha does the footwork for the business deals," said Hank.

"What about the driver guy, Marion, where did he come in?" asked Jack. He figured since these guys were on a roll he would just milk it a little.

"Oh, I think Yuri just thought he needed a driver for show. He picked those two up from some mob guy up in Chicago. I don't even think he liked them. He likes you though, Jack," said Will.

"Really? He said that?" asked Jack.

"Yeah, He thinks cowboys are cool. You gotta give the guy credit. He's a pretty good judge of character," said Will.

"Thanks Will," said Jack, "I'll take that as a compliment."

"Don't get too excited Jack," said Hank. "Will's an awful judge of character."

"What?" asked Will. "I'll have you know I'm a great judge of character, with the exception of the day I met you of course."

"What about that girl that tried to rob you in Cancun that one time?" offered Hank, "and the hooker in Singapore. You thought she was a Peace Core volunteer." Hank began to laugh uncontrollably.

"Oh, Shut Up!" said Will. "You're memory isn't what it used to be..." The fight was on. The two friends argued for fifteen minutes over trivia known only to them. Jack surmised from the conversation that the two had met in the Air Force and had become inseparable while at White-man Air Force Base in Missouri. The two men finally quit bickering long enough to enjoy Hank's Tex-Mex stuffed pork chops. Jack decided that it was a good thing that he liked hot peppers; the chops were smothered in them, inside and out.

"That's the only reason we're not fat as ticks," said Will.

"Yeah, the hot peppers burn up the calories for you," said Hank. "I didn't think to ask if you like hot stuff."

"I do," said Jack, "but I may not be in your league, yet." He rolled an ice cube from his glass around on his tongue.

"You'll get there," said Will. "Hank'll see to that." Will looked at his wristwatch. "I'm ready to hit the hay," he said. Jack checked his own watch. It was only 8:30.

"You leaving early?" asked Jack.

"We have to do a preflight and get the damn flying machine out of the hangar again," said Hank. "Besides, we both like to read."

"What are you reading?" asked Jack.

"I'm reading a John Sandford novel," said Will. "I like his character Davenport."

"The guy's kind of a philanderer. Don't you think?" asked Jack.

"Yeah, but it's kind of fun. He's starting to settle down in this one."

"What about you Jack?" asked Will. "What do you like to read?"

"Oh, I like them all. I guess Louis L'Amour was one of my favorites. But I really like Tom Clancy and Jack Higgins."

"Those are hard to top," said Will. He looked at his watch again. "I'm going to bed."

"Hey," said Jack, "what if I need to get my bike? Is the hangar going to be locked?"

"Yeah," said Will, "Yuri insists on that. I don't have an extra key. The jamb is kind of wide, though. You can get in easily with a pocketknife if you need to. Just look at it. You'll see what I mean."

"Okay," said Jack, "I can deal with that."

The pilots went to bed and Jack went out to the garage and came back with the owner's manual to the S600 Mercedes. He found it in a cabinet with the manuals for the other cars as well. He thought he would familiarize himself with it since he was the chauffeur now. It was hard to get to sleep when he had so much to think about. He thought about compartmentalizing everything and tried hard, but sleep was elusive. He finally got up and decided to walk around a bit. It was pitch dark. He would have played a game of pinball, but he was afraid of awakening his roomies. Suddenly, he heard a noise and looked outside the window. A black Mercedes had pulled up to the garage. Jack saw light flood the driveway and the car as the garage door went up.

"What the hell," he thought. He might gain some brownie points. He walked to the little walkway that led to the garage and opened the door.

Sasha was just getting out of the Mercedes two door. He looked intently at Jack. Jack stared back, holding his ground.

"Who are you?" asked Sasha.

"I'm the new driver," said Jack, giving the man a friendly smile. "I figured I should protect my territory."

Sasha smiled back. "I am glad to see that you take

your job seriously, Jack is it?"

"Jack Wallace. I don't believe we've met."

"Call me Sasha."

"Pleased to meet you." Jack thought the man looked tired.

"If you'll excuse me I am running a bit late," said Sasha. He pulled a briefcase from the back seat and disappeared into the house.

Jack stood there and thought for a moment. He was considering going around to the back of the house and looking in the greatroom windows. He wasn't sure if he might be on camera if he did so. He decided that it wouldn't help much if he couldn't hear the conversation. As he stood there thinking, the door went up again. This time it was Tino driving the four door. The trunk was full of groceries, so Jack thought it only natural to help carry them into the house. Tino looked at Jack, no doubt wondering what he was doing in the garage this time of night. Jack picked up two bags and followed the small man into the kitchen.

Jack tarried long enough to hear voices in the study, but he couldn't make out the words. It sounded as if Yuri and Sasha were arguing. Jack went back for more bags. When he came back in, Sasha was leaving the study. He looked frustrated and Yuri followed him to the hallway. Yuri's face showed no hint of emotion. With the groceries all in, Jack went back to the guesthouse.

Upon his return Sasha approached Yuri in the study. "What is this? You hire one of the cowboys as a driver. Is that necessary or even a good idea at this time?" he asked.

"I needed him for the funeral. Besides, you forget about Elena. We can't have her underfoot, but we can't ignore her either. She likes this Jack. He can entertain her for us," said Yuri with calm resolve. "I have checked him out thoroughly. He is nobody. I am more anxious about someone following you back here than a simple cowboy."

"I take all precautions. I am well trained, or have you forgotten?" Sasha was indignant.

181

"Calm down, Sasha," said Yuri. "Don't be so paranoid."

"It is my job to be paranoid," said Sasha. He stared at the floor trying to regain his composure. Sasha didn't like arguing with Yuri, but sometimes Yuri took chances that were unnecessary.

"This will all be over soon," said Yuri.

"Is this quite necessary?" Sasha asked. "I mean, why now?"

"It is now or never, my friend," replied Yuri. "If we are to profit from this, it must be soon."

"I know, I know," Sasha said, interrupting. "The tritium deteriorates. Stability goes. We could even be in danger now."

"Are you becoming a sentimentalist, Sasha?"

"No," said Sasha, "I just hate the fundamentalists. I do not like being a party to further their cause."

"We won't further their cause if we carry out the plan that I have in mind."

"Yes, but what if they escape?" asked Sasha.

"We will do our part. The Americans are perfectly capable of minimizing the damage."

"Very well," said Sasha. "I must get some sleep." He started for the door of the study.

"Alone, my friend," said Yuri. "We will be leaving early."

"Yes," said Sasha, an unasked question in his eyes. "Alone."

Yuri followed him to the hallway, and then stopped. He went back to the study and poured himself a vodka. He would be glad when this was all over, no matter how it turned out.

CHAPTER TWENTY-SIX

Saturday morning came early for the pilots. Jack got up and went with them. They were out in the hangar readying the aircraft for its flight. It was interesting to watch the way the two men inspected the jet. It reminded him of some of the more conscientious cowboys he had known. They would curry their mount and run their hands over him before and after a hard ride. It was a ritual of affection as much as inspection.

The small tractor pushed the pristine craft out of its confinement. The process reminded Jack of a tender pushing a beautiful yacht out away from its moorings. Will was already in the cockpit and Hank showed Jack aboard. As Will started preflight checks on the engines, Jack got a look at the cabin. The accommodations were more confining than what he had expected, but the finish was top notch. The leather seats and fine inlaid wood gave the craft a highbrow feel, much like an expensive automobile. Headroom was lacking, but when he sat down in a plush seat, Jack found it quite comfortable.

"First class accommodations, aye?" asked Hank.

"Yeah," said Jack, "pretty cushy ride."

"It beats hell out of traveling commercial," said Hank.

Tino appeared at the door looking around intently. Jack looked out the small portal to see the EZ Go with its trailer. The sparse luggage could have been easily carried by hand, but sat in the center of the little trailer. Jack started to exit the plane, when he saw an accordion curtain pulled closed right beside the door. Hank saw him eyeing it and pulled it back.

"That's the head," he said, indicating a small toilet. "Not much privacy."

"I'll say," said Jack. He stepped on out of the plane.

"So how do you like our little air taxi?" asked Yuri at the bottom of the stairs.

"Very impressive," said Jack. Yuri was smiling and obviously proud of the aircraft. Sasha stood beside him. His face showed no emotion. Anna was walking toward the plane. She was beautiful as ever, dressed in a dark suit, very businesslike.

"We shall be back tomorrow night," said Yuri, "You will take care of my niece?"

"Of course," said Jack.

"Tino will see that she does not starve. Perhaps you can see that she does not get bored."

"I'll certainly try."

"Excellent," said Yuri disappearing into the plane. "The day is perfect."

Jack looked at Anna. "Is Elle up?" he asked.

"Why yes," said Anna. "She is eating breakfast. She will be expecting you." She turned and got on the plane without another word. Sasha followed. He did not acknowledge Jack at all.

Jack walked toward the big house as the engines on the plane warmed up. He had reached the patio when he heard the whine of the aircraft behind him begin to increase in pitch and volume as the pilot maneuvered the jet out onto the runway. The plane was swinging past the house on its way to making its turn at the end of the runway as Elena appeared on the patio beside Jack. She was waving and Jack could see hands moving in answer behind the small windows of the plane. The craft taxied to the turnaround and then launched itself down the runway. It took off in a surprisingly short distance and was soon shining in the rays of the morning sun in a clear blue sky.

"So," said Elle, "are you ready to go?"

"What?" he asked.

"You're taking me to the girl's camp, remember?"

"Oh, yeah," said Jack. "Do you want to go on the motorcycle?"

Elle's face lit up. "You bet!" she said. "I've gotta change. I'll be ready in a jiff."

As she walked off, Jack thought what a fine young lady she seemed to be. She was wearing sweatpants and Jack's old KU shirt. He smiled to himself and walked toward the guesthouse.

In the kitchen, Jack got a cup from the cupboard and reached for the carafe of the coffee maker. A small sack of gourmet coffee beans sat beside a grinder near the machine. The smell of the freshly ground coffee was intoxicating and Jack poured himself a cup from the insulated carafe and went to the fridge. A small yellow note was stuck to the door of the refrigerator. In neat handwriting was an explanation of some substitutions Tino had made in the grocery shopping. The writing had a feminine look to it and the note signed with a simple "T" at the bottom. Jack grabbed an apple from the fridge and tossed a piece of bread in the toaster. He pulled the cell phone from his pocket and punched the speed dial.

"Riley," came the voice on the other end.

"It's Jack. They just took off. Tino's still here though. He went to Jackson last night."

"Then we wait. Keep an eye on him. Get a look at that hangar though if you can," said Riley. "Be careful."

"I will," said Jack. "I'm taking Elle over to Ethan's this morning."

"Call me when you find something, Jack. Anything at all," said Riley.

Jack closed the phone.

The old Sportster sat outside the hangar where Jack had pushed it when the plane was being prepped. The hangar was locked. The pilots explained that Yuri was insistent on this. "All the more reason to give it a closer

185

look," thought Jack. He gave his bike the once over, not unlike the pilots doing their preflight checks. Elena came walking up dressed in faded jeans, a pair of lace-up roper boots, and the KU shirt. The neck of the sweatshirt draped open just enough to reveal the end of the girl's collarbone.

"Do I look like a biker chic?" she asked.

Jack laughed. "No," he said, "You look more like a cowgirl. That's a lot better as far as I'm concerned."

He went through the ritual of starting the bike and they were soon on the road towards Pinedale. It was a beautiful day. The air was cool and, when they reached the highway, Jack felt Elle's grip tighten around his stomach. He felt her small body pressed against his back. He looked around at her. She wore sunglasses and her dark hair was whipping around her face. "The wind is cold!" she said, gripping him tighter yet. She wore a huge smile. Jack was suddenly very glad that he had lost the spare tire that had developed during his "lawyering days". Jack was wearing a hooded sweatshirt with pockets. He reached down with his left hand and guided Elle's hands into the pocket on the front of his shirt. "Much better!" she yelled over the noise of the wind. The thought crossed Jack's mind that if he had been riding an Ultra like Will's, this fine looking young lady would not need to hold onto him like she was. Perhaps the old scoot did have its advantages.

They passed through town where Jack noticed a couple of drift boats on trailers. Apparently, fishermen were starting to float the Green River. Jack suddenly had a feeling of being left behind. They reached the county road that went to Ethan and Betty's and turned down it. Elena relaxed her grip somewhat. The washboard surface of the road demanded a slow pace. They finally got to the ranch gate and turned up the lane.

As they approached the house, a couple of dogs noisily announced their arrival. Jack saw two teenage girls walking from a cabin. Upon seeing the motorcycle they ran for the main lodge as if to spread word of an invasion. Jack pulled the bike up to the yard gate and shut it off. Elle got off and ran her fingers through her thick black hair. Jack leaned the bike on its side-stand and they entered the lodge.

"Come get some breakfast," called Betty from the kitchen. She looked up from mixing pancake batter with a smile that lit up her whole face.

"Hello, Jack, Ellen," came the voice of Ethan, getting Elle's name slightly wrong. The older man was seated at a table next to the kitchen drinking coffee.

"Please, call me Elle," said Elena. She walked over to the table.

"Sit down," said Ethan. "Breakfast will be ready in a minute." He looked at Elle. "Have you come to teach these kids to ride dressage?"

"Sure," she said enthusiastically. "I'd love to. You have dressage horses?"

"I've got three that will be able to do it. You may need to remind them a little." He grinned at her. She smiled back and the two began talking about horses and riding like two old professionals. Jack was impressed with Elle more than ever.

Ethan turned to Jack. "I've got a new helper. I think you might know him."

"Oh, yeah, who's that?" asked Jack curiously.

"He should be in soon. You'll see." The older man offered no more clues, but grinned knowingly.

Betty brought Jack a plate full of pancakes and bacon. He was glad he had not eaten much before he had come. "Are you going fishing Jack?" she asked. "The Green's clearing up and I hear there are some guys starting to float it."

"I hope I can try it soon," said Jack with sincerity. "I'll have to stop by the Outdoor Shop and see what they're hitting on."

Just then the back door opened and a tall lanky boy walked up behind Jack and threw an arm around his neck as if to choke him. Jack instinctively grabbed the arm with his hands and pulled down. Before the boy could react, Jack was on his feet behind him with the arm pushed up between

187

the boy's shoulder blades. "Ouch!" yelled the boy, "I give up!" Jack let him go immediately and reached out to shake his hand. "I should have known better than to do that to you," said Reid Wilcox.

"I saw you coming," said Jack. "How are you Reid?"

"I'm doin' great," said Reid. "Mom and the kids are at Disney World and I'm enjoying my freedom."

"Glad to hear it. Have you talked to your mom?" asked Jack.

"Oh, yeah, about every other day. She's a worrier you know. They're staying with aunt Alice. She's tickled to have them there. It's hard to believe how lucky they were to get those free tickets and everything going through so fast. You know, with the airport security nowadays."

"Somebody must have been looking out for them," said Jack. If the boy only knew. "So, what happened to the parts store job?" he asked.

"That's my day job," said Reid. "I'm helping Ethan on weekends and evenings, days off, that sort of thing. Gotta keep the old CJ in parts you know. I've got a top ordered."

"I've been there," said Jack. "What do you have him doing Ethan?" Jack asked the older man.

"He's in charge of waterin' the hay meadows," said Ethan. "And anything else needs doin'." He winked at Reid.

Elle had been sitting through all this conversation with interest. Jack had noticed Reid stealing glances at the pretty girl and Elle had certainly noticed Reid.

"Elle, I would like you to meet Reid Wilcox," said Jack. "You two are probably about the same age, I'd say."

"My pleasure," said Reid sticking out his hand. "Where are you from?" Reid was polite as always.

"Boston," said Elle. The girl seemed to be at a loss for words. Jack thought that this was a good sign. He didn't know if he should be jealous or not, but the handsome young Reid was making quite an impression on the girl.

"We've got another here from Boston," said Ethan. "She's thirteen. You'll like her."

"Wonderful!" said Elle. "I'd love to meet her...and all the girls."

"I'll introduce you," offered Reid. "Those girls should be here by now. Come with me and we'll roust them out."

"Okay," said Elle. She looked at Jack as if for approval. He just grinned and told them to go on. The two left through the front door.

"Looks like they hit it off," said Ethan.

"I'm glad to see it. She needs to get away from there," said Jack.

"What do you mean?" asked Betty, with a worried look. She sat down at the table cradling a cup of coffee between her hands.

"Oh, nothing," said Jack. "It's just a lonesome place for a girl her age." He realized that his tone had revealed more than he had meant for it to.

"She's welcome here," said Ethan. "I'll give her a job as a counselor today. She's got a lot of maturity about her. Be glad to have her. We're one short anyway."

"She can stay in the first cabin with Sally and Jules. Those two girls could definitely use a little guidance," said Betty. "The other two girls staying there are about ready to kill them." She laughed.

"I think that would be a big help," said Jack. "If it works for you all."

"Sounds like we've struck a deal then," said Ethan. "If Elle is agreeable. Have you talked to your dad lately?" he asked, changing the subject.

"No, I haven't," said Jack. "The neglectful son has not checked in."

"You better give him a call. He wants to come out fishing," said Ethan. "He's been talking to your sister."

"I'll do that," said Jack. Maybe in a couple weeks, he thought. He certainly could not let them come out here now.

The three talked some more of Jack's family until the girls began to file in for breakfast. The campers were

189

introduced en masse to Jack. He could not begin to remember all their names.

"Are you sure Reid is safe amongst all these beautiful women?" he asked Ethan. The girls all giggled and some blushed. It was obvious that Reid was a popular item already.

"He is now," said Betty looking out the window. Reid and Elle were in earnest conversation on the porch. Each seemed enthralled with the other.

"Maybe so," said Jack.

The whole thing had turned out for the best, Jack supposed. He would have to make a trip back over with her stuff, but at least she would be a safe distance from...well, from whatever was going down. Was anything going down? Yes, Jim Palmer didn't die for no reason. Jack had to continually remind himself what these people were. It was hard not to like them.

He rode back into town from the Grants' place alone. He once again saw fishermen lining out trips. It was easy to pick them out; they dressed as if they were modeling for L.L. Bean and they gathered around shops that sold flies and float tubes. Jack was envious. How did he get mixed up in this subterfuge? Why not just let somebody else do it? He could be wading the Green or the New Fork.

As quickly as it had appeared, his anger subsided. It wouldn't have worked anyway, not after all that had happened. He wouldn't have been able to enjoy it. Jack really only had a one-track mind. He would grasp an idea and worry it in his mind like a terrier with a rat. He just could not let go until it was finished.

As he started to go on through town toward the ranch, he spotted the pay phone at the quick shop. He pulled in and stopped. He filled the tank on the motorcycle and went in to get a new phone card; they were a lot easier than pumping in quarters. He dialed his folks' phone number with no answer. He tried his sister's number and the machine picked up. "Hey, sis," he said, after the beep, "just wanted to check in.

Hope everyone is well. Catch you later." He hung up the receiver and felt a sudden overwhelming sense of loneliness. This happened to him on occasion. He knew it would pass, but that didn't seem to make it easier to deal with. He thought of Kate and the kids, he thought of Anna. There was nothing there for him, not at either place. He knew that.

Jack had unconsciously sat down on the bench by the phone. He was aware that someone had walked up, but he wasn't paying attention. He looked up to see a girl, a young woman actually. She was petite and pretty. Her hair was dishwater blonde and she was smiling, just looking at Jack. She set down a large backpack, which clinked with a metallic sound. She brushed back her hair with a muscular arm. Her sleeveless T-shirt showed off her strong shoulders. She could have been some sort of athlete, Jack supposed.

"Hey," she said, "why so glum?"

"No good reason," said Jack. "Going backpacking?"

"Yeah, waitin' on my buds." She indicated that they were inside. "We've got rocks to climb."

"Sounds like fun."

"Come with us. We could use a man along. Some-one to do the heavy lifting."

She wasn't serious, Jack thought. Two other athletic looking young ladies appeared from inside the store. All three hoisted backpacks, which were leaning against the building. "Good luck," said Jack, "and be careful up there."

"We will, thanks," said the blonde, "and you cheer up. It'll get better." They walked away. Jack wondered where they would spend the night. They would probably hitch a ride somewhere. He would have given them one if he had a car.

Jack straddled the bike and started back to the ranch. "There are too many Wade Archers out there for girls to be traipsing around the mountains like that alone," he said to himself. He thought of his sister, Jenny, and smiled. She wouldn't have put herself in that position in the first place, but Wade Archer would have been no match for her. The thought made him smile.

191

CHAPTER TWENTY-SEVEN

When Jack pulled up to the side of the guesthouse, he had an idea. He parked the bike and walked over to the side door of the big house and pushed the button by the door. It took a few moments, but Tino finally appeared.

"Tino," said Jack, "Miss Elle is going to spend the night over at Ethan Grant's ranch. She may take a job there, helping out with the campers." The man nodded his understanding. "She needs some clothes. Do you think you could gather some of her things together?" Again Tino smiled and nodded. "I'll take them over..." Tino was pecking at his own chest with his index finger. "Would you be able to take them over to her?" Jack asked. The little man indicated that he would. "Okay then," said Jack. This was easier than he had thought. He stepped inside the house and scribbled a crude map to Ethan's on a piece of paper, handed it to Tino, and went back to the guesthouse.

Jack went to the drawer where he had put his socks and pulled out the cell phone.

"Riley." The voice on the other end was now familiar.

"Joe, it's me," said Jack. "I've got the place to myself for an hour or two at the most. Do you know any more about the security system?"

"Yeah, I got hold of the outfit that installed it. The house is wired. I don't think you better try it on your own."

"What about cameras?"

"There's just the one at the front door," said Joe. "Apparently the lady wanted some privacy out back by the pool."

"That's good. I'm going to check out the hangar. I don't have a key, but Will said I could get in without it. Must not be any alarm there."

"Good," said the agent. "Call me when you finish. I'm not going anywhere."

"Got it, and thanks." Jack closed the phone and put it back in the sock drawer.

Jack waited until the little butler was gone. He walked around to the back and looked down at the old ranch house and bunkhouse. No one was visible. He walked casually over to the hangar and looked at the latch. Will was right. There was plenty of room for the blade of his Leatherman between the door and the jamb. He opened the knife and ran the blade behind the latch. He felt it grab the taper of the bolt and the door popped open. He entered quickly and closed the door behind him. He was inside the main part of the hangar where the two Harleys sat in shadow off to one side. Jack ignored them and scanned the place. A few skylights lent a dim greenish glow to the inside of the building. Jack saw a big, red roller cabinet of tools along one wall next to the little tractor. He could not imagine the pilots working on the Lear themselves, but maybe they did a little minor maintenance. He opened a drawer on the tool cabinet. It contained a complete set of Snap-on wrenches that looked like they were brand new. Perhaps the pilots just got the tools because Yuri was buying. He noticed a full set of torx bits. Anyone working on or accessorizing a Harley would need these. Now he understood.

A small office area had a couple of old, gray, metal desks in it. The desks looked as if they were not being used. He opened the drawer on a file cabinet. It contained a large stack of airplane and pilot type magazines. Jack smiled when he saw a copy of the Harley-Davidson accessories catalog. A couple of files contained maintenance updates and flight records. The desks themselves and the cabinet had the look of government surplus items. Back in the main part of the hangar, Jack saw a large military-looking dolly of some kind that was pushed back into a corner. It had a diamond-plate steel floor and four rubber tired wheels on swivels. It was definitely built to carry a heavy load. Gray paint now covered the cart, but it had not stuck very well and Jack could see olive drab showing in places. Jack looked up toward the skylights. A large beam ran along one side of the building. His eyes followed the beam over to a massive pivot. He recognized it immediately. Many of the better farm shops in Kansas had just such an item. It was a shop crane. The pivot allowed the beam to swing a full 180 degrees out from the wall. About halfway down the length of the beam rested a large electric winch with a massive steel cable and hook hanging off it. An electrical pigtail hung down to eye-level from the winch. It had three buttons on it: Up, Down, and Lock. The winch too had the look of army surplus and still retained its olive drab paint.

"Now what do you suppose they would need a shop crane for?" Jack asked himself. A crane like this was usually used for working on heavy machinery. He could not imagine why it would be used in an airplane hangar. He grabbed the control pigtail and pulled. The crane swung easily out into the space above the front of the hangar. He pushed a button on the side of the unit and he heard the whir of an electric motor. The winch was slowly rolling its way out to the end of the big "I" beam about twenty feet above the concrete floor. He stopped the motor and started to swing the crane through its arc.

Jack stumbled. He caught himself on the winch control. "That blasted ring gets me every time," he said, looking down at the iron ring that he had tripped over. The pilot himself had wondered why they had tie-downs inside the hangar. It was a common thing for planes kept outside. Jack followed the lines in the concrete where the floor had been sawn after the slab had been poured to control cracking. The two iron rings were situated squarely in the middle of two large slabs of concrete. Jack knelt down and examined the edges of the cut. The crack was a bit wider than a normal saw cut. Jack had worked construction on and off while in college to have some spending money, and as an excuse not to study very hard. He was quite familiar with pouring concrete. There were chips and gouges along the otherwise sharp edges of the line. Jack felt himself start to sweat. He stood back up and grabbed the winch control. He pushed the button that read "Down" and a louder motor sound emanated from the big winch as the hook began to drop. He pulled the swingarm around and positioned it directly over the iron ring. When the hook was almost touching the floor, Jack slid it into the ring. He ran over to the door and looked out the window next to it. Seeing no one, he ran back to the winch and pressed the "Up" button. The motor whirred and the powerful winch groaned as it took up the slack in the cable. A couple of popping noises sounded as the weight of the slab was transferred to the I-beam. The huge slab of concrete began to move.

Jack was sweating profusely now. It wasn't from exertion. It was fear...adrenalin; he was close to something. He stopped the winch when the lowest corner of the slab hung about a foot off the floor. He could see a dark cavern underneath. The concrete slab was not perfectly balanced. The higher corner of the slab hung about three feet off the floor. Jack looked over toward the tool cabinet. A trouble light on a reel hung out from the wall. He grabbed the light and pulled, stringing out the cord. He pushed the button, turning the light on, and peered down into the void beneath the concrete slab. "Holy cow!" The words escaped from his mouth involuntarily.

Visible in the light of the handheld lamp was a row of bombs of some sort. They were a dull gray in color and had the typical lozenge shape with fins. Several crates of something labeled in Cyrillic were stacked there also. A metal ladder led down into the basement vault. Jack laid the trouble light on the floor at the edge of the cement, so that it shown down into the pit. He eased down the ladder, descending the ten feet or so to the concrete floor of the basement. In the center of the area was a cylindrical metal object on a stout-looking cradle. The cylinder had circular chrome steel handles that made up each of the ends, allowing two people to carry it between them with ease. The thing reminded Jack of the old hospital-surplus autoclave from his father's surgery. But this was no autoclave. It had some Cyrillic writing on it in red paint and a star and sickle. The markings next to these were unmistakably the internationally recognized symbol for radiation in black and yellow. Jack approached the device with something like reverence. It had a keypad recessed into one end with a digital display. A key slot resided next to this and a pair of keys hung on a plastic lanyard from a ring on the device. Jack's mouth was dry. He took a firm grip with each hand on a handle and lifted. He strained as the device lifted off its cradle about an inch. "That's more than a hundred pounds," he told himself, setting it back down gingerly. Jack looked back to the end with the keypad. He took out his Leatherman and opened the knife. He cut the plastic lanyard and put the pair of keys in his pocket. He was still looking at the bomb, wishing he had brought the cell phone with him, when he realized that the light was getting dim. He looked up at the top of the ladder.

"Oh, Shit!" he exclaimed, as panic gripped him in the chest. The distance between the concrete slab and the floor of the hangar was about an inch. The trouble light, lying just outside the pit, was slowly disappearing. The winch had settled and allowed the slab to drift back down into its resting place in the floor. He had forgotten to set the lock on the winch. Jack frantically looked for something to jam into the slit. As he grabbed at the crating in front of him, the light disappeared completely. He heard the clunk as the slab settled into place. The resulting darkness was absolute, like the darkness of a cave. The only sound Jack heard now was his own breathing.

So this was it. The jig was up. How could he have been so stupid? He had finally found the bomb that everyone in the world was looking for and he had blown it. He was entombed as a result of his own carelessness.

He sat down on the bottom rung of the steel ladder. Jack was not one to give up, but this seemed hopeless. The concrete slab over his head weighed literally a ton. He had seen nothing, before the light went out, to use as a lever. If someone found him, it was not going to be anyone friendly. Perhaps the pilots? They might get him out without feeling the need to kill him. That was assuming that they themselves were innocents. But that would be when? Tomorrow night? As Jack sat, feeling like a fool, he heard a hum and felt a slight breeze on his face. At first he thought that the winch was running and that someone was out there, but he soon realized that the sound was not the winch. He lifted his hand in front of his face. Although he could not see anything, he felt the air movement. He followed it to its source on the far wall of the bunker. The air hissed quietly from a louvered vent on the side of the bunker. He felt around the edges. The vent was a good 18 inches square.

"There might be a way out of here yet," he said to himself. He had his trusty Leatherman in his pocket. He felt around the corners of the metal panel. It had slotted screws. He started to work on the screw, when he had a thought. The air coming out was warm. That meant that he would end up at a furnace of some sort. It made sense that the bunker would be climate controlled. If you built this place to store munitions, you wouldn't want moisture to ruin the stuff inside. If it had a forced air furnace, then the air had to get out. He wished desperately for a flashlight, when he realized that he had one. On his keychain he had attached a tiny micro light, one of those with the Xenon bulb that you just squeeze between your thumb and index finger. He had gotten it for Christmas a couple of years ago and had almost never used it. He dug in his pocket for his key ring. It felt strange, fumbling through several keys; it was hard to tell what something was when you couldn't see it. He found the little light and gave it a squeeze. Jack was amazed at how much light it put out in the blackness. He shined it around on the bombs and crates. He walked over to the far wall. Sure enough, a grate identical to the one on the other side covered a hole in the concrete. He let the light go out and opened his Leatherman. He pinched the light on momentarily to look at the screws. "Damn," he whispered to himself, "Tap Con." That would make it tough. The blue paint on the screw heads told Jack that they were bored and screwed directly into the concrete. He didn't think they would back out easily. He tried the flat-blade screwdriver from his Leatherman tool. It was tougher in the dark but he didn't know how long a light the size of a nickel would hold out. The blade of the screwdriver kept slipping out. He opened the tool to use the pliers. The screws were hex-head as well as screw slotted. The screw turned. After the first few revolutions it came out easily. The next two screws were at the top of the grate. Both broke off just beneath the head after a quarter turn. "That works too," said Jack. The final screw came out and the grate fell to the floor.

The noise made Jack jump in the quiet of the bunker. He squeezed the tiny light revealing the inside of a sheet metal duct running straight ahead for about 15 feet. Jack realized now that he would get out, even if he had to use the can opener on his tool. No sheet metal was going to stop him. He decided to put the grate back on the two broken off screws sticking out from the concrete. The job turned out to be harder than he thought. The duct was not big enough to turn around in. He could reach back and get the grate with his fingers but it took him a full five minutes of maneuvering to hang it on the screw studs. He finally felt it catch and breathed a sigh of relief in the darkness. He began to crawl down the duct on his belly. About half way to the end he felt air coming in from the side. He turned on his light. On his right side was another grate. He poked the little bulb of the tiny light between the louvers. The air was coming from another bunker. "The other iron ring," he thought. He could see similar crates to the ones he'd seen in the other bunker. In the center of the little room he could see another device identical to the one in the first bunker...another nuke. Jack crawled on. He came to the end and realized that a glimmer of light was emanating from somewhere above. The duct went up. Jack rolled onto his back and made the turn. He stood up in the duct and could see a louvered grate a couple of feet above his head. He reached up with both hands and shoved his fingers between the metal fins on the louvers to get a good grip. With a grunt he pulled himself up to where he could see out and got the side of his boot to hold on a seam in the sheet metal. Holding himself there, he peered out between the louvers and could see the hangar floor about a foot below his chin. The blower on the furnace shut off and it got quiet. He reached up and hooked a hand over the turn where the duct went into the furnace. Jack pulled his knees up into his chest and against the inside of the duct. The metal banged and distorted under the pressure. He pulled hard and managed to get himself up another couple of feet. He now had his knees against the louvered grate. He was sweating now as if he had run a marathon. He grunted and gave a mighty shove with his knees and the screws holding the grate screeched as they pulled free from the sheetmetal of the duct. Jack hooked his elbow in the furnace inlet and swung his sweat-soaked body out onto the hangar floor.

He was out! For a moment he just lay there on the floor trying to catch his breath. The metal grate falling had made an incredible amount of noise on the concrete floor. Jack hoped that Tino had not made a quick trip of it. He suddenly felt the need to put things back as he had found them and get out of there. He jumped up and went to the tool cabinet. He found a Phillips screwdriver and replaced the grate, straightening out the damage as best he could with a ball peen hammer also from the tool box. It would take a pretty observant person to notice the change. Jack grabbed the winch control and ran the cable out to unhook it from the eye. He then ran it back up to its resting length and swung the crane back to the wall. He looked back around. The trouble light lay on the floor beside the slab. He picked it up and pulled on the cord until the spring-loaded reel caught. He walked it back into the coil. There, everything was as it had been.

Jack jumped as he heard a noise. It was the slight "zip" sound of a key sliding into a lock. His head swung toward the door. He could see a shadow across the window nearby. Jack ran for the far corner of the hangar and went into a slide, like a runner stealing home. He came to a stop behind the big army-surplus bomb carrier that he had seen earlier. He lay quiet, listening. The door had not opened yet. The knob was shaking and rattling. Jack had worked for his uncle painting rental units one summer in high school. The uncle had an old key machine to make copies with. It didn't do a very good job and you had to shake and twist on the keys he copied to get them to work. The fumbling now, on the other side of the door, reminded Jack of the imperfect keys.

The knob finally turned and the door opened. Jack was surprised to see Tino. The little man looked around the hangar as if seeing it for the first time. Tino looked at the shiny key in his hand and put it in his pocket. He then went into the office and checked it out, much as Jack had done. Jack could hear the drawers sliding open and shut on the file cabinet. What was going on here? Tino wasn't looking for Jack, but he was looking for something. The little man came out of the office. He looked around and found a ladder that went on top of the office. He climbed up on top and checked out the few boxes that were stacked up there. He wasn't finding anything, at least not what he was looking for. He came back down the ladder and checked out the tractor. He looked at the empty bomb carrier where Jack was hiding. As he walked over to it, Jack could see Tino's expertly shined leather shoes. Jack silently slid underneath the carrier. He was afraid to breath. He could feel his pulse in his ears and he hoped his pounding heart was not audible to Tino. Jack knew that if Tino found him, the whole operation was blown. The little man walked away.

When Tino had checked out everything, he gave the place one last look and walked back to the door. Jack heard the click of the lock as the door closed. He waited a moment and stood up. He moved quickly to the window and looked out. Tino was across the runway, heading for the house.

"What the hell was that all about, Tino?" he asked himself aloud. Jack considered his predicament. He had to get to that cell phone and call Riley. Could he just walk out the door and run over to the guesthouse and call? What if Tino saw him come out of the hangar? He surveyed the inside of the hangar again. He saw, in the back wall of the building, a door. It was off-white like the insulation that covered the entire interior of the place. He hadn't noticed it before. He quickly walked over to it and turned the knob. It took a shove to open the door, as some bunchgrass had grown up next to it on the outside. The door obviously was not used very often if at all. Jack stepped out into the sunlight. He reached back in and turned the lock button so that the door would remain unlocked, pulled the grass back out of the way, and shut the door.

Jack looked around him. He saw an old International Harvester pickup with a snow blade hanging on the front of it. The old truck was rusted and the red paint was faded to a rose color. A couple of empty oil drums and a few clumps of sage kept the old "binder" company. Next to the drums sat two cargo containers with faded blue paint. Jack opened the nearest one. It was empty. The containers had numbers that might make it possible to trace back to where they were shipped from and the writing was in Cyrillic, but Jack wasn't going to worry about that right now.

Jack figured he could walk straight away from the hangar, keeping it between himself and the house, until he got to the base of the big knob where the cemetery was. A small arroyo drained the area close to the base and he could follow it until he was totally out of sight. He stepped quickly to carry out his escape. He didn't run in case anyone was looking. He simply walked like a man with a purpose.

Up on the knob Hamad leaned across the old granite cross looking through the spotting scope. "Fahad, a man just came out of the hangar from the backside. He is coming this way!"

201

Fahad lifted his head off the headrest of the reclined seat of the Jaguar and opened his eyes. He hopped up and ran over to where Hamad stood peering through the scope. "Did he see you?"

"I don't know, but he looked up here. He looked right at me when I saw him through the glass."

Fahad looked through the spotting scope. "He must have seen you. He is walking directly toward us. He is coming up to investigate." He glared at Hamad.

Hamad had walked back to the Jaguar. He had the trunk open and was shoving a 30-round, banana-shaped clip into an AK-47 rifle. "Then I will stop him."

"Can you do it from here?" Fahad was skeptical. Both men had shot the Kalashnikov rifles extensively at a camp in the mountains of Afghanistan. Hamad had been the only one who could hit a silhouette at 200 meters with anything resembling consistency. The man walking toward them was just about that distance now.

"Yes." He said it with confidence as he wrapped the rifle's canvas sling around his left wrist and grabbed the forearm of the gun. He ratcheted the action with his right hand and laid the gun across the arm of the granite cross. A scope would have been nice, but was not necessary. Hamad's grip was firm and steady. He brought the sights in line with the man's chest. The gun bucked in Hamad's hands as he fired two shots. The man went down. Hamad smiled with satisfaction and looked up from his rifle at Fahad. The other man was looking through the spotting scope.

"Good shooting cousin," said Fahad. He was folding the tripod and moving as he spoke. "Let us get out of here, quickly." They crouched as they hastily made their way to the car.

Down at the old ranch house Charlie and Abe were halfway through the door with an old overstuffed green couch. They had the thing wedged in the doorway. Abe was cussing, wondering how the hell anyone had ever gotten it in there in the first place. The couch was just one of several pieces of furniture that they would be hauling into town for Nadine Palmer. "Sounds like someone's shootin' up on the ridge," said Nadine. "Jim wouldn't have liked that. He didn't tolerate people huntin' without askin' first."

"Not huntin' season," said Abe with a grunt. The couch was coming loose now. They had it almost out the door.

"Somebody takin' a shot at a coyote, prob'ly," said Charlie. The couch hit him in the chest as Abe gave it a hard shove going down the steps from the porch. "Take it easy, Abe. You're gonna knock me down."

"Sorry," said Abe. "I wonder where Jack is? I thought he was gonna' help."

"If he was around, he'd be here," said Charlie.

Jack had almost made it to the ditch. He felt sure that no one had seen him. He heard the slap of the bullet milliseconds before the report of the rifle reached him. A rock exploded behind him, then something hit him in the head and he saw an explosion of lights, like fireworks, just before everything went black. Jack's limp body fell into the arroyo and rolled to the bottom.

Leroy Donovan had set up his surveillance post in some willows next to the irrigation ditch, where it came onto the property. It wasn't the best place to watch from, but it would be impossible to detect from the house. Riley had insisted that he have a view of the big knob to the north as well. The agent had carefully placed his chair in the shade of a willow. This would reduce possible glare from any shiny objects like the lenses of his binoculars. His position would be invisible from the air as the jet made approach to the runway. Leroy also planned to take a little nap and wanted to do it in the shade. The chair was a folding canvas job with arm rests from Sam's Club and the agent settled into it.

Leroy had planned to retire from the Bureau and move to Florida with his wife, Lisa. He was tired of Ft. Collins and cold weather. He hated the snow. It bothered his arthritis and he just got a lot colder now than he used to. September 11th had changed everything at the Bureau. He himself had been swept up in a new wave of patriotism and a sense of importance in his job. Lisa still had her job at the hospital. She was a good nurse and really enjoyed her work. She wasn't quite ready to retire yet. Leroy had told her that she could get a job in Florida. Lord knows the place is full of geriatrics needing good nurses.

"Stick it out for a couple more years, Leroy," she had said. "You like what you do and you aren't as old as you think you are."

"I don't feel old," he had replied, "but I want to enjoy retirement. I want to go fishing in the Keys. I wanta' have some fun before this old body falls completely apart." He had been wearing a hearing aid for a few months. That was one of the things that had started the retirement talk.

"You always said Florida was full of 90 year old white folks, and that there was nothing uglier than a 90 year old white woman." She had teased him.

"I think that was Redd Foxx," he had said.

"I think it was you," she had said.

"Either way it's true. But I ain't gonna be lookin' at them," he had said. "I'm gonna be lookin' at you. I'm gonna' be looking at you on the beach. You're the best lookin' woman your age...any age," he added quickly.

"Be careful, now," she had said.

"You know what I mean. I just wanta' show you off." And he did. Lisa was a beautiful woman and had kept her figure. She was younger than Leroy and looked a lot younger that she really was. Leroy was proud of her. Heck, he was proud of himself for having married her.

There was nothing going on at the ranch. Leroy was beginning to think that the Denver office was right. That this was a waste of time. He didn't like the Russian. The guy was probably a crook, but not exactly a threat to national security. Leroy thought that they should just go in and bust them. Clear up this whole mess about Jim Palmer and the goons from Chicago. But he knew that Riley often played hunches and Riley was usually right. Leroy liked Joe Riley and had known him for a long time. It was the old guys like Joe that kept Leroy from getting out. They used to ski Jackson Hole together with Jack Wallace's uncle. Now, with arthritis and bad knees, about as close as they got to the slopes was talking about it over beers.

Leroy hadn't noticed the watchers on the knob. His eyes were closed beneath his sunglasses as he had succumbed to the warm day and the comfortable chair. He should have heard the shot, but he didn't. He had turned his hearing aid down when a camp-robber jay kept squawking at him, trying to get to the rest of his peanut butter cheese crackers.

CHAPTER TWENTY-EIGHT

"So what are you thinkin'?" asked Hank.

"I'm thinking I'll have another Diet Coke," said Will motioning to the waitress. They would have been drinking Budweiser, but they had to fly out again tomorrow.

"You're not worried?" asked Hank.

"What's to worry about? We can get jobs with any of the executive jet leasing companies that we want. Besides, Yuri says he's going to give us a generous severance pay. Might be enough to just flat out retire."

"You gotta be kiddin'. You wouldn't know what to do with yourself." Hank lined up on another ball on the pool table.

"Oh, I don't know," said Will. "We've had a lot of time off anyway. We never had any trouble finding something to do."

"Yeah, but we had income. We knew we had money coming. It's easier to spend when you know there's more coming."

"Yeah, maybe so. We might need to pick up a few jobs here and there. Nothing fulltime." Will was watching a guy at a table trying to pick up a girl half his age. He figured that unless she was a hooker or he was a movie producer, the guy was pissing in the wind.

"Your shot," said Hank.

The two pilots had come into McCarron airport and Yuri and his entourage had been whisked away by limousine to the Golden Nugget Hotel. Will and Hank had shut the plane down and taken care of the paperwork at the airport.

They had followed to the hotel in a cab and put their bags in their room when Yuri knocked on the door. Their boss had somberly explained that he would be on an extended stay in Poland, starting a new company, and that he would not need their services or the Learjet for that matter. He was gracious as always. He was courteous and complimentary, but the sad fact was that the balloon had burst. The dream job was gone. It was over.

Will had set a limit of three hundred dollars for himself at the crap tables. They had walked to the Four Queens where he had quickly dropped a hundred. From there they had gone to Fitzgerald's. Will had lasted a little longer but another hundred was gone by lunchtime. They had wondered on, away from the buzz of Fremont Street and found a little bar with a pool table. The place had some dollar slots and Hank had spent the sum total of ten dollars at the one-armed bandits. Now both pilots had settled for the pool table. Both men were wishing that they could have a few cold ones to soften the blow that Yuri's news had given them, but they were flying in the morning.

"I never did like Vegas," said Hank. "Whole damn place is full of hustlers and bug-eyed gamblers. Closest thing they have to real people is the dealers and most of them are weird as hell."

"Gotta be some normal people here," offered Will.

"Not so's you'd notice. Well, maybe the hotel doorman or some of the working class."

"Everyone else is out here to get rich. Or just to screw off." Will was watching the bald head of the guy at the table turn red as the girl told him where he could put his hotel key. "I guess we're just part of that working class out here. Everyone else is having fun, on vacation. We gotta work. It would be okay if we hadn't just got the ax."

"Yeah, I guess it was too good to last. We had fun for a while..." A loud "smack" stopped him mid-sentence. The girl at the table had just slapped the bald guy. She walked away in a hurry and the bald guy laughed and ordered another drink. "Jeez," said Hank. "I ever get that

207

pathetic, do me a favor and shoot me."

"Don't worry," said Will. "You'd never have gotten that far."

"Oh, thanks," said Hank indignantly. "I needed that."

Back in the suite in the North Tower of the Nugget, Yuri addressed Sasha while Anna was in her bedroom. "So, tell me, Sasha, who exactly is this meeting with?"

"His name is Steve Balducchi. I don't know who he is. He's an intermediary," said Sasha. "I don't like him at all."

"So why are we talking to him. Where is this Al-Rahman? Doesn't he do his own talking?" Yuri was sounding frustrated.

"The guy isn't even in the country, Yuri. You know that. He does not speak English or Russian, so he always deals through someone else."

"I am uncomfortable with this. I do not have good feelings about this trip. I cannot even say why," said Yuri with a frown. He looked up at Sasha from the couch where he sat with eyes that seemed to ask for reassurance.

"I have much the same feelings. I wish it were not so." Sasha did not dispel the dread that seemed to have taken over Yuri.

Anna stepped into the room. "Are we going out? Is this going to be an early dinner?"

The two men exchanged worried glances, then Yuri smiled. "Anna my dear, sit down. You must learn to relax. Our dinner engagement is not until 7 this evening." He walked to the minibar and picked up a glass. "Would you like a drink?"

"No," said Anna, "I don't think so. Maybe I will go down to the casino and play some blackjack."

"Yes, yes," said Yuri, a little too quickly. "Go and gamble a little. You have some fun." He poured himself a vodka. Absolut was as good as he could get on short notice.

"Will you come with me Sasha?" asked Anna.

"Yes, I can come with you for a little while," said Sasha looking at Yuri for approval.

"Please," said Yuri waving his glass. "Go and have some fun." He pulled a wad of bills from his billfold and handed it to Anna as if she were a child headed for the movies. She took it without a word. "We will meet back here at 6," he said to Sasha with a trepid look.

When Sasha and Anna had gone, Yuri sat down on the couch with his drink. He could see far, as he looked out the window. Las Vegas was a big city now. He liked the downtown area better than the strip. At least he used to. All this Fremont Street light-show stuff was a bit much. He had avoided the strip because it was too much like Disneyland. This city was always changing. Like a snake shedding its old skin only to replace it with a newer, shinier version of the same thing.

Yuri swirled the ice in his glass. He was becoming morose. It was getting more difficult to keep going with every passing day. He had nothing to live for. Not since his wife, Elena, had died. She had died so horribly, so senselessly. She had simply been in the wrong place at the wrong time. Yuri's Elena had been visiting a maiden aunt in Belarus when the poorly trained technicians at reactor number 4 at the Chernobyl nuclear facility had performed a dangerous test, causing the now infamous disaster. They had put the facility on the map in the worst possible way. The panic that ensued was not handled well. This was typical Soviet policy. The radiation cloud, which swept over Belarus, in itself, was not what had taken his Elena. No. It was a panic-stricken bus driver who had slammed his vehicle into the taxi when his Elena was leaving her hotel. At first it seemed that her injuries were minor. Perhaps they were. But with the evacuations, the hospitals being what they were, a few broken ribs and a punctured lung had turned into pneumonia. The hospital staff had feared that she was contaminated with radiation. They were overworked and afraid and did not check her often. They falsified records.

They let her die before Yuri could get her out and move her to a better facility. She died needlessly for lack of treatment. All because of secrecy and cover-ups. All because of a cold war perpetuated by the United States.

Yuri swallowed the last of his drink and poured himself another. Perhaps what he was doing was wrong. He didn't really care anymore. He had tired of the game. He thought of Anna and then of his niece, his Elena's namesake. He had lied to Anna. She knew nothing of the consequences of what he proposed to do. Even Sasha believed that it would never be allowed to play itself out. Yuri searched his heart for some flicker of emotion. Nothing. He hated the United States. He hated the Soviet Union as well. He felt like his whole life had been one big betrayal of trust. He didn't hate the people. He hated the governments. The bureaucrats, who wielded more power than they could control, were the only ones who would suffer. Like Chernobyl, this too would pass. This too would just be another page in the history books.

At the blackjack table Anna sat watching the cards go down. She did not know why they were in Las Vegas to begin with. Yuri had her selling calls on all their stock holdings and even selling short positions. It was as if he were anticipating a big drop in the markets. It was as if he knew...something. Anna worked daily with the different accounts. She knew that they were held in different names, in different countries in fact, to launder questionable deals as well as to avoid tax consequences; but this looked fishy even to her. What was going down? Yuri had never kept her out of the loop like he did now.

"You need to put your chips out." The voice was Sasha's.

"What?" she said, confused, as she came out of her reverie.

"The dealer split your aces for you, but you need to cover the bet."

"Oh," she said to the dealer, "I am sorry. I was daydreaming." The dealer simply smiled and nodded as he continued around the table with the cards. They were playing a ten-dollar table, which only had two other occupants. One was an older fellow with sad eyes and a bad comb-over. He seemed more interested in the free drinks than the game. The other person was a well-dressed woman in her late twenties who was watching the happenings at a nearby crap table with more interest than the game in front of her. Neither seemed to even notice as Anna's inattentiveness repeatedly stopped the game. Anna finally looked up at Sasha, ignoring the cards in front of her altogether. "What is going on Sasha?" she asked suddenly. She simply stared at him. Sasha looked away.

"Not here," he said to Anna. "Let us go for a walk." He picked up their chips and tipped the dealer. They got up from the table and walked toward the door exiting onto 1st street. A hot wind hit them as they reached the street and walked toward the canopy on Fremont.

"Talk to me Sasha."

"You don't want to know," he answered.

"You are wrong, Sasha. I do want to know. I *need* to know."

"It is complicated," said Sasha, offering nothing more.

"Something is going to happen," she said. "I know that Yuri has information. I know that Yuri stands to profit from it. But what he is having me do... I think that whatever is happening is going to be tragic."

"Perhaps."

"Are you involved?" She waited for an answer that did not come. "Are *we* involved?" His silence was the answer that she had hoped she would not hear.

Sasha did not know what to say. He could not tell her what Yuri's intentions were. She simply would not understand. She was being left out for her own protection. This woman, whom Sasha had thought he loved, was not stupid. She had developed a conscience, which he himself did not possess. She had in fact become rather distant in the last couple of weeks. Was she figuring out that Yuri was involved in something that she could not tolerate? Or was it something else? He suddenly felt his face flush with anger and embarrassment.

"Who is this Jack fellow?" he asked suddenly.

"What?" Anna was confused at his change of direction in the conversation.

"This cowboy. Who is he?"

"What do you mean? He is just a cowboy, he drives the car." She realized that she was blushing a little now as she thought of Jack. Was that all he was to her?

"Are you in love with him?" Sasha stopped now and faced her. Fremont street was not crowded, but there were people walking and standing all around them.

"No!" She said it a little too quickly.

"Are you in love with me?" The question was abrupt. Anna could not look at Sasha now. She knew the answer was no, but she could not voice it. She felt her face getting hot. A tightness in her throat would not allow words to come out at all.

Sasha looked away now himself. He was angry and jealous. Anna still had her back to him. "Our meeting this evening does not concern you. The pilots will be escorting you to dinner." His voice was flat, without emotion. She did not turn around as Sasha walked away from her. A tear rolled down her cheek.

Twenty feet away a tanned figure in white tropical pants and a bright orange floral-print shirt held a brochure promising all kinds of carnal pleasures in front of him. His concentration was not on the flyer at all. What had he just witnessed? A lovers' quarrel? He dropped the brochure into a nearby trashcan and walked away pulling out his cell phone. "Ponytail's comin' in," he said into the phone. "I'll stick with Snow White." He turned back around and leaned against a post. He took off the short-brimmed straw hat that he was wearing and ran his fingers through his greasy, black hair. The woman was still standing there in the street.

CHAPTER TWENTY-NINE

Steve Balducchi was a small time hood. He dressed the part and even acted it sometimes, but he was nobody. He wouldn't even get an honorable mention with the real muscle of this town. He had no idea how these people had gotten his name and he didn't care as long as the money was good. And what did he have to do besides kill a little time and pass some information. He could do that while enjoying a fine Italian meal with a couple of Russian hoods. It might even be a job opportunity, a chance to step up the ladder.

He looked down at the menu in his hands. Maybe start with some spinach soup, a little antipasto, then go for the linguini alfredo with the lobster tails on top. What the hell, this was Stephano's and someone else was buying. Balducchi ordered another whiskey sour and popped a couple of Rolaids. If this fire in his belly didn't go out soon, it was going to be hard to enjoy all this rich food. He felt for the manila envelope in his pocket. It was too thin to have any cash in it. Oh well, a little bullshit, entertain these Ruskies, and he could hit the crap tables with the three thousand the guy gave him.

Yuri and Sasha entered Stephano's and were directed to a table with a white, linen tablecloth, where a man sat in a black suit. The man sat down his drink and stood up as the two approached. He thrust out his hand like a too eager salesman. Sasha reluctantly took it as he looked the man over. Balducchi's suit was rumpled and the blue of his beard gave him a shifty appearance, even though he was freshly shaved. A single dark eyebrow dipped slightly at the bridge of his nose as it spanned the width of the man's face. His round stomach strained at the single button of his coat as he sat back down. Yuri simply looked at the man with disgust. Balducchi flagged a waiter from a different table and insisted that he take a drink order from his "associates". The two Russians exchanged looks.

"The people I represent," Balducchi began, "want you fellows to know that you are very important to them." Again the men exchanged looks. "They would like to express regret at being unable to make this meeting in person." Balducchi was beginning to sweat. This was a tough audience. He had expected a couple of dopey Russians like he'd seen in the movies. His stomach churned as the Rolaids tried to overcome the new waves of acid being dumped in. "I've taken the liberty of ordering for us," he said. "The lobster tails and linguini are superb."

"What is the information that you have for us?" asked Sasha as the drinks came.

"I have the nuts and bolts, so to speak, of how you will be paid for services rendered," said Balducchi. These guys really cut to the chase, he thought. The Russians sipped their drinks and exchanged some words in Russian. Maybe the older guy couldn't speak the language. Yeah, that's the deal. The soup came and Yuri continued to sip his vodka. He made no attempt to pick up a spoon.

"What is it that you propose?" asked Sasha.

Didn't this guy ever smile? What was he supposed to propose? He wasn't prepared to talk about the deal, whatever it was. "I have some numbers for you," he said patting his breast pocket. "This will explain everything." He pulled out the manila envelope and handed it to Sasha. The Russian took it without dropping his gaze from Balducchi.

Sasha opened the envelope and scanned over its contents. He started to say something to Balducchi when a group of waiters appeared at the table singing a version of *Volare*. Sasha leaned over to Yuri and spoke to him while the smiling Balducchi leaned back trying to look happy with the singing. When the waiters finished he clapped and thanked them. Another flurry of waiters engulfed them before anyone could speak and set large plates of linguini before them. Each plate had two lobster tails perched atop the pasta. Balducchi thought that this would surely impress these guys.

Sasha and Yuri stood up without even looking at their food. "Our business is concluded," said Sasha, slipping the envelope into his coat. "Good evening to you."

"Wait...Aren't you gonna'..." Balducchi spluttered as Yuri and Sasha walked away from the table without looking back. He looked down at the food and suddenly realized that he would be stuck with the bill. This was going to cost him at least a couple a hundred, probably three. He shrugged and picked up a fork. He stuffed his mouth full of the succulent lobster tail. The waiter came up and asked him how the food was. "Sgood," he said, around a mouthful, "I'm gonna need a box though."

In the elevator Yuri spoke, "Is the information legitimate?" His lips were tight, his jaws clenched.

"Yes, but nothing that would have required our presence here."

"Then this is a decoy," said Yuri. "Call the pilots and ready the plane at once." Sasha nodded and pulled out his phone. Sasha knew that Yuri was thinking that he, Sasha, had allowed someone to find their location. He had been so careful, but it *was* the most likely explanation.

Anna was barely picking at the Cobb salad in front of her. She was rather enjoying the company of Will and Hank. They were such nice, carefree men. They didn't possess that dark aura that seemed to surround Yuri and Sasha of late. They reminded her of some of her marks over in the republics. She had seduced men such as these out of information that they barely knew they possessed. She felt a wave of shame come over her. It hadn't seemed wrong then. It was her job. It was for her country. But it *was* wrong. She could see that now...now that she had been out in the world so to

215

speak. She thought of the middle-eastern terrorists who had recently caused so much grief to this country. How could they believe that what they were doing was the will of God? The communists had tried to purge God from the system. People were so much more vulnerable when they had no moral compass. The fanatics of Islam had gone even further. They had cleverly disguised their own will for that of Allah.

Anna's thoughts were interrupted by Hank waving a hand in front of her face. "Did I lose you? I think you missed the punch line altogether." He had just finished telling a rather crude joke about hillbillies from the Ozarks.

"Oh," she said, "forgive me. My mind is somewhere else tonight."

"If you missed that joke," said Will, "you were lucky." He looked wryly at Hank who was stuffing the last bite of prime rib in his mouth. If he had a retort he wasn't able to deliver it.

"So, where is it that you're going? Poland?" Will asked Anna.

"What?"

"Starting the new business. You know...in Poland." Will was looking at the dessert menu.

"I don't understand?" Anna obviously had no idea what Will was talking about.

"The boss said," spoke Hank, "that he was going to Poland to start some new business and that he didn't need us anymore. He laid us off." Hank was a little blunt, as if Anna was partly to blame.

"This is the first I have heard of this," said Anna, real surprise on her face.

Will and Hank looked at each other, both thinking the same thing. Was Yuri lying to them? The cell phone on Will's belt vibrated. He plucked it off its clip and flipped it open and answered. "I'm not sure we can do that," said Will into the phone. "They were going to check the hydraulic pressure on the starboard aileron. They may not have completed...Okay...I'll call and check. I'll find out and call you right back." He punched off the phone and began fishing in his billfold for the card the mechanic had given him.

"What's up?" asked Hank.

"Yuri wants to leave ASAP. I gotta call and see if they've got the pump checked. I told the guy he had until 10 tomorrow." Will dialed in a number. "Yeah, is Sam still around by any chance?" He was talking into the phone. "I see. Do you happen to know if he got done with the Lear jet?… That's great. Can somebody check us out then?… Yeah, we're leaving tonight. Great, thanks." He put the phone back on his belt. "Guess we better go pack." He was looking at Hank.

"I never unpacked," said Hank. Anna was just staring off into space. She was trying to comprehend what was going on. The waiter came by.

"Check please," said Will.

The people at the airport didn't seem too upset about the short notice. They got this sort of thing fairly often in Las Vegas. Everyone seemed to think that they were someone special here and deserved special treatment. The people who worked here simply smiled and pocketed the sizable tips that fell their way. Money always made bullshit easier to deal with. Will and Hank took care of loading the bags, as the omnipresent Tino was not along this time. As soon as it was loaded, the Learjet taxied down the runway as a sandstorm approached from the south. They were lucky to get off, according to the woman in the tower. The occupants of the cabin were quiet, as it was past midnight already.

They had reached an altitude of 17,000 ft. when Yuri came up and squatted between the pilots' seats. "I've been thinking," he said. "I really don't want to sell this airplane. I have no intention of selling the ranch and I had an idea." He paused.

"What would that be?" asked Will. Hank remained unimpressed. He was still upset with Yuri for pulling the rug out from under them.

"Why don't you two lease the airplane from me?

217

You could take on whatever charters you like. I have many business acquaintances that would use your services. I may occasionally need those services myself." He paused again. "I will make you one hell of a deal." The way he said "hell" sounded funny coming from Yuri. He was trying to speak their language, or perhaps he was trying to speak Hank's language.

"That might work out," said Will. "If the lease isn't too steep."

Yuri looked at Hank, who was still staring straight ahead as if he hadn't even been listening. Yuri liked these fellows. He didn't want their relationship to end on a sour note. He hoped that this gesture would ease their transition. He would have to let them think about it for a while. "Anna can work up an agreement on the laptop. We can print it out when we get back home. You fellows look it over and see if it meets your approval." He felt better about the whole thing now. "Think it over," he said and went back to his seat in the rear.

Anna was resting her head against the headrest. Her eyes were closed but she was not really sleeping. She wanted to ask Sasha, again, what was going on. She knew that he would not tell her, especially with Yuri within hearing distance. Sasha was asleep in a seat facing hers, his long legs propped up on the seat next to the window. She knew him well enough to know that he could sleep through just about anything.

Yuri came back and sat down beside Anna. She opened her eyes to find him looking at her.

"Are you asleep?" he asked.

"What is going on Yuri? Why are we in such a hurry to get back?" she said, opening her eyes to the dim light of the cabin. He knew that she was not asleep.

"The people whom we deal with are not always savory."

"And?" Anna was not going to let it pass.

"And they may try to steal from us." Yuri knew that he was going to have to let Anna know a little more.

218

"Steal what Yuri?"

"Some years ago," he began, "I acquired some military weapons." He paused. Anna merely looked at him, waiting. "As you know, the current market trends have been unfriendly to us. We need to market the weapons while buyers exist. I guess you could say it is as simple as that. Make hay while the sun shines." He waited for a reaction.

Anna looked relaxed. She was not upset as he had anticipated.

"Is it all about money?" she asked.

"Not entirely," he replied. "But, yes, it is about money."

She wanted to ask him if he was willing to sell these weapons to those bastards from the Middle East. She wanted to ask him if he needed money so badly that he would betray the Americans who had probably done more to make his success possible than anything else. But she knew that it was pointless. She knew that Yuri blamed the Americans as well as the Soviets for the death of his wife. She knew that he was dead to shame or conscience or whatever you wanted to call it.

"What you are doing is wrong." She said with authority. She knew that it wouldn't change things, but she wanted him to know what she felt.

"I know that this is what you believe," he said. "I do not even disagree with you. I just do not give a damn any more." He sat back in the seat as if the conversation had ended. In fact, it had ended.

The two sat silently for several minutes. Yuri spoke again, "I need you to craft a lease agreement for Will and Hank. I would like to lease the aircraft to them for...for something minimal. Just enough to make it legal. I wish them to be able to use the jet for whatever they wish for as long as they wish. Will you do this for me?"

"As you wish," said Anna in a crisp, businesslike tone. She pulled her laptop from the cabinet beneath the bar and opened it. She could not sleep at this point anyway.

219

The Learjet touched down in the wee hours of the morning. The runway lights were accessible remotely, so they didn't even have to wake Tino. By the time everything was shut down and the passengers had disembarked, the sun was trying to come up in the east. The two pilots were exhausted, but neither was actually ready for bed. They were discussing what to do when Yuri came out of the house and came over to them. "Here is a copy of the lease agreement. You two take as long as you wish. I just want to give you this opportunity. You have been such good fellows. Go to breakfast. The Wrangler will be open in less than an hour. Look this over and let me know." He fished a set of keys out of his jacket pocket and handed them to Hank. "Take my car, I insist," he said, pressing the keys into Hank's hand.

Hank took the keys and Will followed as he headed toward the garage. They got into the pearl white T-bird and backed out of the garage. "I'm surprised that Jack didn't hear us come in," said Will. "His bike is here and he doesn't seem like the type to miss much." They drove away into the gray light of dawn.

Joe Riley was puzzled more than anything. He had given Jack instructions to call him after looking at the hangar. He had heard nothing since then. He had to assume that Jack hadn't had a chance to look the place over yet. Riley had a pretty good idea of what might have occurred and was annoyed with the prospect. He had seen Jack return from the Grant place without the girl. He had also seen Tino go and come back. He had surmised that Jack had been roped into helping move Mrs. Palmer's furniture by the other ranch hands. He had seen the pickups leaving with loads of furniture and boxes. That was the only logical explanation...unless something bad had happened. It wouldn't be the first time something totally off-the-wall had interfered with an op. He remembered one sting operation in Kansas City. They had devoted a lot of manpower and time to set up a local mob figure on a racketeering charge. The sting was all set. The men in position waited and waited. The mark came and went. Their undercover man had slipped on the ice and banged his head on a storm drain. He had slept through the whole thing at the emergency room. No one had seen it but some good citizens who had called the paramedics.

Cecil Albertson was Joe Riley's night crew once again, now that he was back from his brother-in-law's funeral. He was glad to have an excuse to get away from his in-laws early. Cecil was not normally a field agent, although he had spent most of his career as one. He was more involved in public relations than anything else now. He lived over by Lander and ran a youth camp in conjunction with the Indian reservation and the Bureau's Public Relations branch. Riley had begged for men and this is what he got. Cecil was appreciated nonetheless, as was the faithful Leroy Donovan, between his power naps. Joe had been lucky to find Jack to recruit or he would have really been shorthanded.

Cecil liked the job, sneaking around at night. He had been demoted to the youth camp thing when he had gotten in trouble for some ethnic joke e-mails that he had forwarded all over the place. He guessed that his immediate boss at the time, a Puerto Rican woman of about 50, had taken it personally. She had shipped him out to the reservation. It was that or quit altogether. Lately he had been thinking that he had made the wrong choice. He didn't like dealing with kids. He didn't like it at all. This little gig for Riley was more like it.

He pulled out the night vision glasses and scanned the quiet ranch once more. He didn't expect to see anything, not this time of night, at least not of the human persuasion. He was having fun identifying coyotes and livestock. He felt like one of those documentary film guys, the ones' who name the creatures in the pack. "Wild dogs of the Serengeti," he said to himself, watching three coyotes zigzagging back and forth trying to cut a trail. The coyotes were right at the edge of the runway. They were within 30 yards of their unseen watcher. "This is pretty cool," he thought. Suddenly the runway lights burst on. Cecil let out an oath and jerked

221

the glasses away from his eyes. He rubbed his eyes involun-tarily, cursing as he did so. Why couldn't the Bureau buy the kind with flash suppression? He was temporarily blinded, but could hear a jet approaching. He looked at his watch but couldn't see it well enough to read it. He thought that it was getting close to 5 a.m. He had better go ahead and call Riley. He would want to know about this. He pulled out his cell phone, flipped it open, and put it to his ear after punching the speed dial. Instead of hearing the ring of the motel phone on the other end, he heard a series of beeps. He pulled the phone away from his head and looked at the display. "Low Battery" flashed on the screen, just before the unit turned itself off.

"Christ," said Cecil, "this thing just won't hold a charge anymore. Oh, well, these people aren't going anywhere." He decided to watch who got out of the plane. Then he would just run in to town and get Riley at the motel. He looked at his watch. By that time the Wrangler would be heating up the grill and he could get some breakfast and a good cup of coffee.

CHAPTER THIRTY

Jack moved his head. Pain shot through him like a searing iron behind his eyes. He was lying on his left arm and couldn't seem to move it at all. He didn't try to move his head again, but reached up with his right hand to the side of his face. He closed his eyes and felt. The side of his face was tight. It was caked with dried blood. His mouth was dry and he couldn't feel his tongue. He tried to swallow. His tongue felt like something that didn't belong there; it was a huge dry lump in his mouth. With his right hand he pushed against the rough ground beneath him and tried to pull his left arm out. The arm was without feeling. He slowly rolled toward his left side, off of his arm. He now lay on his back. He opened his eyes and found himself staring into a clear night sky. The blood flow was coming back to his left arm now and it was tingling. It hurt, but his head hurt worse. He felt intense throbbing in his temple. A warm trickle of blood ran down into his right ear. He just lay there for a few minutes, waiting, hoping the pain in his head would go away.

He opened his eyes again. Had he slept? He tried rolling across his right shoulder to the prone position. His left arm was working now. He pushed himself up and brought his knees under him. As he picked his head up, a wave of nausea swept over him. He began to wretch and the pain came swooping back down on him like some predatory animal. His head pounded and he again passed out.

What was that sound? Far off, the sound of church bells echoed across the valley. The sound seemed to come and go. Jack felt hot breath on the back of his neck. He moved his head. A sudden snort and the roll of rocks startled him. In the cold gray light he could see Buck standing over him. The horse looked puzzled. The smell of the man was familiar, but the smell of blood was strong. "Hey, Buck," Jack managed to say in a hoarse whisper. The big buckskin stepped forward again. Steadying himself with one hand on the horse's foreleg, Jack slowly got to his knees. If Buck were to shy away now, Jack would go down in a heap. Reaching up to get a handful of the horse's thick black mane, Jack managed to pull himself to his feet. The pain in his head had subsided. He was thirsty and most of all cold. He leaned against the big horse. The warmth of its body felt good. Jack tried to think. He remembered being in the hangar and trying to sneak away from it out the back. He remembered a shot and then nothing.

The sound of water caught his attention. It was the gurgle of water running through one of the little irrigation gates. He let go of the horse and stumbled toward the sound. Laboriously he climbed up out of the arroyo. The sky was getting lighter and he looked out across the meadow toward the big house and the hangar. The jet was back, parked outside the hangar on the tarmac. How long had he been out? He walked on toward the source of the water sounds. Jack dropped to his knees at the little ditch and lowered his head down to the flowing water. He drank a little and decided that he wasn't going to throw up. He steadied himself by grasping a large clump of grass next to the ditch and drank again, deeper this time. The water was so cold that it hurt his head. Buck had followed him and was also drinking from the ditch right beside Jack. As the cold water reached his stomach, Jack began to shiver. He realized that he had to get back to the house and get warmed up. He was very close to hypothermia. He splashed water up on his head. He gingerly bathed the side of his face and temple. He could feel a wound in the short hair above his ear.

Jack knew that he had been shot. He had no idea how lucky he had been. Hamad was an excellent shot, but he had failed to take into account that he was shooting down on his target. The relatively low muzzle velocity and the looping trajectory of the 7.62 mm round, coupled with about a two-hundred foot drop in elevation, would have required aiming at Jack's feet to hit him in the chest where Hamad had aimed. As it was, gravity had not had as dramatic an effect as it would have on a level shot, and the first bullet whizzed by Jack's head. The second had cut a furrow in his scalp with enough force to knock him out.

Jack got back to his feet without the horse's help this time. He felt better now, still extremely cold, but better. He stepped across the ditch and headed for the guesthouse. He kept the hangar between himself and the big house, but he figured that it was early enough that no one would see him. He got to the corner of the hangar and pushed the wire down on the fence, stepping over. Buck had followed him and seemed to be expecting something. Jack reached back over the fence and patted the big buckskin's neck. "I'm fresh out of oats my friend. You'll have to catch me next time."

He knew of no other way, so he just started walking across the runway toward the guesthouse. He felt very much exposed. There were no lights on in the house. Jack made it to the guesthouse and quickly let himself inside. The warmth of the kitchen felt good. He went directly back to his bedroom. The doors to the pilots' rooms were open and the rooms were empty. Jack wondered where the other men could be this time of day. He went into the bathroom and looked in the mirror. The side of his head was dark with dried blood. He took a finger and traced the wound, which ran at an angle above his right ear. He turned on the water, letting it get hot, and with a washcloth he gently bathed the wound. It took some time to get the blood out of his hair, even though the hair was short. Jack turned on the shower and stripped out of his clothes. As the steam began to roll out the top of the stall, he climbed in. For a few moments he just stood there and let the hot water run over his neck and down his back. He was finally beginning to get warm again. He washed his hair as well as he could without stirring up

225

the gash in his head. He didn't want to get it bleeding again.

Jack climbed out of the shower and toweled off. He suddenly realized that he had to get the cell phone and call Riley. He had been so intent on warming up, that he had not done this immediately. With a towel wrapped around his waist, he walked over to the dresser and pulled open the drawer. He reached under the pile of socks. Nothing. The phone wasn't there. He swept his hands all over the bottom of the drawer, knocking socks and underwear out onto the floor, but there was no sign of the phone. "Damn!" he said, realizing that he should have hid it somewhere more secure. He went to the closet and grabbed his old backpack. He dug to its bottom, already knowing that he would not find the old Colt. He was right. The Colt was gone too.

"Is this what you are looking for?" The voice startled Jack. He looked up to see Sasha leaning against the bedroom doorjamb. He had the cellular phone in his hand. "Get dressed," he said, without emotion.

Jack's mind was spinning fast as he pulled on a pair of jeans, some socks, and his old Vasque hiking boots. He pulled a hooded sweatshirt on over his T-shirt. Was this what he would be wearing at his execution? He thought about it, but he didn't really care. "It's not over yet," he told himself. As he finished dressing and started toward Sasha, he found himself looking into the barrel of a small automatic pistol of some kind. The hole was not as big as his old 45. He guessed it to be a 9 mm.

"Put out your hands," said Sasha. Jack did so and Sasha produced a pair of handcuffs. Sasha put them on Jack's wrists with his left hand, keeping the 9mm pointed at his chest with the right hand. Jack simply looked at the man's face. He was wondering what the Russian was thinking, what he was going to do. "Go." Sasha waved the pistol.

Jack went ahead through the hall and to the kitchen. He was thinking about grabbing something to attack Sasha with, but he couldn't see how it would work with the handcuffs. Sasha was being careful. Jack had no way of knowing that Sasha was Spetnaz as well as KGB trained. Jack's meager knowledge of self-defense was no match for the man.

Sasha told Jack to walk to the house when they got outside. As they were crossing the short distance to the main house, Jack heard a vehicle coming down the driveway. Sasha heard it too and he shoved the gun into Jack's back. For a moment Jack thought about trying for the gun, but Sasha pushed him on through the door of the main house as voices sounded from the front. Once inside the door, Jack found himself shoved sideways just inside the doorway into the dark kitchen. He felt the gun pressed hard against his lower lip. He tasted blood.

"Not a sound," said Sasha through clenched teeth. The kitchen was open to the adjacent hallway by a large pass-through with a countertop running most of the room's length. Wooden blinds in dark mahogany, matching the other woodwork, were dropped down now, so that the kitchen was in darkness, but the blinds were open enough to see through the opening into the hallway and across the greatroom. They waited in silence.

CHAPTER THIRTY-ONE

The old jeep came bucking and jerking up the driveway, finally smoothing out, just in time to stop again in the circle drive. It came to a jerking halt and heads rocked forward, then back, as the motor died. "Clutch, Elle, clutch!" Reid was saying frantically, holding himself away from the dash with his hands on the little grab bar above the glove box.

"Oh! This is so hard!" said Elle, turning off the ignition key.

"You're doing alright," said Reid. "You just have to get a little smoother on the clutch. You'll get it. Don't worry."

"Yeah, Elle," said a voice from the little jump seat in the back, "you did fine until we got to the driveway." Two girls, dressed nicely, sat in the rear of the jeep. Reid had taken special efforts to wipe the dust off the seat so that they wouldn't get their clothes dirty. He had also made sure that Elle drove slowly on the gravel, so the passengers did not get dusted on the trip.

"My Uncle must have come back early," said Elle, noticing the jet beside the hangar. "Do we have time to go in?" She looked at Reid.

"It's pretty early, they may still be in bed," he said. "Besides, I wanted to buy you girls breakfast before church."

"Okay," said Elle, "I'll just go get my clothes changed. Come with me Reid. You can meet Anna." Reid got out of the passenger side of the jeep and stood beside Elle as she punched the doorbell button.

Tino appeared, smiling as usual. "Hi, Tino," said Elle. "Reid, this is Tino. He runs the place." Tino smiled and shook the hand that Reid offered him. The girl brushed past Tino into the foyer. Reid followed her across the greatroom where she stuck her head in the door of the study. Reid could see the glow of a computer screen and a distinguished looking gentleman peering into it. "Uncle?" Elle called to the man.

Yuri looked up, startled. "Elena," he said, punching a button on the keyboard that caused the screen to go black. "You are up early." He was looking at Reid, puzzled.

"I'm staying over at the Grants' girls' camp. Didn't Jack tell you?"

"We got in early this morning," he said, realizing that he hadn't even given the girl a thought. "I haven't talked to Jack yet. Who is this young man?" He was almost smiling as he looked at Reid.

"Oh, I'm sorry," said Elle, turning to Reid. "This is Reid Wilcox. He works for Mr. Grant. He's taking a couple of the campers and me to breakfast, and then to church." Reid shook the older man's hand. "This is my uncle, Yuri Aleksandrov," she said formally.

"Pleased to meet you, sir," said Reid, sounding almost military.

A weak honk came from the horn of the old CJ at the front of the house and Elle said, "I've got to change. The girls are waiting." She hurried off to her room.

Reid stood in awkward silence as the man before him seemed preoccupied with thoughts of his own. The silence was broken as Anna came from the hallway where Elle had disappeared. She was tying the belt on a silk dressing gown as she held it tight around her waist.

She looked up at Reid. "Hello," she said, in a tone that practically asked "Who are you and why are you here?"

"My name is Reid Wilcox, ma'am." Reid offered his hand. "I brought Elle by to change clothes for church."

"Oh." Anna looked a little out of it.

"You're welcome to go with us," said Reid. "All of

you." He looked back at Yuri.

"Thank you, but no." Yuri turned to the study. "If you'll excuse me," he said and walked back to his computer.

"Oh," said Anna, fiddling with her hair. "Perhaps some other time. I'm sorry. We just got in and I'm not very coherent."

Elle came out of the hallway. "Anna, you've met Reid?" She came up and gave Anna a big hug.

"Yes," said Anna, hugging the girl, then both turned to look at Reid.

"Isn't he cute?" said Elle, using a stage whisper.

"Sounds like you're talking about a horse or something," said Reid, turning red.

"I'm just teasing you," Elle said with a laugh. "We better go; the girls are going to wonder what happened to us." She turned and kissed Anna lightly on the cheek. "I'm glad you're back. I have to talk to you...tell you stuff." She moved to the door with Reid following closely. "Reid's teaching me to drive a stick, too," she said as she opened the door.

"That's nice. Be careful." Anna was still not quite at full speed. She had not slept on the plane. She looked out the door and waved at the other two girls before shutting it.

In the kitchen Jack could see out the partially opened blinds. He could hear the conversation. "Keep your mouth shut," Sasha had said quietly, calmly. "If you make any trouble, I will kill you. I will kill the girl. I will kill the boy." The two waited in absolute silence as the conversation in the greatroom took place. Jack prayed for the kids to get out. He just wanted them out of harm's way. This would all be over soon.

Once outside Elle and Reid hopped back in the jeep. Reid was going to drive now. "Wait!" said Elle. "We forgot to ask Jack. You said he would go with us." Elle jumped back out of the jeep and ran around the corner of the house. She ran up to the still open door of the guesthouse. She hesitated and then rapped on the door. It swung further open and she looked inside and raised her voice, "Jack," then louder, "Jack, are you awake?" No reply. The door to the main house opened and she could see Sasha's face as he stuck his head out.

"Jack is not here," he said. "He went to town."

"Oh." Elle looked perplexed. Sasha was standing behind the door as if he was hiding something. Jack was being held with his back to the wall just beside the door. The muzzle of the gun in Sasha's hand pressed hard against Jack's throat. Jack could smell the man's cologne as a slight breeze came through the open door. "Alright," said Elle, "Maybe we'll see him in town." She walked back around the house and got in the jeep. Jack was relieved to hear the little six-cylinder buzz off down the drive.

Sasha shut the door and swung Jack in front of him by the hood on his sweatshirt. The Russian shoved Jack out into the greatroom "Yuri!" he called.

"Sasha," came Yuri's voice from the study. "Sasha these accounts are not accessible. I can't try to access the Swiss one again with the wrong code or we will be shut out of it altogether." Yuri was getting up and walking toward the door of the study, still talking. "The Cayman account had a good password but no balance. What is happening..." His voice trailed away as he came into the room and saw Jack. Sasha had the muzzle of the automatic resting on the back of Jack's neck. Just then Anna came in from the hallway, dressed in a white shirt and knee-lenth jeans. She froze. A look of horror came across her face.

"Sasha! What are you doing?" Her voice was shrill, panicked.

"Your boyfriend has betrayed us to his Arab friends!" Emotion was strong in Sasha's voice now. His eyes were ablaze with hatred.

"How do you know this?" asked Yuri. His voice was calm, no emotion.

"*Someone* is leading them to us," said Sasha. "I thought it might be him, so I searched his room when we landed." Sasha pulled the cell phone from his pocket. "I found a phone. This one communicates with a satellite link."

"Is this true? Have you betrayed us to the Arabs, Jack?" Yuri wasn't letting anyone know if he believed it or not. Jack simply looked at him. He thought of Anna and felt shame. He was ashamed that she might think that he was a terrorist sympathizer, but he didn't want to tell them what he was. Not yet, anyway.

"And I found this," said Sasha. Jack expected to see his gun, but Sasha pulled out a sheet of yellow legal paper. The sheet was crumpled as if it had been wadded up and thrown in the trash. Sasha had smoothed it out. In neat, rather feminine handwriting, the note read: 'Have not located device. Must have radiation detector ASAP." The note started to continue and then stopped abruptly.

Tino had been watching all this in his normal state of silence. No one would suspect him. He had been writing the note that he would pass to his contact in Jackson, when Hank had burst in on him in the kitchen of the guesthouse. Tino had wadded the paper and thrown it into the trashcan. Hank had given Tino his list for the grocery in Jackson. Knowing that he would empty the trash, Tino hadn't given the paper another thought. He had simply made a new note when he was alone in the car. He had not yet located the nuclear device. That had been his assignment when the network had approached him so many weeks ago. They had offered him an incredible sum of money. They had given him ten thousand American dollars to show their sincerity. Soon, he would no longer have to cater to these arrogant people.

His newfound employers had not yet provided him with the radiation detection equipment he needed to locate the bomb. He had fed them information, always communicating when in Jackson for groceries. He had not used the cell phone for fear that Yuri could monitor the digital messages that he sent. It was, after all, Yuri's phone. The people he was working for had, only Saturday, given him a number to call should he find the device. He had asked them to get him the Geiger counter then. They had indicated that they were trying to acquire one and that they would get it to him soon. He had led them to the ranch, but they needed to know if the bomb was here before they came in. Tino was certain that the device was on the ranch, but he didn't know where.

Jack was thinking fast. Why the note? Where had he seen that neat style of writing before? The writing was bigger, but the style was the same as...he remembered the note on the refrigerator. It was Tino! It had to be Tino! Jack turned his head slightly and looked over at the butler. The little man's eyes widened in shock, as he realized that Jack had figured him out. Jack looked at Anna. Her eyes pleaded with him for some explanation. He once again turned his head to Tino. The little man calmly reached behind his back, underneath the little butler's jacket and brought out the big Colt automatic. "Tino, there is no need for that." The voice was Yuri's. He didn't have a clue that Tino was the problem and started to move towards the little butler.

"It's Tino," said Jack. "Your little Filipino butler sold you out."

"No," said Yuri with a forced laugh, "Tino would not do this." Yuri was looking at his butler when the little man raised the pistol and shot him.

Anna screamed. Sasha had dropped the gun from Jack's neck and was turning it on Tino when the little man swung the barrel back toward the other two men. The sound was deafening as the big 45 bucked in Tino's hand for a second time. Jack had shut his eyes involuntarily when the gun had swung his direction. He ducked away, expecting to be shot, but felt nothing as the blast went behind him. Anna saw Sasha's head nod forward as the big slug struck him in the chest. She saw it all as if in slow motion. His black ponytail flipped forward and struck him in the face momentarily as he fell backwards. Sasha's body landed on an antique Armenian table that sat next to a large leather sofa. The table collapsed and splintered under his weight. Jack turned to look and Sasha met his eyes. The man tried to speak, looking at Jack. He managed a couple of grunts and a gasp, then his eyes seemed to glaze over and his head fell limp.

Anna wanted to go to Sasha, but she couldn't get her legs to move. She brought her hands to her face and her knees buckled. She was sobbing and shaking, kneeling on the handmade Tibetan rug. An oath came from the other side of the room. Yuri was clutching his left arm and cursing in Russian. He stole a glance or two at Tino, but concentrated on the pain in his arm, where the 45 slug had shattered his elbow. Jack looked over at Tino. The little man was still holding the big Colt, pointing it in his direction. A tendril of smoke rose from the barrel of the gun, which looked even larger in the hands of the diminutive butler. Tino switched hands with the gun and pulled his cell phone out of his jacket pocket. Jack could hear the beeps as he hit the buttons on the phone. Tino punched one last button and a longer beep emitted from the phone. He folded the unit and put it back in his pocket.

Tino came forward and took a wide birth around Jack. He had switched the gun back to his right hand. He knelt beside the still form of Sasha and reached into the man's pocket. He switched hands again and tried another pocket. This time he came up with a key. Tino stood up and looked down at his own knee. He had knelt in a pool of blood. The blood had soaked into the finely pressed crease of the knee on Tino's black pants. When he looked back at Jack, his teeth were clenched. The soiling of his pants seemed to bother him more than killing a man. He motioned to Jack with his free hand. Jack started to step toward him, when the little man became frustrated and slapped at Jack's cuffed hands. Jack held them out. Tino held the gun in his left hand and the handcuff key in his right. Jack wondered if he should try for the gun, but as he thought of this, Tino pulled the gun back out of reach. The thought had crossed the butler's mind also.

Tino reached out and dropped the key into Jack's

right hand. Jack looked at him wondering what he intended to do. With the key Jack unlocked the cuff on his left wrist. He started to move the key to the other hand when Tino slapped his wrist again. The little man held out his hand and Jack dropped the key into it. Tino looked over at Yuri, then back at Anna. He reached down and grabbed Anna's arm. She just looked at him and didn't respond. Tino gritted his teeth and swung his foot out, kicking Anna in the back. She yelped and he pulled on her arm again. She got on her feet and allowed herself to be pulled over to where Jack stood. Tino deftly clapped the open cuff on Anna's wrist. Jack and Anna were now shackled together. The little man backed off and motioned with his head toward the door. Jack and Anna began to move toward the hallway leading past the kitchen. Tino pointed the big gun at Yuri and waved it, indicating that he too should follow.

As the little procession funneled out the back door, Jack heard the squall of tires and the rev of an engine. A car was coming up the drive fast. Jack was hoping to see Riley and a dozen SWAT guys come sweeping around the corner. He heard the noise quiet slightly as the car jumped off the paved drive and started through the grass. All four of them stopped momentarily as a big black car came flying through the yard, wiping out a well manicured shrub before screeching to a halt on the edge of the runway in front of them. Jack's heart sank. The car was a black Jaguar. The same black Jag that had bumped them in Jackson that day with Elle in the T-bird. The two men in the car were Arab. They got out and one of them walked up to the little group. Tino was smiling and nodding. "Phony little bastard," Jack thought.

Hamad looked at Tino. "Where is it?" he asked. His English was heavily accented. Tino merely shrugged, which seemed to irritate the Arab. "Who can tell us?" Hamad asked. Tino shrugged again, then pointed toward Yuri.

The Arab looked at Yuri and reached inside his coat. He pulled out a 22 caliber pistol and waved it at the man. "You will tell me where the bomb is."

Yuri looked back at him, breathing fast with the pain in his arm. "You can go to hell," he said, suddenly defiant.

The Arab raised the pistol and fired at Yuri's left leg. Yuri jerked and staggered, howling in pain. The bullet had pierced the muscle just above the knee. The Russian managed to keep his feet. He cursed at the Arab in Russian.

Hamad swung the pistol toward Anna, who merely looked at the man, then at Yuri. "No!" said Yuri. "I'll tell you." He made a head motion toward the hangar. "It's there. Under the floor." Yuri seemed suddenly defeated.

Hamad turned and said something in Arabic to Fahad, who stood beside the car. The other Arab reached through the open driver's door and popped the trunk. He then went around, raised the lid, and pulled out two Chinese knock-offs of Kalashnikov rifles. The guns were of the newer, lighter weight variety, with folding stocks. He slung one over his shoulder by its sling and held the other in his hands. He slammed the trunk lid shut and pointed the rifle in the direction of the Russian. He ran the action of the gun, putting a shell in the chamber.

"You will show us," said Hamad, addressing Yuri. He gave the pistol in his hand a couple of quick jerks toward the hangar, which stood open; the plane was still sitting outside. Yuri began to limp painfully in the direction of hangar. The others followed. Fahad handed one of the rifles to Hamad, who slung it over his shoulder, and the two Arabs fell in behind the group.

Once inside the hangar the group gathered around the moveable slab of concrete, which served as the lid to the bunker. "It is here," said Yuri, pointing at the ring in the floor.

Hamad looked around. "The winch," he said, pointing up at the crane. He turned to Tino. "You," he said, "Operate the winch."

Tino looked at the man; he was not smiling now. He appeared not to like being ordered around by the Arab, but he walked over to the winch, stuffing the Colt in the back of his pants. He reached up to the control pigtail, which hung slightly above his head, and thumbed the button that ran the winch out to the end of the crane's beam. The electric motor growled loudly in the empty hangar. When the winch had reached the length of the beam, Tino pulled on the control and swung the arm of the crane out over the floor. He pushed another button, running the cable out until the hook could reach the ring on the floor. He reached down and slid the hook into the ring. The butler then reached back up to the control and began to take up the slack in the cable. The crane groaned as the weight was transferred to its beam. The slab began to move. When it had cleared the floor, Fahad reached out with a free hand and pushed on a corner of the concrete. Tino did the same at another corner and the crane began to swing. Light cascaded into the bunker as the slab moved away. Fahad looked up at Hamad with a huge smile on his face. He spoke in Arabic, praising Allah. He was obviously pleased with what they were looking at. Hamad's eyes were fixed on the device in the center of the bunker. The other ordinance surrounding the nuke did not interest him.

"Is the airplane full of fuel?" he asked, looking at Yuri.

Yuri didn't answer immediately. Hamad swung the gun up again. "Yes!" said Yuri, "Yes, we refueled in Salt Lake. We were chased out of Las Vegas by a storm." He seemed beaten. He wanted to avoid more pain.

Fahad started to go down the ladder into the bunker but words from Hamad stopped him. He came back up. The two Arabs seemed to be arguing in Arabic. Hamad looked at Tino. "You," he said, "get in the pit."

Tino just looked at him. He made no move toward the bunker. The little man was beginning to wonder if his usefulness was about at an end. Hamad gestured towards Anna. "Her," he said. "Take off the wrist shackles. She can hook up the cable."

Tino moved toward Anna and pulled the handcuff key out of his pocket. He unlocked the cuff. She began rubbing her wrist where the cuff had been. Tino started to walk away when Hamad said, "Wait. Cuff that one to the crane." He gestured toward the huge base of the freestanding crane just behind Jack.

Tino led Jack over to the concrete and metal base. Jack reached around the base as if hugging a huge tree and allowed Tino to apply the cuff to his other hand. As the cuff racheted tight, Jack got a look into the little man's eyes. He saw something there, perhaps regret? Tino smiled wanly at Jack and gave his familiar nod, before he turned and walked away.

"You," said Hamad to Anna, "down there". He pointed to the bunker. She moved to the edge of the pit and sat down, looking back at the Arab with hatred in her eyes. She got her feet on the top rung of the ladder, turned around and began to descend into the bunker. Fahad had unhooked the cable from the concrete lid and swung the crane back over the bunker. He reached out for the pigtail and squeezed the button with his left hand, lowering the hook into the void below. His right hand held the rifle, now pointing into the bunker at Anna.

When it reached her, Anna grasped the hook and attached it to a ring on the center of the bomb carriage. Fahad took up the slack and slowly raised the bomb off its cradle. The device spiraled slowly as it came up out of the bunker. Fahad pulled on the control pigtail and swung the bomb out over the floor. He lowered it gently onto the concrete. Fahad rushed up to it and suddenly became angry. He spoke loudly in Arabic, gesturing towards the display end of the bomb.

Hamad looked at Yuri, his eyes aflame. "The key," he said. "Where is the key?"

Yuri's eyes were wide. He was in trouble. He did not know that the key was missing. Yuri knew that the Arabs would never believe that.

"I have the key." It was Jack who had spoken. Yuri was confused and it showed on his face. How would Jack have the key? Anna was coming up the ladder. She had stopped climbing when Jack had spoken.

238

Hamad turned to look at Jack. "Where?" he asked.

"In my pocket," said Jack.

"Get it," said Hamad, speaking to Anna. "Get it and bring it to me." Anna climbed on out of the bunker and walked over to Jack.

"My right hand pocket." She reached in his pocket and pulled out a stubby key. She walked over to Hamad and gave him the key. He examined it and put it in his pocket.

Hamad and Fahad spoke rapidly to each other in Arabic, and then Fahad walked over to the bomb. "Come here," he said looking at Tino. Tino walked over to him. "Help me," said Fahad. Together they picked up the bomb, one on each end.

"Open the door to the airplane," said Hamad to Anna. He pointed the pistol at her. "Now!" he shouted, as she hesitated. She moved ahead of Tino and Fahad, walking quickly over to the plane. She reached up and pulled the latch on the door. The stairs came down slowly. Tino and the Arab set the bomb down and Fahad pulled the stairs downward to their stops. Fahad pulled the rifle sling over his head, held the rifle in front of him, and went up the stairs. He peered about the cabin and then set the rifle down inside the door and came back down. With one foot on the stairs he reached down with one hand and grabbed the chrome handle of the bomb. Tino grabbed the other and the two men picked the device up. Fahad climbed the steps clumsily still holding onto the pistol with his free hand and Tino followed. The bomb bumped heavily on the top step as Tino could barely handle his end of the device. Fahad, having good footing now, dragged the bomb on into the plane. It's chrome cradle screeched loudly against the aluminum threshold. The Arab grabbed both handles now and pulled the device on around into the isle, away from the doorway.

Tino was backing away from the plane and Anna had walked back to the hangar. She stood beside Yuri, who was looking pale, balancing on his one good leg, and holding his arm, wondering what would happen next. Fahad stuck his head out the door of the plane and spoke loudly to Hamad, again in Arabic. Hamad spoke back and Fahad reached down and picked up his AK from the floor of the plane. The muzzle came up immediately and two shots rang out. Tino slumped to the ground. The little man had received his payment in the form of two rounds in the chest. Hamad had turned the other rifle to Yuri and squeezed off a shot, hitting the Russian in the chest. Anna was screaming and turned to run as the rifle came around to her. As she took a step backwards she fell into the bunker. Two shots rang out at the same time, but the bullets simply exited through the back wall of the hangar.

Hamad let out an oath and continued to fire, swinging the gun around at Jack. Seeing this coming, Jack had swung around to the backside of the pedestal of the crane. Bullets riddled off the base of the concrete structure. Jack could feel fragments of concrete striking his exposed, cuffed hands.

Another shot rang out. The sound was deeper than the ones from the rifle. The firing stopped and Jack could hear Hamad yelling, obviously in pain. Jack heard the deeper bark again. He recognized it this time and stole a glance around the base of the crane. Hamad swung around to where Tino lay stretched out on the runway. The little man was struggling to get Jack's big Colt up again. Jack could see blood soaking through the back of Hamad's jacket high on the shoulder. The Arab let go with another burst of gunfire, screaming at the little man in front of him. Tino's body jerked as the bullets riddled his body. He finally dropped the pistol and his head fell to the ground.

Jack could hear Fahad yelling from inside the Learjet. He could here turbines whining and one of the big jet engines barked to life. Hamad turned again to look back at Jack. Jack remained still behind the crane. Hamad looked at his bleeding shoulder and dropped the AK rifle to the floor of the hangar. He pressed his left hand against the wound and turned and staggered quickly to the plane. Jack saw him mount the stairs and then pull them up to shut the door. The second engine fired.

CHAPTER THIRTY-TWO

Since his cell phone battery was dead, Cecil had left his post and gone to report to Riley. He had seen Leroy's sedan at the Wrangler and had stopped in to talk to him. Leroy had called Riley with the news that the jet had come back. Riley had expected this news as the Las Vegas office had informed him of the suspects' unscheduled departure from McCarron airport. The two pilots came into the restaurant while Leroy and Cecil were talking and sat down at a table near the agents. The two appeared to be deep in conversation about a document that they were passing back and forth. Leroy had seen each of the men sign the paper just before their food came and they put it away. Realizing that they needed to cover the ranch, Leroy left the Wrangler in a hurry, leaving Cecil to pay the bill.

Cecil was waiting on his food when Reid Wilcox, Elena, and two younger girls walked into the restaurant. The group was dressed as if they were going to church and they sat down near Cecil. He couldn't keep from overhearing the conversation.

"I was hoping Jack would be here, since he wasn't at the ranch," said Reid.

"Something was strange with Sasha. I don't think I like him very well," said Elle. "When he stuck his head out the door to tell me that Jack had come to town, I could have sworn he was hiding something." She took a sip of her orange juice. "I just have a bad feeling about this."

The conversation continued, but Cecil had heard enough. He left money on the table and ploughed out the door, jumping in his sedan and scratching off in the parking lot. The hotel where Riley was staying was only a few hundred yards away and Cecil brought the big car to a screeching halt in the parking lot, attracting scornful looks from an older couple that had stopped at the quick shop for coffee on their way to Sunday school. Cecil rushed inside the hotel.

"That man needs to slow down, Henry," said the woman as her husband handed her the Styrofoam cups filled with coffee through the car window. "My soul, I wish people would observe the Sabboth."

"I don't know Mildred, that fellow looked scared. I hope nothing's wrong." The man's face showed genuine concern. Before he could walk around to the other side of the car, he saw the same man and another fellow come racing out of the hotel. The other fellow was on a cell phone and the two jumped in the car and careened out onto the highway.

The couple eased out onto the highway and headed for their Sunday school meeting. They met the sheriff's car headed west, lights on, hitting the gutters that crossed the road so fast that the car bottomed out throwing a shower of sparks out underneath. "I think a prayer for those fellows would be prudent, Mildred."

Back at the Circle "A", Leroy was rushing to his surveillance post. He could see people in the hangar, but the light was not good enough to make out what they were doing. An unfamiliar black Jaguar was parked haphazardly near the back of the house on the edge of the runway. Leroy was surprised to see an Arab-looking guy come out of the hangar with the little butler. They were carrying something between them that appeared to be heavy. It looked like a generator or something. He called Riley.

"We're on our way," said Riley, "something is going down. I think our man Jack may be in trouble."

"I haven't seen him at all, but some guy with a rag on his head is loading something into the jet."

242

"Don't approach them," said Riley. "I've got choppers coming with an assault team. They are already in the air."

"I can't get any closer," said Leroy. "I'll have to go back to my car to...Holy cow! What was that? Shots fired! I repeat! Shots fired!"

"Step on it Cecil! All hell just broke loose!" Riley turned back to his phone. "Get to your car Leroy. Get up there fast."

"The plane's moving Joe. You better get here fast or we're gonna' lose 'em."

Riley looked over at Cecil, who was actually smiling. His heart rate had just doubled. He reached into the back seat, pulled out a riot gun, and checked the loads. "God help us Cecil. I'm afraid we may be too late." The smile disappeared from Cecil's face.

CHAPTER THIRTY-THREE

Jack felt helpless. The plane was going to take off, and he was handcuffed to a tower of steel buried in the ground with concrete poured around it. Where was Riley? He looked at Yuri lying far out of his reach and wondered if he had a phone on him. Jack's phone was probably on Sasha's body up at the house. "Anna!" he yelled. "Anna, are you there?" She had fallen about ten feet to a concrete floor. She was probably hurt pretty badly. He yelled her name a few more times, but heard nothing in reply.

Jack sank down on his knees. The jet was going to fly out of here with a nuclear bomb. It had plenty of fuel to reach, where? Washington D.C.? And he was stuck. He let his head fall back. He looked up wondering why God would let this happen. In looking up, he realized that the crane stood entirely on its own. "I wonder..."

Jack stood up and slid his cuffed hands up over the concreted portion of the base. He hooked the chain that ran between the cuffs over the lip of the heavy steel cylinder coming out of the concrete. He bent his elbows and lifted the weight of his body off the ground. He swung his left knee up over the top of the concrete and pulled himself up. He now was perched on top of the concrete base. The crane's tower was made of a series of telescoping heavy metal cylinders rising twenty feet or so in the air. At the top was a big I-beam that ran slightly beyond the base, with a short, thick gusset welded on each side. Jack's hands were sweating just enough to make them feel sticky as he grabbed the painted surface of the tower. He began to climb, gripping the base with his hands and legs wrapped around it, like a monkey climbing a palm tree after a coconut. The handcuff chain clinked against the base each time he reset his grip. With a few short bursts he was at the top. He managed to stand on the lip of metal where the last cylinder came out of the one below it. The tough soles of the old Vasque hikers gripped it easily. It was a stretch, but he managed to work the handcuff chain out over the end of the I-beam. Now he could hang off the I-beam and pull himself along it like a sloth on a tree limb. He was hurrying now. He could hear the plane rolling away down the runway. It would soon be turning around to make an attempt at taking off. His head throbbed and he could feel blood seeping from the wound on the side of his head. Jack's feet slipped about halfway out on the beam. For a moment he was hanging there, but he quickly recovered and swung back up. He made it to the winch. Now what? He wrapped his legs tightly around the beam; he was going to have to get his hands over the end of the beam. Hanging upside down, he hugged his shoulder into the greasy cable and stretched out his arms. The chain caught momentarily on the end of the beam. Jack gave a couple of hard jerks and it came free. His wrists ached where the cuffs pulled on them. Now he had just the cable between his cuffed hands. He was still hanging upside down. The blood was rushing into his head as he hung there. He was working feverishly. He worked the sleeves of his sweatshirt up over his hands, so that they acted as gloves as he gripped the heavy cable. He gave his torso a mighty twist and let go with his legs.

The cable was greasy, but big enough to get a grip. When his body swung down, his legs hit the bottom portion of the cable. He was going too fast. He could feel the cable sliding through his hands. Even with the sweatshirt he could feel little wires stabbing into his hands from the cable. He hit the concrete floor feet first and went down hard. The big hook struck him in the knee. He was hurting, but he was down!

Jack slipped his cuffed hands around the hook. Now,

245

where was the handcuff key? He picked up the AK 47 where Hamad had dropped it and ran outside. He could see the jet at the end of the runway; it was just ready to turn around. Jack knelt down and feverishly rifled through Tino's pockets. There. He found the key and his spare magazine for his 45. He pocketed the clip and quickly inserted the key into the left handcuff, then the right. He was out of his shackles. Now what? What could he do, just stand here and try to shoot the big Learjet down as it went by at a hundred miles an hour? He had to call Joe Riley. He thought of Tino's cell phone. As he fumbled in the jacket, looking for the phone, he heard his name. He looked back into the hangar and saw Yuri struggling to roll onto his side. Jack ran over to him. He could see over into the pit. Anna was lying motionless on top of one of the wooden crates. Jack knelt beside Yuri.

"Jack," Yuri said weakly, through a froth of blood on his lips. "You...must...stop them."

"I'll call the authorities, Yuri," said Jack.

"No," said Yuri, "if they shoot the plane down..." He paused so long that Jack thought he had died, but then he spoke again. "The bomb is unstable because it was not maintained. It will detonate on impact."

"Oh God!" said Jack. "I can't let that plane get off the ground." He thought of running down the runway to get closer so that he could shoot into the cockpit before the plane got moving, but it was too far. It was probably three quarters of a mile. What could he do?

Jack ran back outside. The jet was facing this way now. It looked suddenly menacing as the heat waves coming off the pavement distorted its image. Jack bent over Tino's body and pulled the old Colt from the dead man's fingers. He ejected the clip in the gun and replaced it with the full one, then he put the gun in the pocket on the front of his sweatshirt as he wondered what to do. He had to get down that runway and get closer to the plane. He could shoot at the tires. He could shoot at the engines. It was just too far away.

246

He looked back in the hangar and there was the answer. Hank's big Road King waited patiently on its side-stand. Jack ran to the bike and twisted the ignition. The lights came on and he heard the fuel pump. He was in luck. The ignition wasn't locked. Jack swung his leg over even as he thumbed the starter. The big V-twin engine roared to life. The metal banana clip gouged the paint of the gas tank as Jack rested the rifle across his legs. He slipped the canvas sling over his neck and pulled in the side-stand. He instinctively punched down on the brake pedal with his right toe, until he realized the shifter was on the other side. "Think, Jack," he told himself. The transmission clunked into gear and the big bike lurched forward as Jack twisted the throttle. The rear wheel slid sideways on the slick, painted concrete of the hangar floor as Jack gunned the bike out into the bright morning light. The big motorcycle swung out and lined up down the runway as Jack took it through the gears.

At the end of the runway, Fahad sat in the left seat. He was looking down at the instruments and arguing with Hamad. Although they had studied the Lear and both had flown other planes, they were not exactly familiar with this one.

"What is that?" Hamad said in Arabic. Fahad looked up.

"Shit!"

"Go!" said Hamad, "GO! GO!...GO!" The man was screaming at Fahad, who was pushing the throttles forward. Hamad stepped out of his seat. He was going back in the cabin for the AK rifle.

The motorcycle was approaching fast as the jet began to move. The scene looked like a horribly mismatched game of chicken. Jack figured he could hit something now, so he set the thumbsrew to lock the throttle, swung the muzzle of the Kalashnikov up, and sqeezed off a couple rounds. He was aiming at the cockpit.

The two rounds tore through the aluminum over Fahad's head as he screamed at Hamad to do something!

Jack dropped the muzzle down toward the tires as he

squeezed the trigger again. The bullets tore through the windshield of the bike, startling Jack as pieces fell away. He felt a piece of the windshield hit him in the knee as he hurtled on down the airstrip.

Hamad held on to the back of Fahad's seat as he stared out the windshield in disbelief. He heard more shots and then a loud pop as one of the tires blew. He held the rifle in his hands but what could he do? Shoot through the windshield? He began screaming back at the panicking Fahad to get the plane off the ground.

Jack was close now. He let go another burst at the tires. He had heard at least one of them blow out. The plane was gaining speed and Jack began to veer off out of its way. He pulled the muzzle up and aimed at the port engine. He let go with the rest of the clip. The rifle was empty. He slowed the bike and threw the AK to the pavement. He reached into the front of his sweatshirt and drew out the Colt. With as steady an aim as he could muster on the motorcycle, Jack emptied the full clip of the 45 into the cockpit. He was aiming deliberately at Fahad.

The jet was coming so fast now that Jack almost laid the bike down trying to dodge the leading edge of the port wing as it passed him. He felt the blast of heat from the big jet engines as he swung the bike around to follow the plane. He had no idea what to do next. He simply hoped that he had done enough damage to stop the plane's departure.

Inside the cockpit the two Arabs were screaming at each other. Fahad had taken a bullet in the knee and was having trouble using the rudder to steady the plane. Hamad was yelling at him to get off the ground. The big engines labored hard to get the craft up to speed as the blown tires were creating a tremendous drag while gravity continued to hold the craft to the pavement. The front wheel had just started to lift, when a loud bang resounded through the craft and thick, black smoke began pouring from the port engine. The front wheel came back down hard, and the tire, having been nicked by a bullet, blew out. Fahad screamed as the craft careened off the runway and bounced down a slight

embankment where the dirt had been moved during construction.

Hamad fell down between the seats as the craft
bounced down the slope. He was facing aft when the front
wheels dipped into the irrigation ditch and the plane came to
an abrupt halt. Hamad stared in horror as the sudden stop
caused the heavy bomb to slide forward down the short isle.
The digital display and chrome handles charged at him, but
he could not move. All he had time to do was scream.
Hamad caught the weight of the bomb in his chest. Ribs
buckled and splintered, sending fragments tearing through
the man's lungs. An involuntary grunt came from Hamad's
mouth, followed by a froth of blood. If Hamad was to be
surrounded by virgins, he was about to find out.

"Holy Cow! He did it! He did it!" Leroy whooped
and jumped into the air. "Go Jack Wallace! You the man!"
He had seen the unlikely duel on the runway. He now
watched as federal agents and choppers came swarming out
of the woodwork. Riley pulled up beside him and as soon as
he got out of the car, Leroy grabbed him and gave him a bear
hug. He was so hysterically happy that he could barely get
the words out of his mouth to tell Riley what had happened.

Fahad, momentarily stunned, twisted in his seat to
look at his cousin. He popped the latch on his seatbelt and
started to climb over his fallen partner. Pain shot through his
knee and he yelled out involuntarily. He managed to get aft
of the bomb and he pulled and jerked at the heavy device,
dragging it away from Hamad. The cabin was quiet now.
Fahad had pulled the throttles back to their stops, when they
had left the runway. The fuel pumps were silent, and the
steady "Whap, Whap, Whap" of a helicopter could be heard.

"It is not finished!" Fahad screamed. He pulled at the
inert form of his cousin, dragging the dead man out into the
space by the door. He began to fumble through the man's
pockets. He soon pulled out the worn, stubby key and held it
up to look at it. He could hear commotion outside the plane.

The helicopter had landed. It sounded as if another were coming now. "We will not leave this world alone, cousin."

With the intention of setting the timer for a few seconds, Fahad took the little key and tried to insert it into the control box. It refused to go in.

The keys to the bomb were still in Jack's pocket; Anna had given the terrorist the spare key to Jack's old Sportster. Fahad pushed harder and struck the chrome handle above the box, hurting his fist. He screamed his frustration at the unyielding device. He picked up the rifle where it had fallen from Hamad's hands. He stood with difficulty; his knee was grinding shattered pieces of bone upon each other from the damage inflicted by the .45 slug. Fahad released the latch on the door and shoved it open. The stairway went down slowly and sunlight poured in. Fahad stuck the AK out the opening and triggered off a few rounds. The morning sun was bright in his eyes and he couldn't see what he was shooting at. His firing was answered quickly as federal agents returned fire. The bullets wracked his body and Fahad fell forward, tumbling out of the aircraft. He lay still in the bright green grass of the hay meadow.

It was over.

CHAPTER THIRTY-FOUR

Jack sat astride the Road King in the middle of the runway. He watched the helicopter land in the hayfield and the exchange of gunfire that followed. The commotion finally died down and the agents had entered the plane. He slipped the bike back into gear and swung around to the hangar. Another helicopter was landing now and he could see a stream of marked and unmarked sedans pouring in the long driveway. He parked the bike and moved quickly to the bunker. Anna still lay motionless, stretched out on the crate that had broken her fall. He went to the ladder and climbed down. He went to Anna and felt for a pulse. As he touched her neck, she stirred. Her eyes fluttered open and she looked at Jack.

"Oh, Jack," she said, her chin crinkling up as tears welled up in her eyes.

"It's okay," he said. "It's all over."

"I'm so sorry," she said as the tears rolled down across her cheeks.

Jack could hear men entering the hangar. He looked up out of the pit as a woman appeared. She wore the blue uniform of a paramedic. "One down here," the woman said to someone. She began to descend the ladder.

Jack looked back at Anna. Her eyes had closed again, but came open when Jack looked at her. She reached out a hand and touched his chin. She let her thumb rub along the stubble of beard. More tears rolled down her face. The paramedic was there now, talking to her. Another man was descending the ladder and a stretcher was handed down.

251

Jack climbed out. Anna was not badly hurt but she had bounced her head off the crate and very likely had a concussion.

Jack looked around and saw that another team of paramedics was working on Yuri. They had an oxygen mask on him and had set an I.V. Jack couldn't help but think that they were wasting their time, that Yuri would never survive. He surveyed the carnage around him as yet another chopper landed on the runway outside. Joe Riley was walking towards the hangar now, with Leroy Donovan. Leroy was grinning ear to ear and was talking excitedly.

"Congratulations Jack," said Leroy as they came up to him. The agent grabbed Jack's hand and pumped it. "I just want to be the first to shake the hand of a bona fide American hero. If you hadn't of stopped that plane...jeez...I hate to think of what might have happened." Jack just stared at him dumbly. He had to fight down a sudden urge to throw up as the realization of it all began to sink in.

"Yuri told me that the bomb is unstable..."

"Don't worry, Jack," said Riley. "There's no radiation leakage yet and a special team just landed to take care of the thing."

"Looks like one of those terrorists cushioned the landing for the bomb," said Leroy. "Kind of an Al Qaida airbag."

"There's another one," said Jack. The smile immediately left Leroy's face. Jack led the other two men over to the bunker and they looked down into it at the array of armaments.

"Jesus, Mary and Joseph!" Leroy was shaken. "How did they ever get all this stuff inside our borders?"

"My guess is that it's been here for years," said Riley. "They must have just brought in a couple of containers directly off a ship."

"I think you'll find another bunker just like this under that other slab," said Jack pointing to the other ring protruding from the concrete, deeper inside the hangar. "I think I saw another nuke in it, but it was pretty dark."

"Sounds like you got the deluxe tour," said Riley. He looked at Jack knowing there was more to that story.

"I'll tell you about it sometime," said Jack, with a slight grin.

Another helicopter landed outside the hangar. This one was a life-flight for Yuri, who was still holding on by a thread. The stretcher was loaded aboard, along with federal agents and paramedics, and the chopper took off again. As Jack and the two agents watched it leave, they saw a white T-bird, stopped at the edge of the runway where county deputies had set up a perimeter. Riley reached for a hand-held radio clipped to his belt and spoke into it. "Let them come on in, Jake. Leave the car and they can walk in here. We're going to have to talk to them."

Will and Hank came walking toward Jack and the agents. They both looked sufficiently stunned at the carnage. Will was looking down into the hole under the floor of the hangar in disbelief, but all Hank could do was stare at his Road King. The big bike sat there in the door of the hangar with it's windshield shot to pieces.

"I borrowed your bike," said Jack.

"Yeah, I reckon you did." Hank turned to look at the jet, sitting nose down in the irrigation ditch. "I think our retirement plans just took a nose dive, too." Will looked up from the bunker at him. He pulled the envelope with the lease agreement in it from his pocket.

"I suppose this is just a piece of worthless paper now," said Will. None of the other men knew what the two pilots were talking about.

"You two fellows are going to have to answer some questions," said Riley. "Don't make any immediate plans."

"I gathered that might be the case," said Will. "Good God, is she alright?" Will had spotted Anna who was being carried out on a stretcher to an ambulance.

"She'll be fine," said Riley. His radio crackled and he turned away to answer it.

"I'm thoroughly confused," said Hank. "What the hell happened here, Jack?"

253

"I'm not really sure myself," said Jack, "I just came out here to do some fly-fishing and visit some friends. Things deteriorated from there."

"I guess that old saying that 'if something is too good to be true...' is right," offered Will.

Riley suggested that the pilots get some sleep before they were grilled by the FBI's best. The pilots were shuffled off to town and put up in the Pinedale Inn, under guard. Jack was left to his own devices. He thought about just taking off on his bike, but realized that he had obligations to Riley and the law in general. He was pretty much in a daze when he mounted his old Sportster and motored to Jackson. He left word with Riley where he would be.

CHAPTER THIRTY-FIVE

Jack walked down the corridor of the small hospital in Jackson, Wyoming. The smells of disinfectant reminded him of his father's clinic, with the notable exception of a lack of dog smell. He came to the room that he had been directed to. He didn't have to read the number; a guard was posted at the door.

"I'm sorry sir, but this is a restricted area," the guard said robotically, putting up a hand to stop Jack. Reporters had already been bird-dogging the room. "No one will be admitted to see the patient."

"Is she awake?" Jack asked.

"I'm sorry sir," said the guard, "but all information regarding the occupant is classified."

"My name is Jack Wallace. Is there any way that you could call Agent Riley..."

"Oh, I'm sorry Mr. Wallace. You have been cleared to visit, sir." The guard changed his demeanor; he was a young black man in a black suit and tie. He was obviously a federal agent. "May I shake your hand, sir?" the agent asked.

"What?" asked Jack, incredulous.

"I'm with the Bureau, Mr. Wallace. I've heard the story and I'd like to shake your hand and thank you, sir."

Jack stuck out his hand. "I'll shake your hand, but I'm no hero."

"But you are, sir." The man had a military air about him. "If that plane had gotten in the air..."

"I just did what anybody would have done, given the

255

circumstances."

"You go right on in, sir," the man said, "take as long as you like."

"Thank you."

Jack walked into the room. The door closed behind him. Anna was sleeping. Jack could see an I.V. in her arm and noticed a bag of Ringer's solution hanging near the bed. She looked so peaceful that Jack decided not to wake her. He sat down in a chair beside the bed. Anna's eyes fluttered open even though Jack had made no sound. Almost immediately, she began to cry.

"Jack, oh, Jack," she sobbed. "I had no idea..."

"It's okay, Anna, I..." Jack hesitated. He didn't know what to say. Should he tell her that he thought she was innocent? He didn't. At least not completely. Should he tell her that he thought he was in love with her? That seemed ridiculous even to him.

"Please leave me," said Anna. She seemed suddenly to have plenty of resolve.

"What?"

"Go away," she said.

"Anna, I want to help you. If I can."

"It is not possible."

"But you didn't really know what they were up to. Did you?" He looked into her eyes, searching for the answer that he wanted.

She turned her head to look at him. "Do you think anyone in your government is going to believe that?"

"No... well maybe...I don't know..."

"Jack, please, I stuck with Yuri all these years because I knew nothing else. He treated me well, like a daughter or something..."

"Anna just tell them the truth. This isn't the Soviet Union. People here *want* to believe you. Just be honest."

"They won't believe a thing I say."

"Anna, Yuri will probably back you up."

"Dear God," said Anna, her face paled even more. "Yuri is alive?"

256

"Yes, he is going to live...and I think that he will ex-onerate you."

"Oh, I hope so," she said through trembling lips. It was too much to hope for at this stage of the game. Anna reached out and clasped Jack's hand. "I've always done what I was told." She brought Jack's hand to her cheek and rained tears down upon it.

"I know," he said. "I don't blame you."

Anna, in a sudden display of emotion, pulled Jack's head to her own and kissed him, like a mother kissing a child on her deathbed. "You're a good man, Jack. If only..." Her voice faded in a flood of tears.

"You get some rest," he said. "I'll talk to you later."

She slumped away from him. Jack walked away from the bed and moved quietly out of the room. He felt like he was abandoning her. He was not sure that he was glad that he had come...not at all.

Jack climbed aboard his motorcycle and pulled away from the hospital. As the highway turned south out of town, he once again was greeted by the smell of barbecue smoke. He realized that he hadn't eaten for over twenty-four hours and that he was ravenously hungry. But, somehow, he didn't feel like eating. He stopped at a convenience store and bought a pre-packaged sandwich and some peanuts. He ate quickly in the parking lot and motored on south. Clouds had rolled in and a light rain hit him in the face, speckling his sunglasses, but it felt good to Jack. Let it rain.

CHAPTER THIRTY-SIX

The old two-door station wagon looked out of place as it took its time bouncing over and avoiding rocks the size of grapefruit in the primitive road that followed the course of the river. The day was picture perfect with the sun just peaking up over the eastern side of the valley, pouring warmth over an otherwise cool morning. The old car was a light blue Chevy Nomad with a white top. After some extensive rebuilding, it looked today just as it did when it rolled off the showroom floor in 1955.

The car turned off to the right onto an even rougher track that led down to the river. The driver eased the old classic up beside a picnic table and parked. Joe Riley stepped out from behind the wheel and went around to the tailgate. He pulled out a pair of Gore-Tex waders and donned them. He was sitting on the bench of the picnic table meticulously tying on a dry fly to a fine tippet. He wore an old slouch hat, which had a pair of magnifying lenses clipped on it. Riley was looking through the lenses, working at his task, when he heard a voice behind him.

"Forget your bifocals, old timer?"

"Don't need bifocals, Jack."

"How are you, Joe?" Jack sat down on the bench next to the man.

"I'm doing well, thanks. You alright?"

"Never better," said Jack. "I guess I could be better, if I could get a fish to take this bead head."

"Let me get this thing tied on and I'll show you how it's done."

"The Nomad is looking pretty cherry. I'm surprised you would submit it to this poor excuse for a road." Jack was admiring the timeless style of the old car.

"No more surprised than I was to see *that* when I got here." Riley nodded toward a brand new Harley-Davidson Road King in vivid black leaning on its sidestand. "I expected to see the old Sportster. You didn't sell it did you?"

"No," said Jack with a sheepish grin, "I couldn't do that. I shipped it back to Kansas with a load of horses." Jack sat down on the bench opposite Riley. "How's Yuri?"

"He's recovering nicely. He's actually providing a lot of good information. I was pleasantly surprised."

"What was he going to do with all that stuff? Was he really willing to sell to whoever had enough money?"

"I don't know Jack. I think he planned to run a shell game on the Arabs. The other bomb was a fake. The fact that he had the real thing, though, makes it awfully hard to cut him any slack."

"What about all that other stuff? There were several crates of RPGs. That would have been a disaster if those had gotten loose."

"Yes, that's why I'm surprised at his cooperation. He'll never be turned loose again."

The two men were silent for a moment. The constant gurgle of the river only a few feet away was like soothing medicine to Riley, who had spent the last few months under a great deal of stress. Riley finally spoke. "She won't be going to prison, Jack." Riley looked up to see Jack's reaction. He couldn't tell if the man was pleased or not. "We got an anonymous phone call from Las Vegas that tipped us off to a couple of offshore accounts. We froze them immediately. It had to be her, Jack. Anna's the only possibility. She gave us the account numbers." Riley was silent for a moment. "I think she called as soon as she found out what they were doing."

"So what then? Is she a free woman?"

"Not for a while, but eventually, she'll be released."

Jack looked up at the rim of the valley across the river. "I always feel like I'm being watched when I'm fishing here." Riley looked up at the rim, too. "I half expect to see about a hundred Indians sitting there on their ponies, looking down at me when I'm in the river." Riley's fly was tied on, and he was ready to try the fishing, but both men just sat there.

"What now, Jack?"

"I guess I'll go back home for awhile. At least to visit." It had been a month since the events at the ranch had taken place. Jack had continued to hang around until all the paperwork and interviews were done. He had been helping Charlie in the meantime, wondering what would happen to the cowboys and the ranch. It seemed that the government had seized all of Yuri's assets. That was expected, but it affected a lot of people who had nothing to do with the illicit arms deal. The ranch would probably be sold at a fire-sale price to someone else that didn't really care about the cattle business. Maybe Charlie would get lucky and they would let him run the place without any interference.

"What did you do about the plane, the Learjet?" Jack asked.

"I've convinced the attorney general that the contract that Smith and Jones had is valid and was done before the bust. Of course it's going to take a lot of money to repair the jet after you worked it over, but Will and Hank will be able to use it and run their own charter."

"Sounds like they got their golden parachute after all. I'm glad to hear that."

"Yeah, they were extremely lucky. This asset seizure thing is hard on a lot of innocents. When the government gets its hands on something it can sell...well, those two gents are very fortunate."

"So," Jack hesitated, "What exactly is going to happen to Anna?"

"They've already taken her back east to Washington D.C. for a while. The woman is a wealth of information on money laundering and a real genius with computer networks.

260

She must have hacked into every computer in the Eastern block at one time or another. I don't think Yuri had any idea what she was truly capable of. My guess is that she'll end up working for us or maybe Langley will get her, but either way the government will keep her on. She's too valuable to let get away." Riley looked at Jack, waiting for some kind of response. "She's been asking for you."

"She has huh?"

"She's a very lonely woman, Jack. She doesn't have anyone except Elle...and you." Jack turned to look at Riley. The agent had a wry grin on his face. "Go see her, Jack. You'll be glad you did."

The two men walked into the river and spread out to begin fishing in earnest. Jack had barely finished stripping out line in order to begin casting, when he looked up to see that Riley had a fish on, in practically the same spot where Jack had been earlier. The agent held up a fine cutthroat for Jack to see, before he released it.

The two men fished quietly for the rest of the morning, each catching fish occasionally. They met back at the picnic table when the sun was straight overhead.

"What about you, Joe?" Jack asked. "Are you going to retire like you threatened?"

"No," said the agent resignedly, "I wouldn't know what to do with myself."

"Back to Denver then?"

"Yes, probably. Leroy is moving to Florida. Just a transfer. I think his wife talked him out of retiring. She told me she wasn't ready to have him around the house full time," Riley said with a laugh. "I've been asked to do a little training on some new agents...and work on some recruiting..." Jack looked up. There was something in Riley's tone. "I'm authorized to offer you a job, Jack."

"Me?" asked Jack. "I'm not qualified for anything."

"I think you've proved that that's not true. But I want you to know up front that they liked your undercover work. That's what they would use you for. Dangerous stuff, Jack." Riley couldn't judge Jack's reaction, which was good, he supposed. Jack was cool under fire. He would have to be if he took this job.

"I'll have to think about that one."

"Take your time," said Riley. "Call me in a week or so. You've got my number if you have questions you need answered." Riley was stripping off his waders and getting ready to leave.

"You know, all I wanted to do when I came out here was to get away from the rat race. Maybe I was just bored to death. I really don't know."

"I'd say you jumped out of the frying pan and into the fire."

Jack laughed. "I'll say."

"Well, take care," said Riley, "and give me a call."

"I will," said Jack. Riley started up the Nomad and drove slowly back up the trail to the road. Jack watched him go. He knew even then that he would take the job.

CHAPTER THIRTY-SEVEN

Jack turned up the now familiar driveway, and a blue-heeler dog came bounding out to meet him, barking up a storm. The new bike was quiet. Jack had not had time to make any modifications yet. He pulled up to the yard gate and leaned the bike on its stand. He took off his jacket and laid it across the seat of the bike. Bud came bounding out of the house.

"Did you see it? Did you see it?" He was looking around for something. Just then Jack heard the distinct cackle of a motorcycle on the county road. He and Bud watched as the bike turned up the driveway and came toward the house. The old Panhead lurched to a stop and died right beside Jack's new Road King.

"Clutch! Reid, clutch!" said Elle from the buddy seat behind Reid. It was a picture right out of the fifties. Reid had a short-billed leather cap on and a bomber jacket, while Elle had a scarf wrapped around her neck to keep the wind out.

"I don't know if I'll ever get used to this foot clutch," said Reid.

"Sure you will," said Elle. "You'll get the hang of it," she teased. She climbed off the old motorcycle and ran to Jack, giving him a big hug. Then, as if she had just noticed, she turned around and looked at the Road King. "You got a new motorcycle!"

"Yeah," said Jack. "You two better try it out. See how far Harley-Davidson has come in fifty years."

"You serious?" asked Reid.

"Sure." Reid and Elle, still dressed in vintage motor-clothes, hopped on the Road King and headed down the drive.

"I guess if you'll drive, Jack," came Kate's voice from the front porch, "I'll take the buddy seat and we'll go chaperone those two."

"You serious?" asked Jack.

"Absolutely," said Kate, slipping on her jacket and sunglasses.

"Alright Mom!" Bud exclaimed.

Jack got the Panhead started and Kate climbed on. Jack let out the clutch and the old bike cackled as it labored to catch the disappearing Road King. They went down the county road and turned toward town when they got to the highway. Reid and Elle were way ahead of them now. Jack gave the bike its head once he got it in high gear. The hand shifter was a little awkward for him too. They had gone only a mile or so, when the old bike coughed and sputtered. Jack pulled off the highway and coasted to a stop on the shoulder. Kate was laughing uncontrollably.

"Is it really that funny?" asked Jack smiling. He was looking down into the empty gas tank. The petcock was already on "reserve".

"Look where we are, Jack," said Kate. Jack looked around but didn't see anything all that unusual about the spot. "This is where it all started." She pointed across the highway at the other shoulder. "Right there is where the Suburban broke down the day you stopped to help me." And so it was.

Jack could see the Road King turning around in the distance. "How's Bud doing?" he asked.

"Oh, he's fine now. Ornery as ever."

"Kate, I'm sorry that I couldn't tell you what was going on..."

"Forget it Jack. I probably would have had a heart attack if I had known."

Reid and Elle pulled up beside the stranded motorcyclists and they all had a good laugh. Gasoline was retrieved and they all got back to the ranch, where Jack was saying his goodbyes.

"Oh, Jack, you'll come and see me in Boston, won't you?" Elle was saying. "Reid's coming out for Thanksgiving," she added, looking expectantly at Kate.

"Sure, I'll be over that way...sooner than you think," said Jack.

Tearful goodbyes were said all around and Jack straddled the motorcycle and headed once more down the highway. It was back to Kansas for a long visit with his family and then...well...Jack had never been to Washington D.C. in the fall.